Totally Bound Publishing books by Judy Jarvie:

Sassy with Sir
Scoring with Sir

Sassy with Sir

SCORING WITH SIR

JUDY JARVIE

Scoring with Sir
ISBN # 978-1-78651-961-0
©Copyright Judy Jarvie 2016
Cover Art by Posh Gosh ©Copyright May 2016
Interior text design by Claire Siemaszkiewicz
Totally Bound Publishing

SCORING WITH SIR

Dedication

Thanks to Ashantay Peters—crit partner
extraordinaire, fabulous writer and great friend.
Thanks to Lynn Morgan-Hill who lit the spark for Sir.

Chapter One

"Dis me and you're roadkill."

"You and whose skankwad army, loserboy?"

It's a gray Monday morning and I can't miss the yelled swearing across the school car park. My iPhone's Bruno Mars megamix can't sweeten the F-bomb napalm by the third years at the tennis courts. I long to flee but I still have hours of teaching torture ahead.

Today will herald a watershed in my life. Because I — Izzy Tennant, English teacher at Netherfield Secondary School in Barnet, North London — have a secret. Over the years, I've hidden the real me behind the mask of an oh-so-nice and proper English teacher. But at heart I have dark, private appetites. I may teach the classics of literature to kids that don't give a stuff by day, but at night I'm an insatiable erotica-holic.

Little do I realize that my fantasies are about to ignite with a man who can liberate these passions.

This is the story of my journey.

With *he who must be called Sir.*

* * * *

If David Attenborough studied chavvy North London school kids, instead of mating penguins ice-bonking for hours, he'd explain the brawling teenager ritual. I've consumed insufficient coffee to try. I beeline for the school's back door but the yelling mob turns and charges straight toward me.

"Is it true, Miss Tennant?" asks Darren Blackwater. He has the name and look of a repugnantly splendid extra in *Game of Thrones*. One you hope will get impaled before the ad break. From what his mother said at open day he's no stranger to sticky ends — he gets a little too much solo bedroom exercise and I don't mean kickboxing his punch-bag.

"Tell us," Eddie Childs butts in. "They're sayin' 'es comin' 'ere? We're askin' you cos, for a woman and a teacher, you know most about football."

I yank out my iPhone earbuds, succeeding in thwacking myself in the teeth. I remember not to swear but shouldn't bother — none of the pupils pay me such regard.

"I've nothing to impart. And no time at present, boys."

But Darren, Small Lord of the Blackwater and perpetrator of much school evil, is not mollified. "Ethan's brother said we're gettin' a new PE teacher and 'e's famous. Tell us if it's true, miss."

My tooth's throbbing. I'm more interested in calculating if I've brought painkillers or my dentist's number.

"I don't know anything about a new teacher."

"Ethan's bruvver said, miss," says Darren, "'E 'erd it from Matt Riley. 'Is mum's a cleaner an' she reads stuff on the desks. An ex-premier league player as head of phys ed, she says."

"If Matt's mum's so good at surveillance, who is he?"

Always answer a challenge with a question. This is my 'teacher's gold' tactic. "Tell Matt Riley he should employ his mother's reading habits himself if he wants to pass English."

I walk away, feeling like Khaleesi in *Game of Thrones* and pretending I look like her. Then I hear words uttered from behind a hand.

"Told ya she don't effin' know. Told ya not ta bovver!"

It's Mickey Peters. The boy who dented my car bonnet with a cricket ball. I pounce like a cougar.

"Peters!" I yell and his rigor mortis response gives me a delicious trickle of thrill. "Another word and it'll be detention and Mr. Rogerson's office. If I hear another curse, I'll be mentioning Matt Riley's mother. Then you'll have Knuckles Riley at your door and he's only weeks out of detention center."

They pout at me but I'm already high-fiving myself from atop my high horse.

"If I knew about the school's latest staff member, do you think I'd tell a car smasher? Disperse now."

I'm only through the door when Jack Carson, school janitor, corners me breathlessly. Creosote Carson, as he's affectionately nicknamed, is out of puff.

"Are you still seeing the doctor about your emphysema, Jack? If not, you need to go and get checked out."

Jack stops me with a hand. "Izzy, love, we're getting a new teacher."

I'm more worried about his dicky ticker and the wheeze like my nana's busted accordion than school staffing. "I know. Apparently he's a premier league footballer. As if." I roll eyes.

Jack stares with squished-up eyebrows. "How in feck's name did you know that, girl?"

Jack has fingered more gossip pies than Betty Crocker—he's a loveable Columbo with a wood preserver and chutney-stained coat. I hate to see him thus disappointed.

"Heard it from the future prison inmate reserves in the car park."

"Then you'll already know the worst."

"I know the bare minimum, Jack. It's best with Viagra Rogerson in charge."

Jack's jowls wobble at me. "The new sports head—he only used to play for feckin' Spurs, Izzy. Sacrilege! And us Gunners lifers—a viper in our midst."

I take this as my cue—Mother of Dragons, Daenerys Targaryen, could play this no better. I throw down my bags and breathe deeply, closing my eyes. Then I stare at Jack with the iced fire of Boadicea.

"Oh fuck. Bollocks. Crap. Piss. No!"

In the religion that is Arsenal Football Club, at the cathedral that is the Emirates, I am bishop in training to Carson's cardinal of fan worship.

Being a loyal season ticket holder for two decades solid does not come without fortitude and sacrifice. Nor does it allow for a high-caliber Tottenham Hotspur ex-striker to come waltzing into our school staffroom without comment.

We're reeling—and I don't mean doing *Riverdance*—as we head past phys ed toward the English corridor.

"Who is it?"

"You don't wanna know, girl."

"I do. You can't not tell me." Much as I'm dreading the answer, there's no avoiding it.

"Brilliant finisher—two hundred and five goals in two hundred and fifty games. He joined Spurs juniors in 1994…"

"Naff off, Carson! Don't play *Question of Sport* with me at eight-forty-two on a Monday morning or I'm liable to kick you hard. My shoes are killing me, I set fire to the toaster this morning and my key broke in the back door again. Spit it out in the name of Arsene Wenger."

He pouts but his stare goes soul deep, so intense I see the name before he speaks.

"Darby. Will bloody Darby!" we say in unison.

I take a step backward to hold on to the wall for support and my ankles feel wobbly. Which reminds me, never buy wedge heels from Debenhams, even in a blue cross sale. Bunions on BOGOF.

"That's bad. He was good," I whisper.

"I know. Better than good."

"Head of PE?"

"It's a maverick move." Carson offers me a stick of gum, but I decline. He pops one in his mouth and I'm hit by a minty waft of school days memories. And the recollections aren't as welcome as I'd wish them to be. I shiver.

"When does he start?"

"Not sure—the copies of his contract are faint but I'll check again. I 'av my magnifying glass soaking in Sparkle now."

"Matt Riley's mother needs dealing with," I mutter and kick the loose skirting board where I'm standing. The shoes now have a split seam.

Carson pulls me close. "I won four balls on the National Lottery on Saturday and invested the spoils in multi-buy Oreos. Pop by my lair at break. I might 'av it cracked."

I bite back my professional itch to correct him — it's a basement dumping ground next to the boiler room with a wasps' nest in the corner. It isn't a lair — or, for that matter, a place accustomed to hygiene. But if stinking of something stale and foreboding qualifies as a lair — then a lair it sadly must be.

"Oreos noted. We'll meet later." I tap on my nose. "At least Darby was a class player. If he has to come — better that he be top drawer. But why Netherfield? Why teach when you've scaled football's heights?"

"He said, and I quote from the application form, 'for grass roots experience of an inner-city school and to apply opportunities for social inclusion for youth in sports, specifically football'."

I'm tempted to ask if Matt Riley's mother is a code cracker spy in her free time. The woman needs a lesson on the purpose of dusters.

"Why doesn't he go for club manager or coach?"

"Running a bookies would be better than this game, girl. But his mysteries will be revealed in time." Jack's phone blasts a vintage chorus of *Happy Days Are Here Again*. "Time is a wily mistress." He walks off to attend to his summons.

The bell sounds and I stride away with purpose for the English staffroom. And that's when I glimpse him — halfway down the corridor, deep in conversation with Dodgy Rogerson. He's wearing casual trousers, a waistcoat and an open-necked shirt. I'm grudgingly impressed at how ruddy good Will Darby looks in the flesh.

His hair is dark and curling at his collar. He's bronzed as a gypsy prince who's spent time aboard a pirate ship. The hairs on the backs of my hands prick up and I stand gawping, not wanting to move yet. I'd blame the shoes but I'd be lying.

I'm expecting him to notice me but he's avidly attending to Rogerson's spiel. Not that I think planets will collide or he'd recognize me from the stadium crowd at past matches or anything. I mean, at over five feet seven I'm no pocket Venus, but I think I've nice eyes, decent legs in heels and wavy brown hair that can behave when I remember to condition and drag a brush through it. I continue to stand, and still not a glance comes within a meter of me.

He's starting to make me feel like Lizzy Bennet at the Assembly when *she's not pleasing enough to tempt Mr. Fancy Buns Darcy*. I can't muster a demi-glance here.

Will Darby—post young playboy footballer days—looks eerily like Sebastian Silver in *The Guy with the Silver Tie*. The book that started me reading erotica—my secret hobby. Shit, this is bad.

"Oh, Izzy. The very person. Can you help me with these?"

Our head of department Dibian Hicks barrels toward me with a tower of Krispy Kreme doughnut boxes. It's been many a year since Dibian bent down to clip her toenails. I can't see Krispy Kremes saving her on pedicures or assisting slimming aspirations. She's way too generous with her snack donations.

"Be a doll and open the door. My hands are like fly paper from a breakfast doughnut on the north circular."

"Course." I nod toward the new PE teacher. "Have you spied the sex god in our midst? Sports head's in the building."

Dibian flutters her eyelashes like a flapper girl. "Yes, darling. And I read that he loves a woman with curves! My ship might be in. Before I forget, Izzy—special teaching staff meeting in the staffroom tomorrow lunchtime. Food will be provided. All must attend."

I push the door then rush to decant my stuff and grab my room keys. The mental horror of envisaging Dibian and Will in flagrante delicto derails me from quizzing her on the purpose of the meeting.

Will Darby at Netherfield—it's like finding out George Clooney tap dances. In a tutu and a fez.

In such moments, I find myself asking how one of my favorite literary heroines would react. Lizzy Bennet would grab her bonnet, take a bracing walk then sew a voodoo curse into a sampler. I'll have to be content with thirty hormonal second years and Muriel Spark in ten minutes.

This morning's revelations and seeing Will Darby in the flesh have unsettled me. And put me right off Dibian's haul of sticky Krispy Kremes.

Chapter Two

I'm standing in the car park at lunch break and I've done it again. Lost my keys in the mayhem of mess that is my handbag. It would be funny but it's the fourth time in two weeks.

I'm losing my patience as, no matter how hard I root around, I cannot locate them and my lunch is in the boot while my stomach rumbles a lonesome love-call.

"Effin' gimme a break. Oh bollocks, hide then if it makes you happy!" I say aloud because venting feels helpful. In all honesty, it's a temper hangover from a morning where the kids have been hormonally charged and acting up in my classes.

"I didn't think I was hiding."

There's a pause — I don't turn around. Mainly because I already know who's behind me. I see Will Darby's reflection in the car window.

"Step away. Mad woman talking to her car keys. Nothing to see. Move on without a caution."

Which only makes me jump fifty steps up the nutter scale toward unadulterated lunatic.

"You okay?" he asks. His voice is both deep and soft. A combo made in heaven for chocolate advertisements on TV. Should I suggest he sideline? Then again, now's not the time for incidental chat with a man you've vowed to hate at all costs.

I want this not to be happening but it's too late. So I look over my shoulder and don a waxwork smile. Fate is being an evil bastard, waving its knob at me today.

Will's wearing shorts, a running shirt that reveals the kind of defined pecs breastplates were designed around, and his feet are in track shoes. I can't help but notice his hair-dusted, muscular legs, yet doing so makes me breathe rapidly. A heavy duffle bag is slung over his muscular shoulder and concern flashes in his green eyes.

"I'm Will, by the way. I don't usually do Samaritan but I'm intrigued about talking keys. If it's true, I want to see them with my own eyes rather than on the news or YouTube."

"I know who you are. I'm Izzy, I teach English."

"Now back to the keys." He straight-talks better than Jon Snow on an election night special. "What words did they say to you? Did they talk in unison, or nominate a spokesman?"

I pause for a beat. "That would be silly. And there was no *spokes key*."

He dead-pans and furrows his brow. "Good point—never tangle with an English language expert. Should I call Sky News or leave you to write the press release while I capture the runaway keys with ninja moves?"

Will's teeth are so white. I think it's his five o'clock shadow—at lunchtime too, what a man—that highlights the contrasting dazzle.

I can tell he's enjoying my circumstances. His eyes are twinkling more than a drag queen's tiara. Pishy fate, I damn thee.

I shrug. "I don't have talking keys. I'm in need of sedatives. Or a sword to fall on." God, I do say the most riveting things.

"You work with Dibian. Tell me if I'm wrong but I think she's a bit of a handful. The kind of woman restraining orders were invented for. I saw her grope the janitor in the dinner queue. He didn't seem to mind but that's not the point. I've known football managers that way and it needs to get handled. If you'll pardon the pun."

This is all rather unexpected. I did not bank on Will Darby having a ready wit and a fetching sense of humor.

"She should face a tribunal but there would be so many names, it would take years. It could go back to the Middle Ages—given her witchcraft heritage."

He grins. "I'd pay to watch."

I want to smile but I resist. He is the enemy. I shall not succumb.

"You locked out?" Will motions to the car.

His hair—dark and the kind of curly bobbed hair that many women would kill to have, let alone go daft to run their fingers through—waves in the light breeze. "You can empty your bag in my boot and have a rummage?"

"You often invite women to rummage in your rear?" I can't believe I've said that. I can tell from his face I have and he's embarrassed for me.

He shrugs. "If it works, use it."

"Came out wrong, the thing about your rear," I ramble. "It's been a long morning—had second years from the abyss and one can long-distance spit on my whiteboard." Again. Why am I telling him? Has verbal diarrhea and its nonsensical shabby colostomy baggage taken up an attic studio flat in my brain?

"Bloodthirsty pupils are reason enough to drink in the day. Do you have moonshine in your car boot?"

"Just a hummus and tomato bap. I'd break the glass if it was moonshine."

He nods like a sea captain changing course. "Can't have you hungry. Let's get to it." Will walks toward the enormous ice-white Range Rover by the fence. It's a pop star car, a pimp-my-ride wagon. Big bumpers, big extras, big price tag. Sex guaranteed with random pedestrians. "My boot has room for CSI on your bag. I'm improvising in an emergency."

He deserves points for being gallant. Really, he should've walked off and locked himself in the car.

"Thanks. Sure you don't mind?"

"Mind? I've always wanted to know what English teachers have in their handbags."

I don't know how to reply. I think I've run out of the worst comments I've ever made. Which is a blessing. Silence is hugely preferable. I stare at him as I open my satchel's straps. "There are things in here… Maybe look away now?"

The edge of his mouth quirks up, revealing full dusty brown lips. "Is this a game and you're going to produce a blindfold? Unless you have a machete in there, nothing will daunt me."

"This could offend," I warn.

He closes his eyes and shakes his head. "I played with Vinnie Jones. I can handle scary."

I laugh out loud and my subconscious is mad that I've been such a pushover. I unlatch my bag, tip it up and a plethora of junk spews forth.

"Christ on a bike!" Will's face is priceless.

I pick up my phone case. Its Arsenal crest is resplendent in gold and red.

Will has his hand braced on the side of the boot—I notice long fingers, a brief sensual note my brain bites on to like a rabid vampire. His lemony body wash isn't half bad either.

He's staring at my card wallet now. My credit card holder too is Arsenal FC embellished—a gift from last birthday. Then my Filofax—it's covered in player pic stickers. They're my hot squad heroes of legend—Thierry Henry, Freddie Lundberg and Robert Pires.

Will gently puts his hand to the back of his head. "Shit, woman. You need major detox. Ever consider a makeover at the taste academy?"

I put one hand on my hip—provocative and petulant in response. "I'm considered a gourmand with a fellowship."

The keys appear in the midst of the mess from my bag. They are on their Arsenal cannon key ring. Will picks them up, using the end of a pen he's taken from his pocket. As if he's found a missing finger in the woods and he's retrieving it with a stick.

"There you are. Bad keys. You made Mummy worried," I say with droll, sarcastic voice fully employed.

Will's answer weighs heavy for his soft tone. "You need a bag organizer. Or a change of teams."

I bite my lip. "Only an ex-Tottenham player could specialize in organizing handbags."

Will straightens to his full six and an almost half feet. Wow, he's big. His wave of offended testosterone nearly causes my wipeout. He pulls out a pair of sports wraparound sunspecs and dons them.

"Fighting talk." He's close—his voice a threat-coated challenge.

"You set your stall out with the top league, you play hard rules," I bluster but inside my heart is revving and my nerves are jiving under his watchful scrutiny.

Will's bristling so much he could have his own broom factory. "I don't know about handbags. But you've backed the losing side."

"Nice specs, Mr. Shady. But you're going home in an Arsenal ambulance." It's a famous line—sometimes the old chants are the best.

Will picks up my Arsenal baseball cap. Then my Arsenal sunglasses. The miniature picture of Tony Adams is, I believe, my *coup de grâce*. He shoves them into my bag as I'm piling the other paraphernalia back. Thank God I hadn't got my Gunners spare knickers there but I used them recently as a whiteboard duster. I turn and flip my hair—what else would Beyoncé do? The hair thing and a pivot always win.

"You're something, Izzy the English teacher." Will raises the shades and watches me. He inspects the name on my staff pass that he's pinched and kept in his hand without me noticing.

"Give that back."

"It's been illuminating." He returns it.

My inner rampaging football hooligan is still AWOL. "The pleasure's yours."

I watch him ascend into his pimp wagon and start the engine. He rolls down his window and starts a loud bass anthem. I walk to my rusty but trusty car and click the key fob. I've scored a small Arsenal goal for womankind by proving myself immune.

But Will purposefully curb crawls past with an inch to spare. His tone changes to turbo charged. "Consider this a warning. In future, you'll call me Sir. Unless you pull your Arsenal socks up."

His tiger smile flashes as he passes.

He got the last word. But, next time, vengeance will be mine.

* * * *

By six I'm dog tired, but as I pry off my bunion master shoes, I realize we've brought forward our book club to tonight. This lifts me from my funk.

"You having your porn night?" My flatmate Flo has a long auburn mane of curls that look like it last saw a paddle brush in the nineties. She doesn't deserve the peaches and cream, lightly freckled complexion of a model because I've never seen her wash. She's a local paper photographer and we've flat-shared for five years.

"It's not porn. It's a book club."

"Sleaze club, more like."

"Erotic women's fiction appreciation group is more accurate."

She's stirring her mug in a clunky way that dings my nerves. "Panting for porn. Salivating for sleaze." It's like playing tennis with Federer — she just keeps returning.

"Some of what we read is sensual romance without any erotica at all. It's no different to *Lady Chatterley's Lover*, Nabokov or Emile Zola."

With such a closed mind on my home turf, I wonder why I bother.

"Panting, groping. Bodice ripping and big members." Flo takes a deep slurp from her mug. "It boils down to filthy books about dirty bits." I can smell her hot Bovril. To think she criticizes when she drinks beef-flavored tea—it's positively medieval.

"Janey, Fi, Mo and me. Join us if you fancy." I know full well we'd tear her arguments to shreds in seconds.

"Too much hanky panky. I'm teaching salsa classes for the senior citizens. They need hip action—I need cash. One of my oldies slips me tenners if I pick him for demos."

"*Dancing with the Stars* for octogenarians. Gripping. Hope you've read up on heart attack response technique."

Flo flounces off, her shoulders dangerously close to her ears but she always walks like that, though I never get used to it. I can only hope the elderly dance stars like meat breath and body hair issues. Flo's not called Sasquatch for nothing.

I go to inspect my preparations for the evening ahead. It's the second anniversary of the Dirty Girls' Book Club and nothing is going to spoil our sauce with all the trimmings.

* * * *

Janey's on my doorstep freshly spritzed in her favorite fruity perfume—we're both wearing silver ties as a nod to our fictional hero's bondage antics and we squeal full tilt.

I love Janey Woodside—she's the sister I never had and she works as a support worker in the special education unit at Netherfield. She's blonde, lithe and can get away with an Alice band without people taking the piss and setting it on fire. She's funny and she swears, and she'd be the perfect woman if she liked football and supported Arsenal.

Janey can barely keep still and her eyes are as wide as a drugged-up raccoon's. "I have a good feeling about tonight. The book we've read has been amazing. Can't wait to discuss it."

"I wasn't sure at the start but it got better the further you got in." I recognize my double entendre from Janey's loud snort of approval.

Janey waves her bottle of wine and Fi knocks on the door with Mo behind her. We're all wearing ties. Fi teaches biology and her bonkers dad was our headmaster at primary school. Mo runs her own vegan chocolate shop and makes book club night complete by bringing choc contraband.

She hands me large boxes of chocolates then shows me her phone. "I've downloaded an app. Random Hot Cocks. Look at yesterday's! I nearly died."

I have no time to answer before Fi pushes her face to mine. "I've brought an old flogging cane from Dad's study. He found it during a clear out. Thought we could have fun with it."

We all gather around and touch Fi's cane with mock reverence. Mo's face is ruddy with delight. "We could punish the naughtiest club member?"

I try to enforce some order. "Ladies, please be seated. Pour the wine and grab a pew. As lady chairman I must keep things in hand.

Mo cackles and her ample chest jiggles. "Good luck with that. I've seen what's in Janey's bag."

Tonight Janey is sharing findings on online BDSM supplies' stocklists. Restraints, straddle bars and nipple clamps are featured in the array of brochures Janey hands me. I wouldn't mind but currently none of us has a man.

I seize firm control. "Now may I please draw attention to agenda item one — cock rings."

Chapter Three

Janey's eyes are dilated orbs as she reads from our book of the fortnight.

"We need to find another submissive."

"I've tried, it takes time to put such things in place, Sir," *Salvador replied, taking a sip from his goblet.*

"Not good enough," *Dominico snapped, taut agitation discernible in his features. "Find her. You know the spec. And this time I want the special girl. The woman we saw in the restaurant. Did you find out where she lives, where she works? The brunette? I want her."*

Dominico turned in his black leather chair, his eyes fixed on the door to the pleasure chamber. He caressed the leather-topped desk, then moved swiftly beneath to press the button. The chamber's doors sprang wide.

"Find that girl, Sal. I'll wait no longer. She must be mine. Tonight."

* * * *

We bask in the glowing aftermath of Dominico Blackstar's story—a tempestuous and sensual rollercoaster of a tale. *The Submissive's Journey* has had us raving for the last hour. It is book number forty on our erotica book reading list.

The Guy with the Silver Tie was the book responsible for this campaign. It's two years since that book—part romance, part titillating intro to the heady world of BDSM, part mystery—changed our tastes and sparked an adventure where the Dirty Girls' Book Club covers all the juicy erotica we can find. From the kinky, to the downright stinky—from perv to ménage. Our Kindles have never been so busy, or so steamy. If my fourth year class knew its Cloud contents, I'd be banished from the school library forever, amen.

"Did anybody see our new school pin-up today?" asks Janey, putting her e-reader back into her bag and gathering up her nipple clamp samples.

I'm immediately on high alert. There's only one teacher in the school who gets that title.

Fi replies, "Will Darby. Haven't seen him but it's the special teacher's meeting tomorrow so we might get an eyeful."

"Anyone know what that's about?" I ask.

"Rumors abound, but they're saying some reality show has made an approach to Netherfield." Fiona's eyes are so big at this prospect they're screaming for matching teacups.

I take a double gulp of wine. "As if exams, short staffing and a maniac head aren't enough challenge." I keep mute on the man in question as I don't want to relive my handbag 'show and tell' humiliation in the car park and can't bear admitting the scene.

Janey butts back into the conversation. "He's lovely — I talked to him myself. I think he'll make a great teacher."

"Spurs can't have rubbed off too much then." None of the others understands my Arsenal FC passion. I often feel like my mad, elderly uncle Cyril at a party — my foibles ignored like an embarrassing affliction.

"He's nice as well as dishy, sounds promising. But surely he'll have a bit of an ego after all the years in the limelight, Janey?" Mo speaks through a mouthful of nachos. Somebody's opened up Mo's chocolates and the heady scent of darkest, freshly crafted cocoa magic makes us moan in appreciation. Mo's good — she knows it too.

"He's not stuck up or into himself at all," Janey continues. "Quite the opposite. Rogerson asked him to pose for some local paper pictures and talk to the kids in additional support. He was kind and patient and did some football tricks. He stayed ages — what a cool guy."

"She means she's hot for him," Mo adds.

Janey resists the jibes. "Not my type but three women in special ed fancy the pants off him. They're menopausal so maybe it's hot flushes."

"He played for Spurs. Once stained, forever blemished," I add, stabbing at the veggie nachos, but the others take no heed. Uncle Cyril strikes again.

I'm frankly flabbergasted. He can have a fit arse and a cute wit, plus all the physical trimmings, but I don't want him to be nice and generous with his time. Or kind to disabled children. I want buckets of reasons to stay suspicious.

"So how's your book coming along?" Mo asks me, flipping topics like an acrobat chameleon.

"Slowly. You don't write a bestseller overnight." The erotica book I'm writing as a hobby is a topic close to my heart. As much as the others think it's just for fun, I've got surprisingly serious about it.

Fi snorts. "Come on, we want to read some."

I give a non-smiling stare. "In between marking and prepping kids for their exams, I don't have time. Plus there's my Arsenal commitments."

I shudder. Why did I divulge my deep secret longing to write erotica and first flailing attempts to try?

Oh yes, I recall. It was pinot grigio followed by shots and loose lips. Even though they're my great friends, I don't want to share my naked, sensual side. Laughing about other people's books is okay, but mine? Not so sure. And now here's a double scoop of pressure to go with my unpalatable scrutiny pie.

As much as I want to do this—write saucy, glue your tongue to the floor books—putting it out there for people I know to read is a pole vault of a leap too far—I'm not exactly experienced. Writing your first erotica book when you've never performed such antics in the bedroom yourself is like writing *Moby Dick* without having held a fishing rod.

My lack of rod experience is the toughest issue. My past boyfriends have, in truth, been crap lovers. In fact, I've barely left land, let alone chartered passion's stormy waters or faced my serpent of deepest desire.

In the bedroom domain, all has been relatively tame. Okay, we've got off. I've achieved the big O in a few ways. But more in a groping, brisk as a security frisk at Gatwick fashion, than a 'let's play slow-mo sex games into the dawn' way. Sad to admit and, worst of all, true.

As much as I love my friends, I've never shared my lack of sexual adventure. Maybe it's because they always assume I'm well versed in bedroom arts. And now that we're erotica fans, I'm too far down the line to fess up. I know Fiona's not had many boyfriends either, but even she's had sex in a cupboard at a party. Which puts her one further up the wild scale than me. Maybe I need to think about coming clean about hidden truths?

I stare at the nachos, now reduced to smeared crumbs. Fi picks up her dad's cane and tests it on her twitching palm, then giggles.

"From now on this is the ceremonial book club cane. We'll pass it around for the number of chapters in the book we've read. Whoever is left with the cane must do a forfeit."

She thwacks the cane hard on her hand for emphasis and we all laugh or shriek or both when it swoops through the air.

Fiona passes it clockwise. Twenty is the magic number and we hand the cane to one another like a strange twist on pass the parcel. As we count, twenty approaches. We're teachers—we know damn well twenty is going to land on me.

"You have been remiss, Izzy." Fiona's tone is dark. "Your forfeit will be decided by the group. Leave the room now. Stand at the door, head bowed."

I'm a tad incensed as this is my flat but I play along in the name of fun. When I'm summoned back, I head straight for my wine glass and ask, "Can I keep the cane for my month? It'll be useful for getting that missing sock under the cooker and the thong behind the radiator."

Fiona hands me the cane. "Just make sure you bring us three chapters of your book. Or have a new fling to report on by next meeting. It's been a while since you got action. We expect developments one way or another."

I laugh at their crassness. "Right. Course. Nothing else you want to add? Remember, it could be your turn next month so don't go getting too Russian roulette trigger happy."

"Stand before me, head bowed. Do you accept your challenge?"

"Yes. But what if I fail?"

"You won't. Or there will be extreme penalties."

They've no idea that my book's first draft is complete. I need to edit and polish it and to go back over every sex scene and oomph them all. But the characters are formed. There's a structure, it's complete in draft. But I'm not ready to share it. Or write the blatantly erotic sex it needs. How will I change that in a matter of weeks?

"I will obey."

Like *Lord of the Flies*, our book club has cast a slightly sinister shadow tonight. But on the plus side — that sock and the hot pink thong are coming back! It's been a weird night but one with definite fringe benefits for my knicker drawer. Result!

* * * *

The following lunch break we herd into Netherfield's dirty-beige staffroom over the library for the much anticipated teacher's special meeting. It's reminiscent of when the Bingleys arrive next door to the Bennets' in *Pride and Prejudice*. And they all get hyped and hyperventilate and the smelling salts are on stand-by. Today there's a definite frisson of expectation on the breeze—either that or they've changed the cleaning chemicals in the lavatories.

But when I enter and see a long trestle table erected at one side of the room, with three smiling strangers sitting behind it, I sense something thoroughly out of the ordinary is afoot. Especially when I note that caterers are providing a selection of teas and sandwiches on platters—there's even small cakes and petits fours. In a climate of stringent budget cuts, this screams proverbial jamboree.

Color me intrigued and I'm on my marks to claim a mini éclair.

Behind the table sit three official-looking strangers. One guy has a dashing mustache. The woman in the middle with a BBC lanyard has a bun so tight it was designed for the sole use of international gymnasts. The man at the end is wearing a cravat and large spectacles. I stare at his crested BBC badge with awe.

If that doesn't say 'sit and drink in events like a double margarita', then I'm not a crochet expert with a cupboard full of doilies—strictly confidential info on my handicrafts pedigree, by the way.

Cravat Man smiles at me as I sit and I feel ungracious not reciprocating, so I half smile then look around me as if waiting for a bus. If this were a dating club and I'd been smiled at by a man in a cravat, I'd be crawling along the floor and calling a cab. Though I think it's his will.i.am specs that unsettle me the most.

Our esteemed headmaster Rogerson comes into the room. Francis Rogerson may be our leader but he causes me issues. One, his malignant halitosis and two, his nasal voice that sounds like a persistent unfriendly wasp.

"Izzy."

"Hello, Francis."

"May I introduce you to Tarquin?"

Hell's teeth — did he just say Tarquin?

Cravat Man responds with an even wider smile then gets up, walks over and grabs my hand for an Etonian shake. It feels like a robotic sea behemoth's grabbed me.

"Tarquin Endermann." It must be hard to face the world sharing a name with a monster from Minecraft. He's still shaking my hand. I might need paramedics.

"I'm Izzy Tennant. English department."

"Oh yes. We know about you. You're on my list."

List? Now I'm worried. Rogerson says nothing so I'm guessing he is the author. Fiona sits beside me and stares at Tarquin hopefully.

"This is Tarquin. From the BBC."

"BBC Entertainment Documentaries." He nods.

Entertainment? If he's looking for that, he's stuck his sack down the wrong chimney. I'm riveted to find out what awful, heinous plans he has.

When I gaze at the doorway, I glance straight at Will Darby and he doesn't smile, he maintains a blank stare. Will walks with effortless ease, grace and marked hotness. A man with a body for sculpture and a profile I'd like to lick. I remind myself — ex-Spurs striker. He is tantamount to toxic. Licking prohibited and might need an antidote.

Rogerson leaves us and leads Will to the front row. Will's so close when he passes by I can see his trousers are inky blue cord, and his shirt is a downy plaid, his shoes brogue style. All he needs is an Irish wolfhound, walking stick and a sensible cap. In a photo shoot on a mountainside, we'd all sign up for mantelpiece prints.

Fiona has caught me watching. She winks at me. "New man promise, remember?"

I ignore her because Rogerson brings the throng to order, clanking a spoon on his mug. I perk up like a meerkat—I can't wait for the show to begin.

Rogerson smiles and joy brims from his buttonholes. "I'm delighted to introduce you to the team from *Class Wars* at the BBC. I'm sure you all saw the last series of the hit show where students are mentored in subjects they're failing. Then teachers are mentored to compete against one another in a talent spot finale."

There's a rumble around the room as we all digest this snippet. Frankly it makes me shudder. God. I'd rather watch polar bears shag in a snowstorm. I only hope Rogerson's getting oodles of cash for this crazy number.

Our leader progresses his crusade. "We've been lucky enough to have been approached by director Tarquin Endermann and his talented team. In a weeks' time, we intend to have cameras rolling on a daily basis in Netherfield. Five pupil groups plus a teacher will be mentored, nine additional teachers selected for three mentoring teacher groups. It's a phenomenal opportunity for the school! This year we're upping the numbers of teachers involved due to prior success."

A rabble of excited chatter crescendos. Rogerson soon has to settle the masses. "I'm sure you have lots of questions and Tarquin is on hand to handle all your queries—please, Tarquin, come enlighten us."

We all clap as Tarquin takes over. "For those who missed out, and didn't see our show, where the heck were you? Living in a cave? Seriously, though—our program has earned acclaim and backing for two more series. We want our Netherfield series to be our best. We think you can deliver. We aim to make that happen." He grins like the pro presentation front man he clearly is. "So here's some clips from last year's headline-stealing show. This year we plan to find the stars of your school…" He presses a remote and if this were a timeshare scam set up by marketing monkeys, we'd all be signing our life's cash up because it's that well packaged.

It does look like a great idea, with several real-life characters, some heart-tugging stories and even some highly entertaining moments. Various pupils are chosen — from the troublemaker to the teacher's pet. All are given surprising subjects and inspiring mentors. Two mentors are downright dictator crazy-heads. Each has two months to impress and progress.

The teaching mentoring element usually gets the biggest laughs. Teachers are combined — often with disastrous results. The science teacher who became a belly dancer in the last series caused viral online fuss. He has his own show on Channel Five now.

Tarquin pushes his specs up the bridge of his nose like a trombonist honing his instrument and going for the big notes. He proceeds to explain the show's ins and outs and his big plans for this series. Apparently, he missed out on an award last year and he's hell-bent on getting it this time.

I can see my fellow staffers are pretty happy and impressed by the furore. I, on the other hand, am thinking — please don't let it involve or prey on anyone remotely close to me.

I imagine Dibian Hicks will be a prime contender for the spotlight. There are also a few teachers of a narcissistic disposition — Awesome Annie the music teacher springs to mind. If she were made of chocolate, she'd lick herself to death and go back for seconds.

"We'll be in and around the school from now on and this week we intend to sit in on classes. All pupils will be given permission slips to take home. We will draw up a draft list for our central mentor and mentee roles by the end of the week."

There's a gaggle of questions from around the room. Dibian puts her hand up and says as head of English she'd like to be mentored for a part on the next series of *Poldark*. But she's only having a laugh because she's a big fan of the show. To my knowledge she has every item of Aidan Turner merchandise the BBC has produced. So while her comedy may be coated in a lighthearted chocolate shell, there's a lonely, obsessive kernel of concern at its center.

We're each handed out pamphlets about proceedings. As I'm about to leave, new boy Will Darby stands and smiles at the group.

"I'd like to add, since I'm new here, I'm having a party-cum-initiation ceremony. I'd like you all as my guests at my new home. Next Friday night. I'll put flyers on the coffee tables. I've spoken to Tarquin and his team and they'll be coming along—seems like an opportunity for everybody to get acquainted. Free bar, free food, come casual, dressed up or fancy dress if you want—just hope you all can be there. I'm pleased to be at Netherfield and looking forward to meeting you all properly."

As Will scans the room, I briefly feel—albeit for about five seconds—his green gaze fall on me. Yes, truly, no lie.

He's probably remembering all that Arsenal stuff in my bag and figuring out a way to bar me from the party. I feel heat radiate from the tips of my toes to the top of my head. Its ignition flashes and burns my body like a sparkler taking light.

I don't want to hold eye contact but I don't want to be a prat either. So I raise my eyebrows and use the pen between my fingers to tap on my upper lip. I'm aiming for unimpressed but I suspect I look like a nutter.

I glance back and he's still watching. His stare makes me shiver and I tear my gaze away. I know I'm blushing now and am confused. So right after I've turned away again, I peek and he's still watching. Crap. Oh why did I start this? Now he's walking over.

"Hi, Will."

"Izzy. Sorry if we got off on the wrong foot yesterday."

"Don't worry about it. Thanks for helping out."

"Coming to my party?" Will's question throws me farther than a steroid high shot-putter.

"I don't think so. Prior engagement."

"I'd like you to be there. If only for the sake of someone to laugh at." He grins and it's a 'knock you back on your heels' number. I'm not even wearing my wedges today.

"You'd only want to show me your collection of handbags. I might get jealous."

He's grinning widely now. And there, in an instant, even in this crowded room full of colleagues, the air has somehow become taut with frisky sexual tension. I don't know how we manage to create this. Like some scary baby we clone together out of football angst and charged hormones and repressed competitive sparks. *¡Ay caramba!*, together we're hot. And that's scary.

He doesn't look at me but says softly by my ear, "I lied. I'd like you to come. Punishing you is my guilty pleasure and it's constantly on my mind."

I gulp at those words. Surely he didn't mean...?

I don't even know what to say. The Comeback Queen is sucker-punched. How intolerable!

"Making sure you're at the party is a little personal challenge I've set myself. Let me try," he adds. His grin is so boyish it needs an action figure and a catapult. "Come along and wear your Arsenal strip. I'll get Arsene Wenger there to try you out. I hear he's desperate enough. I do have his private number so it could be arranged."

"I can't risk it, Shady. You and me would only end up doing a shots to the death contest. Or underwater arm wrestling. Let's be sensible and choose to avoid revelry gone wrong."

Will stares at me hard. I watch his Adam's apple move above my eye level. "You can deny all you like but you will be there. I'm good at persuasion. You're something, Izzy the English teacher."

And I'm figuring it's 'something' meaning extraterrestrial. Rather than splendid and worthy of applause and a badge.

"The feeling's mutual. You're something to avoid at all costs."

I do a 'Destiny's Child in a video' pivot and swiftly walk away. *Touché*.

Fiona and Janey bound up at jet speed. They look as if they expect my exuberant joy because they're clearly over the moon at the prospect of a premier leaguer party and a TV reality show circus come to town. Sadly I miss their emotional marker entirely.

"Come on, Izzy. It'll be great! We can bring Mo." Fiona says, "Janey was right, he's so nice. I'll have to buy a new outfit for that invitation."

Janey squeaks because she likes nothing better than an opportunity for retail therapy, especially clothes. "Shall we go to Watford, Saturday?"

I opt for, "Me, at a Spurs player's party? I might be washing my hair. Or embarking on a new project in crochet. And it won't be a dress. It'll be a barricade."

Chapter Four

I'd promised to go and tell Jack Carson all after the meeting—a debriefing over tea and biscuits in his lair.

But as I get nearer, there's barking coughing coming from the basement. Correction—coughing is too mild a word. It's hacking, gut-wrenching noises, like somebody can't grasp enough oxygen to breathe.

I run. Then I stop, take off my heels and run again.

Jack's standing against a wall. When he looks at me, his eyes bulge like some awful cartoon character. And he's still not caught his breath.

"Hell Almighty, mate!" I take his arms and step him back to take a seat. I begin to thump on his back because I quite simply don't know what else to do. At times like this you wish you'd paid more attention in first-aid sessions.

Jack doesn't speak because he can't, but he manages to finally gasp for air like a dying trout. And this dying trout is noisy.

"This isn't good. Would you like a drink of water?"

Jack nods. His expression, eyes not meeting mine demeanor and expression tell me he's embarrassed, and worried as he gasps in air. He hates fuss as much as I hate going to night matches in winter and forgetting my gloves.

"Water," I say, taking refuge in doing something. That was no minor cold slash coughing session—that was an almost turning blue and unable to breathe situation. Perhaps ending up on the floor or worse if nobody had come in. I fill up a glass from the bottle in his fridge. He sips.

"Take your time, Jack." I itch to smooth his hair but I don't. His staunch pride would be mortally wounded.

Jack laps like a baby with a beaker. And some three minutes later, he's breathing okay and is somewhat calmed. His eyes are rheumy but that's only to be expected.

"That chest must get attention from a doctor. Tell me you're not still smoking." I see the familiar bulge of a packet of Rothmans in his upper pocket. I can tell from the smell of him and the color of his fingers that I'm right. "Didn't we have this discussion two months ago? Didn't you promise me you'd cut down and try to quit? You told me you'd stopped."

Jack says nothing. He's sixty-two years old and sits like a belligerent kid in one of my classes, eyes on the floor.

"Shit, Jack."

His voice is a whisper when he answers me. "Wi' my Lilly not being 'ere anymore. And Bobbie gone too. I channeled all my loss into that little pup and made him my world. Walking him got me through losing Lilly. I even talked to him."

Lilly was Jack's dear wife who passed a year ago. They were devoted to each other. She was a dinner lady—her loss left the whole school bereft. Six months ago Jack lost Bobbie, his West Highland terrier, to some mystery illness. I know Jack's grappling to cope.

"Smoking fags won't bring them back, Jacko." My voice has gone other-worldly—emotion is strangling my voice box. The thought of Jack alone and lonely makes me wish I had done more to help.

"You're right. I need to stop."

"So you didn't go to the doctor? Can I make an appointment and go with you? You can't hide your head in the sand on this one."

"Do what you have to."

"First, you're going home. I'll take you in the car…"

"I live three streets away. I can damn well walk. The air will do me good."

I struggle to believe him. He looks weak and those noises I heard on arrival haunt me. "I hate to say it, Jack, but it bloody stinks down here. And that can't be good for your chest. We need to clean this place a bit."

He stares at me with a face so forlorn I wonder if he's going to cry. He rallies and goes to fetch his coat and hat and hang away his overall. I put my shoes on and grab my bag.

"I'm walking you back. And telling Vi your neighbor to keep an eye and an ear out. No complaints. It's that or I camp on your doorstep for the rest of your life." I'm acting big, bad Izzy. But it's only because he's genuinely freaked us both.

"You're a ruddy pain in the backside. You're going to curse some man when he's fool enough to marry you."

"You taught me from the manual, Jacko. Now it's time for my dastardly revenge."

* * * *

"Jack, how are you today?" I've come in early to make sure he's okay before work — I've worried since yesterday.

"I'm fine, girl. Fit as a fiddle. Just needed a good kip." His color's back at least. The smell of tea and fresh, hot toast covers the basement's usual dubious odors and my belly growls an entreaty for pity. I still haven't managed to procure a new toaster — I must correct that soon.

"You okay if I make that appointment at the doctor's later or tomorrow?"

"Said so, didn't I?" he answers behind his mug. "Want a slice, girl?" Jack waves a glistening golden triangle of toasted heaven and brandishes his butter knife.

"Thanks, Jack. I could murder a cuppa as well, if you don't mind."

He's poured in a trice. "I can spare a crust and some super brew, girl."

Jack's tea is so welcome it could have its own doormat and slippers by the hearth. "Cheers, Jack. Coming to next Wednesday's game? You can have Uncle Cyril's seat if you fancy, I have a car space reserved? Recompense for the toast."

Jack nods then smiles and my heart soars. His usual self has returned. And his toast and tea are back to top standard so life is good. But I do have to keep a bit more of an eye on him.

* * * *

It's disconcerting to find Alan Collier waiting beside my classroom door before the bell rings. I don't really know him—he's a religious studies teacher with bad taste in footwear—sometimes sandals—and he wears half-mast trousers on a regular basis. Add warts and a leer and the guy would have the full maxi package.

Despite the fact that we're strangers, I've already decided I don't want to become acquainted. He also has a laugh like a perplexed goose—I've heard it in the staffroom. And his Fiat has a sticker about being 'cock-a-hoop for cocker spaniels'. In the world of football where men mince flesh before words, his dog sticker would merit a good kick in the knackers.

"Hi. Alan."

"Yep. *C'est moi.*"

Close up his lips would suggest a Botox booth on a bad day. I slide my key into the lock. "How can I help?"

"I don't know if you're aware but I'm something of a squash *Meister.*"

I still can't decipher his meaning. "Squash?" Has he earned some teaching module I need to get?

"Twenty medals and corresponding trophies—many say I should've been pro but the sports world's loss is teaching's great gain. My question is, do you play? If so, what level and how about testing compatibility sometime?"

I've never played squash. I never wish to. "Hit a rubber ball in a sweaty glass box? I'd rather wash in bleach and stinging nettles. To put it in first year language, FYI not happening in this lifetime."

Alan stares at me then whips out a leather-bound notepad, unclips a pen and writes a flourish inside it. "A simple no would have sufficed. But I like the feisty fillies best." He grins and it's pure Cheshire cat face.

"What are you writing?"

"All will be revealed. When time holds fullest promise. I'm in need of a new squash partner and a life partner too."

I can't be bothered to ask more. My prejudices are on the money. I pity the spaniels. And their hooped cocks.

"*Au revoir.*"

"Same to you." I shut the door to escape him.

* * * *

I should be marking while my second years answer comprehension under silent conditions, but I find my gaze repeatedly roving to Lydia Salter.

She's got dark copper, straight hair and a smattering of storybook freckles. In character she's pure teacher's dream in an introverted package and Lydia stirs something within me. Her wide-eyed stare and nervous glances. The way her eyes meet mine then dart away like startled neon tetra fish in an aquarium.

"Lydia. You have a problem?"

"No, Miss Tennant." Her head nears the desk as she speed writes.

There's tittering laughter from the back corner. Lydia's pen hares across the desk. She knows she's the focus of the jokes. As do I.

They're the pretty, trendy, crass mob, not that I believe in stereotypes or labels. But maybe it's their trendcentric styling and gadget addiction. Plus the vacuous conversations overheard — not that I'm judging, much.

Lydia acts like she doesn't care but she tucks her fear of being singled out deep as a black cobweb tattoo. I know she's concentrating as a cover. Her ears are almost turning like transmitters.

"Did you see her shoes?"

"Do you think her dad knits her sweaters?"

"Enough." My bark is pure Rottweiler and I stride between the desks to the cluster of conspiring girls. I'm keeping my assumptions battened down lest the smoke curls from my nostrils. "Sophie. Ellen. Heads down and more attention to your work. Final warning."

"We weren't doin' nuffin', miss."

"My point exactly. This isn't an oral task. It's a written one."

"I needed a pencil."

"She did, miss, it's true."

That's how it starts. Pinpointing an object of derision, then a slow assault of words and mind games. It's how I got my armor. Head down, achieve and eventually develop a well-honed wit as a weapon slash diversionary tactic. Even today I disperse the negative attention with a choice barb. Use intellect to intercept. But it's a tactic to deactivate threats. My sarcastic reactions to life are to deflect unwelcome attention. I don't want the scrutiny on my flaws.

"Ten minutes left. Make them count," I warn the class.

Lydia makes my heart beat fast and that old sense of panic rises—it's not a feeling I bear easily. Like a slowly filling pool of angst, the tide of self-doubt rises. But even slow, steady drips can damage a fragile ego.

In my case, my experience of school bullying was drowning by soft but steady character destruction. It made me go into teaching. To stop it happening to others because the negativity hampered my self-belief for years.

At the end of class, I call Lydia back. "If you need someone to talk to — I promise you I can help. If you're finding things hard to deal with."

"It's fine, miss. Honest," Lydia replies with the rushed brevity of an express train flying through a station.

"If you need help, you only have to ask."

"I'm gonna be late for art. Gotta run."

* * * *

By break I've a ladder the length of the M25 running a circular route around my tights. I'd leave it but I have a particularly sinister third year boy front row this afternoon. He might notice the leg hair through the hosiery holes. It worries me that the hair could turn him on.

Fortunately Jack lets me keep a large bag of my rubbish in his lair for emergencies. I rummage in the bag while Jack takes a brief trip out to the recycling bins. There's lady stuff, cough sweets, an inhaler or two, a lippy and eventually my wad of emergency tights. I'm pulling at my tangled hosiery when I'm shocked by a stark face staring into mine. It's Will.

"Izzy. What the hell's that?"

"Um... Hi."

He is staring at the brain model of tights in my hand.

After our recent wars of words, the last thing I want to have to say to him is, 'I'm unknotting a tangle of tights. I need them for my witchcraft.' In his book, I'm already nutter suspect *numero uno*.

"Nothing. What you down here for?"

Will stares more. "Could ask you the same. I'm looking for Jack Carson."

Will is standing in the gantry of Jack's basement that houses the cleaning equipment. He's holding a long fluorescent tube light bulb. I seize the upper hand.

"So how many PE teachers does it take? I'd imagine at least fifty."

He narrows his eyes. "Only one. Me hopefully. If I can get a replacement tube first." He stares at the end bit as if looking for something.

"With that, I can assist you, sir," Jack says, returning from his errand and appearing between us with the leap and flourish of a genie in a pantomime. "Need a hand, Mr. Darby, sir? Would that be a five-foot tube or a six? Would you like me to refresh others while I'm at it and light you up like Blackpool?"

"Five feet—this one will be great."

"I'll fetch it in a jiffy. May I accompany you and undertake the tube change personally?"

For a man who had a near coronary yesterday, frankly I'm irked that he's so into Will. When we first learned of his arrival, Jack was as suspicious as me. He's defected to Team Darby a tad too quickly for my liking.

"Happy to change it, but that's good of you to offer," Will confirms. I sense kindred spirits here—but Jack's my friend and I got him first.

"It's no trouble at all," Jack deflects. "And may I say how nice it is to meet you at last. I sincerely hope you will enjoy your time at our fine establishment. It's an honor to have someone of your caliber join us." Jack sticks out a hand and Will shakes it vigorously. Jack then scurries off in search of Will's tube.

I decide to have a few ego pokes for fun. "You should've let him change the others. You know you want your office floodlit like White Hart Lane. The extra light would help when you apply mascara."

I'm feeling pretty chuffed at this point. Especially when I see his jaw tense and flex.

"I never bring my cross-dressing stuff to work. Might rip my stockings." He looks pointedly at my tights.

Man alive, but the bugger's trounced me with that joke.

Jack comes back looking like a puppy with a Frisbee but thankfully the tube isn't in his mouth.

I still can't fix the tights monkey puzzle so I shove it in my jacket pocket and bail on the Darby fan fest. I'll talk to Jack another time, preferably once my funk's mellowed to moderate.

"I need to get back to class. I found what I need."

Will stares at me intently. Dark eyes, somber expression. Six and an almost half feet of unyielding all directed at me. "You make a habit of losing things, don't you?"

"Fortunately I strap my sanity in with cable ties."

"Just losing it generally." His stare is black as a Halloween churchyard.

The barb hits home. In his shiny onyx tracksuit, he's like a virile, tetchy panther in high-tech breathable fabric. I'd itch to touch but I sense there'd be static sparks. Or fisticuffs.

"There are lost causes everywhere, Will."

"Meaning?"

"Like trying for a sensible conversation with you."

"Or listening to replies. You don't listen. Too busy claiming striker status."

"Like my team. Natural talent rises."

"Aiming for kicks in the goal mouth without teamwork will eventually run you out."

His comment hits home but I'm not about to concede. "Point taken. Speedy goals were never your strong suit."

"I think we need to get back to work," Jack interrupts.

While standing here in these tights, my own allure already drank twenty shots and cried a river of its own mascara. His confidence and distinct lack of empathy jar. He's tagged me as a harridan. Can't he see below my bluster? He thinks I'm that hard? Am I that bad?

I've had enough. Nice to know I'm public enemy number one and Will's not even seen out his first week yet.

"Let's mark this one down as a nil-nil draw," Will tells me.

"Something you were used to."

"Do you ever pack it in?" His tone is iced steel.

Jack stares at me, shocked. His glare's so hard I know he's disappointed. But Will Darby riles me more. Am I worse than I even realize?

"I need to go."

"I think that's best," Jack answers.

We're reading *Brighton Rock*. And right now I feel like I've hit rock bottom too.

Chapter Five

It proves to be a day of gentleman callers. As the bell rings for lunch, Tarquin the Terrible of the BBC appears at my door as the second years straggle through in a gaggle of 'OMG's, 'LOL's and 'wicked's.

"Any chance we could chat over a coffee? I don't mean to intrude on your lunch but I have supplies." He shakes a brown paper deli bag.

I have my own lunch but agree. I'm semi-impressed at his thoughtfulness. I probably would have found it harder to say yes but his friend, the cravat, has stayed home. I dread to consider that it might be one member of a cravat commune of assorted shades and fabrics. I imagine them staging a closet demonstration with 'We Want Out' signs.

"I thought we could perhaps sit at your desk so we've privacy, there are a few issues I'd like to discuss."

I'm uncertain about what he's keen to flesh out but I relent. "Fine."

He smiles like he's found a hundred-pound note in a lucky bag. "I've brought a raspberry tart as inducement."

I resist the urge to clap my hands and say 'goodie'. It's one up from playing squash. But when he removes his jacket, I notice his trousers are higher than Blondie's *The Tide Is High* today. Come back, cravat, all is forgiven.

I want to point but that would conflict with politeness—worse still, he wears them with paisley-patterned braces, lest his trousers escape.

Ah hell.

"Unless you've some other invitation?"

I've got my foil-packaged sandwiches out now. I've pre-empted my escape visa. Unless I can still call the braces ambassador?

"It's fine." I aim to eat this sandwich at luge speed.

"Coffee?"

When I agree Tarquin removes an aluminum Thermos from his bag as if it's a cherished heirloom vase. Then he presents two tiny goblet-style steel cups. Has he mistakenly come to me for a valuation? He fills both mugs with some aromatic coffee blend then offers cream. Soon he's opposite me with his salami baguette suggestively thrust between us. The tarts remain tucked away.

Tarquin smiles—I cannot return the sentiment. I see the waistband of his trousers over the desk.

I blurt out, "Sorry to rush this, but I've marking to finish right after lunch."

The legs of Tarquin's chair squeal across the floor like a badger in labor. I'm wondering if he has regular stalker habits and uses his doll-sized coffee cups for dates with reluctant women.

"What did you wish to discuss?"

"I'd like you to complete my questionnaire." A document is thrust between us before he seizes his baguette and starts to chomp. "This enables us to assimilate the best mix for our mentoring profiles. Our mentor spots are selected via a computer program. It's a technical process."

Impressive. Though, if the software is that clever, he should ask the computer what to wear. I flick through the form. Even the paper smells medicinal and foreboding. Like an ancient apothecary shop — the kind with brains in jars. I'm starting to think Tarquin lives in a tower and keeps a raven as a pet.

He sips his coffee. "Simple questions about likes and dislikes. Aptitudes. Preferences."

I see the form has items including phobias, things I hate, past traumatic experiences and biggest regrets in life. I sip my coffee too. Then wish I hadn't and force it down.

"Do you have any objection to participation as a mentor?"

Having a TV camera stuck up my nostril or indeed at the back of classes would not be my idea of fun. I'd be worried about parental complaints and scrutiny generally. Or, worse, the personal epiphany that my arse really is as large as I fear it to be. But I don't want to be tagged as a dissenter, lest Rogerson gets the hump. I take a gulp of bleh coffee.

"I'd be more than happy to boost the school profile. I do, however, feel that there are others at Netherfield far more skilled and better placed to fulfill your criteria. And, indeed, some much more willing to participate and camera friendly than me."

"You do yourself little justice. I think the camera would find you charming—you have a fifties movie star air about you. Brunette bombshell looks and the wit of a warrior, it's a heady combination." He winks at me and jiggles his eyebrows with scary menace. "I particularly love the fact I can often see emotions warring in your eyes as you hold back your true thoughts."

If he can read my eyeballs right now, he'll see abject terror and a club on the head with my umbrella at his laid-bare, scary attraction vibes. I'm about to interject and get rid of his notions but he trundles on.

"I mean this from a TV production perspective only. Don't run away with the notion I'm about to leap on you with lust. Though there's a few of my crew who've expressed a preference. So, what about a spot being mentored? You have a certain air that the camera would do well to capture," he opines, blinks then sips. "As you know, we need to find true characters to capture for this segment of our shows. It's an audience booster. I'm sure you realize you'd become a household name."

"No. Not in this lifetime. Not with me."

He stares at me as if I've thwacked him with my line-caught trout. I throw in a grin to take the edge off. But he's struggling to come to terms with my firm reply.

"You realize Mr. Rogerson says it's access all areas and we are entitled to pick whoever we wish. It's for the good of the school. Participation could be deemed part of your contract."

"I don't think it would be a good outcome if you chose me. I would get signed off due to stress. I have a history of anxiety issues."

It's a total tosh toss but who cares if it works?

Tarquin twists the cap on his Thermos. His salami baguette's only half gnawed and I've had no whiff of a raspberry pastry. He bags it all and he's soon standing by the door.

"Your goblet?" *The Fellowship of the Ring* will likely need it back. I open the window and throw out the contents. At two floors up, there's a risk I've scalded a first year.

Tarquin takes the cup. "Excellent. If you could return the form by tomorrow midday latest."

I yank his hand and shake hard. "Certainly, Mr. Endermann. I've enjoyed our lunch together immensely."

It takes him by surprise. Hopefully I've put enough mistrust in his heart about my loose cannon potential that the TV cameras will stay far from my door. His expression is a pleasing reward. My objective is bulls-eyed.

* * * *

I must heavily invest in NachtGarten *eau de parfum* because the scent is attracting men like moths to a musty fisherman's sweater. After Tarquin's exit there's another man at my door… It's the cameraman I've seen tailing Tarquin, armed with lots of camera kit and those big tin foil circles that make people look glowing on screen. Whatever they're called. Let's called them magic doofers because that has a ring to it.

"Hi, can I help?"

He smiles at me. "Can you?"

Clearly this man likes riddles. "If you're looking for Tarquin, he's been and gone. He took away the raspberry tart he'd promised me—rather scurrilously.

If you run fast, you might be able to catch him and mug him for it."

He laughs and crosses his arms over a muscular, T-shirted chest.

"I'm Andy. Andy Regis."

"Nice to meet you, Andy."

"I'm chief cameraman on this crazy ship called chaos." He holds out a hand and he has a wry, dishy grin. He's quite good looking in a Jaime Lannister type way with sun-mottled hair, designer stubble and strong shoulders. It must surely be all that camera holding that's bulked him out. I imagine he's something of a chick magnet in his spare time. Yep. Definitely a womanizer who's thoroughly briefed on his own attractions.

"I'm Izzy, what can I help you with?" I say.

"I know who you are. I've been watching. And listening. It's part of my job, believe it or not."

"Star cameraman and stalker too. A thoroughbred all-rounder."

"When it comes to some people who've piqued my interest, I go the extra mile." He smirks at me. "Wanted to say, as much as Tarquin's a knobhead, he's pretty good at his job and underneath he's not as bad as he seems."

"You're his cheerleading squad then?"

"He won't stitch you up on screen—he might come across as the biggest dickhead you've ever met. Let him grow on you. He has a magic touch for knowing the best people to get stories out of—he's usually right. And I think you've caught his eye."

"I'd rather not if I can help it. And as for the growing on me part—do you mean he's like some kind of fungus?"

Andy chuckles. "Pretty much. I was thinking mold. Mildly unpleasant but harmless. And, in fact, he has exceptional qualities that are little appreciated."

"Does he know you go around talking about him behind his back?"

Andy shakes his head. "Nope. But for what it's worth, he knows I'm a shit-hot cameraman so I'm bulletproof. I wondered if you fancied a drink sometime? And wanted to say if you want to talk or need to steer Tarquin or vent in future—just shout and I'll be there. I'll come to your rescue."

"Right now I'm knee-deep in teaching faff. But who knows…? It's good to know there's a knight with a shining camera lens around the corner."

"I'll hold you to that," he says. "And I'll keep buffing my lens, waiting for the call. Maybe a pub lunch sometime?"

"I've never had lunch with a shit-hot cameraman before. Do they pay the bill at the end?"

"For you, most definitely. Say yes, you'll be glad you did. Laters. Gotta go, Izzy. See you soon."

I think I may have an admirer. And I have absolutely no idea why.

* * * *

I've booked Jack a doc's appointment for next evening. I text him because I'm knee-deep in marking at my free period. But I know I'm also avoiding any reprimands about my earlier conduct with Arsy Darby.

I do have guilt about it.

I also suspect I went off my high dive deep end in a too-tight Speedo bodysuit. I let my temper run riot. I should learn to keep the pot lidded.

But what can I do? Buy Will Darby humble-hued carnations? Send him a 'Sorry' balloon?

When I go to my post hole outside the English lounge, a small yellow envelope with my name written in an unfamiliar hand rests there.

I open it when I get back to my desk, with a soda from the vending machine. It knocks me back on my heels.

The dark, masculine script reads,

Madam,
Jack has served us both yellow cards.
He's a good guy by the way. You may be a misguided Arsenal supporter but I fear we've collided in error. You like to joust. I like to tackle, and I do it hard. Apologies.
I hope your keys made a full confession the other night. I also hope you've solved your sticky stocking problem.
Let's agree to keep it teachy clean, hope that works? I will try. Let's see if things improve.
Found a red pen in my car boot. No Gunners crest, though I still think it's yours. Felt a need to buy you a better one. The party invitation remains open. Perhaps we should try out a new entente cordiale there? I still have some Arsenal memorabilia in my collection you might be interested in. (To be clear, I have no handbags. I'm not the total wuss you think I am.)
Believe this as you see fit.
Yours
Sir Shady – W.D.
P.S. I'll keep your pen hostage until we agree a truce.

I retrieve the pen from the envelope. The type and crest featured are of Tottenham Hotspur Football Club. I'd rather use charcoal to mark exam papers. And, believe me, I'm an OCD stickler for stationery protocols. But I smile that he's gently mocking our disputes.

I place the betraying pen before me. Then, in the spirit of camaraderie and pushing limits, I pick it up and mark nine essays.

* * * *

I walk down the corridor, past the sixth year common room, along the big sport hall's wall adorned with photos of past champs. I'm at the staffroom of the physical education department before I quite know what to say.

Am I crazy? Should I leave this?

I find a woman with blonde spiked hair, wearing a neon tracksuit and a static death glare. She's using two-fingered skills to poke her keyboard into a signed confession. She doesn't look up at my arrival, but keeps jabbing.

"Hello?"

Maybe it's a good thing we don't interact. She's uncannily similar to cheerleading's Maleficent, Sue Sylvester in *Glee*.

"Is Will around?"

Still no eye contact, or words. Then a pause. "Who?"

"Your new head. Will Darby? He in?"

She stops typing. Flicks me a glance. "Oh. Yeah, him. No. Dunno where he is."

Professionalism and Netherfield Secondary sports department are galaxies destined never to merge.

"Forget it." Then I reconsider. "Got an envelope?"

I enclose what I had in my pocket with the Spurs pen then address the outside,

Thanks, Sir, entente cordiale accepted. Pen returned after a test drive – it's a touch slow for speed marking.
I. Tennant.

The package will, I suspect, never get to Will. They'll find it in years to come under a pile of festering jock straps.

I'm pretty sure Will getting my note is as likely as me getting a New Year's honor from Her Majesty. For services to clog making.

But I've replied.

* * * *

I'm grinning as I reach my car. Inside the envelope I left is a freshly printed pic from the web from ten years back. He's looking dapper at a swanky cocktail party and was probably papped at exactly the wrong moment. He's holding a clutch bag—probably a girlfriend's. The bag is silver and glittery and the captured moment is priceless. It's pure alpha male does Elton John with enormous reluctance. *Gotcha!*

I've sent him the printout from Google images with his returned pen. We may have a truce. But you can't leave 'a sitter' in the goal mouth.

I'm getting into my car when I hear a voice.

"Izzy. Wait up." Will jogs toward me. His gleaming muscles are on full display in a vest top and shorts that would cause breathing issues for any female who decided to watch. Specifically me.

Will stops right beside my car and lays a hand on the door. "I've something I want you to see."

Is it wrong that I'm hoping it's his new homage to a *Magic Mike* routine? Naughty me—how bad am I? I summon focus, and concentrate on 'professional teacher' thoughts. "How can I help you?"

"Come with me, Izzy. I've something I really want to give you."

* * * *

I'm beginning to feel a frequent flyer when it comes to the boot of Will's Range Rover.

"What do you reckon?" His boot has a large box of vintage football programs and fan items. There's another box of signed shirts and assorted bits too. "I have loads of memorabilia. I intend to auction some of the valuable stuff for the school. Rogerson and I have a plan for that. But I found Arsenal items. Thought I should give you first refusal given your superfan status."

I immediately kick myself for sending Will the handbag jibe and wish I could turn back time. "That's so thoughtful."

He smiles and kicks at loose stones underfoot. "Not a problem."

He doesn't deserve my slight. I see at least twenty programs, many signed. There's a shirt signed by the Arsenal squad of 03-04. It's the season when Arsenal went unbeaten and it had never happened before in modern football. My team was top and I was there every match. But I never got a signed squad shirt. It's awesome.

And Will's standing here offering these – and all the time filling my senses with his musky man meets lemon fresh scent. It's a lot for a woman to take in after a long day's frazzling school shift.

"You have first refusal."

"Golly. Thanks. Tell me how much you want."

"No money needed. Think of it as a bridge-building exercise." Will's smile would deflect attention from a solar eclipse. He has that kind of dynamite grin that makes me want to stand, watch and appreciate.

"Thanks." Our eyes meet and hold. "That's good of you."

He dips his hand inside the box to take out a few programs and one snags my eye, handcuffs my attention and causes my breath to catch. I have to clear my throat. "It's the FA Cup Final program of '98. Ray Parlour and Dennis Bergkamp signed it. My two fave players — as in favorites for technical ability — ever. Wow!"

Will raises an eyebrow. "And yours if you want it. Any of it — keep the shirt too."

I tug it close and marvel at the signatures. I know somebody who'd love to see this too. In fact I know several people. My favorite Arsenal childhood legends touched my life and now I'm holding things they touched. It's like a slice straight out of my childhood and teens and he's handing me a wedge of my heart back to examine and relive. Will's offering the stuff I cherish most in life.

This is not evil dictator behavior. This is white knight with silver spurs.

I'm already thinking frames for my treasures. At least a hallowed shrine in my living room. "I must pay you — these would cost a fortune. For the programs with Ray Parlour and Dennis Bergkamp. And the shirt."

"You can't pay for gifts. They're yours, and keep the rest too, to do with as you see fit."

I shake my head. "I know someone who'd love what's left. And he'd love them even better if they came from you. Somebody who needs a bit of TLC right now. He goes by the name of Jack and he's great at everything from boiler maintenance to light bulbs. Would you do the honors?"

If I thought Will's smile was dazzling before, it's monumental now. "I'll take them down to him now. He'd like 'em, you reckon?"

"He'd seriously love this."

"Brilliant."

I reach out and lightly touch his arm. "He's had losses in his life of late and some health issues. You'd be doing me a big favor, cheering him up. I have to say sorry — I left a note for you earlier. I want to apologize. I didn't mean…"

Will shrugs. "Forget it. You got my note?"

"I did."

"So — truce in place?"

I hold out my hand and he reaches out to clutch mine in his. The back of his hand is hair-dusted and double the size of mine. And why exactly do my hormones find that a sensory stimulating factor? I'm happy to drink in Will Darby's attributes *ad infinitum* while something in my abdomen does the freestyle lambada.

"Thanks."

"To pleasant working relations. Want to seal the deal with a drink after I've been to see Jack?"

I shake my head but a tiny imp in my head is screaming at me. A drink with Will Darby — there's so much I could ask him. About his career, his highlights — and I don't mean hair highlights. Maybe I'll get another shot at it sometime? We've made progress, best not to wreck it. "Don't suppose you'd mind making that offer to Jack?"

Will stares into my eyes with surprise. "If he wants to. Sure. It'd be my pleasure."

I'm the one who's grinning now. "You'll have to set a strict time limit and I guarantee he won't let you pay. Another time?"

"Consider it a date." Will reaches out and his hand touches mine again. Zip, zap and the chemistry's back. "Catch you later."

Crazy butterflies in my stomach are doing loop-the-loop, the whole ride home—I'm Will Darby's new BFF. And Jack's going to be so over the moon he won't shut up for days on end. Sometimes life brings excellent and surprising opportunities. And the thought of Jack's thrill provides me with an internal cozy hug of happiness.

Chapter Six

After a boring night of intensive turbo-charged marking on the sofa, I've surprises in store for me next day.

The first one is Fiona. She swings by my class before morning bell to warn me I'd better get my act in gear on my forfeit — book chapters or finding a man without delay.

"Which is it to be?"

"Not sure. Do I have to commit now?"

"Cutting it fine, aren't you?"

I visually frisk her for signs of more canes or crops. I can't see any but a lot can be hidden inside a biology lab coat so I stay wary.

"Look, I'll try but stop hassling me. I promised to obey, didn't I?"

"You need to take this seriously. We're your friends and we're trying to help you realize your dreams."

Put like that, it sounds sympathetic.

Fiona widens her sparkly blue eyes behind their rimless frame specs. "Personally I'd go for the man—you can use him for research. I'm meeting one myself tonight."

I'm agog with surprise. "Wow, so who's the lucky fella?" I'm imagining someone like Sheldon from *The Big Bang Theory* or a brain surgeon. Maybe they met at Boffin Dating Dot Com?

"Alan Collier's challenged me to a game of squash."

I gulp. And force a smile.

"I said we could have a drink and a bite to eat after," she says. "He's suggested the new French restaurant that is supposed to be wonderful."

"Alan. Right." I'd never had Fiona down as a lover of cocker spaniels but I keep it zipped. "Didn't realize you were into squash."

"I play tolerably well. I've had my eye on Alan. I hear he has a talent with his lob."

I keep smirks pinioned inside me. "Tell me all tomorrow."

"I will."

I push the forfeit and the thought of Fi and Al 'squash dating' well out of my mind. My brain's so fried with her Alan revelation anyway I can't take in much more.

On the back of Fi's visit comes a text from Jack informing me to cancel the health center appointment. He tells me the receptionist got him an earlier time and he's been already. He's been given inhaler medication and told he's okay. I call the surgery to cancel the other appointment I made only to find that Jack's already phoned. I'm a little perturbed that Jack wants me out of the way. But I push away inclinations to mistrust him. If he wants privacy, I have to respect that.

Hot on the heels of this is my biggest surprise of the day. As the pupils herd in in dribs and drabs for morning class, Tarquin arrives in my classroom doorway — expectant efficiency follows him like his cloying cologne. The camera guy I now know as Andy Regis plus a sound man with him make something unwelcome unfurl in my belly. And it's not just the letchy wink Andy gives me.

Tarquin's cravat is back. The high-waisted trousers have gone. Today's cravat is lilac with dots and his shirt has a pale lime stripe and a matching hanky. He holds up a fanned wad of slips as though he's auditioning for *The Mikado*.

"Ms. Tennant. We're filming your class. The necessary permissions have been obtained."

"Not from me."

"I have faith in you and I think you'll perform best when you're unrehearsed."

"You did this to save yourself an ear-bashing more like."

"Precisely. But I'm famed for my insight. Mr. Rogerson has sanctioned it." He takes little heed of my stern face and pays even less attention to my reluctant thundercloud of woe.

"Second year English, isn't it? Studying *Pride and Prejudice*?"

"It is. But…"

"No buts, Ms. Tennant. I have a show to film." He holds up a hand before my face, in a style favored by drag artistes. "Consider this your screen test. *Pride and Prejudice* is always an audience pleaser — let's get to it."

I feel my stomach roll and wish I'd gone to Jack's for toast and tea. Being filmed as you're back-chatted, heckled and giggled at by thirty-odd thirteen year olds is something best faced on breakfast.

Shit, bollocks, fuck.

I feel like Anne Boleyn eyeing up the gallows.

"Your ensemble is fetching." Tarquin gives me a wink. "Fantastic calves for a pencil skirt."

"Come in." I point them to the back of the room. I wish I'd planted a bomb there. Cleaning bits of cravat off the light fittings would be a small price to pay for Tarquin annihilation. Talk about missed opportunity.

* * * *

It wasn't arduous. It was horrific. A car crash in teaching caught on film.

The class were silent, the best-behaved kids they've ever been. So I had to fill time teaching. If I'd had more time and notice to plan and rehearse, I'm sure I would've been fine... The question and answer session I included as an ad hoc brainwave was pure comedic awfulness.

My question about what lay beneath Darcy's issues with Mr. Wickham resulted in an assertion from half the class that Darcy was gay or dealing with his bisexual identity crisis. Let's say if this had been exam day, my teaching career would've been six feet under.

I suspect it'll be total TV gold.

I emerge from my first experience of being reality filmed in a teaching capacity, a shaking wreck with a parched throat and a perma-blush that probably goes from waist to follicles. When they leave I sit back in the chair and draw in a major yoga breath fit to put an elephant in corpse pose.

"You okay?" It's Janey. I feel like a crumpled wreck driven over at speed by a monster truck. She's standing at my class door. Fresh as a daisy and looking like the modern world's version of Doris Day—a-line skirt in a ditsy print, cute cardi and jumper twin set and a small crystal star clasp in her hair. She's more fifties retro than the fifties were for real.

"Janey, I've had a bollocks of a day."

"Oh, doll." She comes to hug me.

"They ruddy came to film me. It was awful."

"The bastards! Didn't you know?"

It's only then that my gaze plops straight onto a letter in the wonky pile on my desk. It's marked with the word 'Urgent' in red ink and signed from Rogerson's PA. *Shite.*

I must've pushed it aside and hidden it in my keenness to print out the best shots of the handbag touting footballer yesterday. *Oh bugger!*

"I swore three times. My bum itched half way through. I kept doing a weird walk to ease it, and must've looked like Quasimodo having a fit."

"You'll have done fine."

"Won't."

Janey's gorgeous, clear blue gaze holds me steady. "Nothing is ever as bad as we fear it is. Nobody's died. It'll turn out okay."

"I feel a bit icky." I place a hand to my rolling stomach. I can hear it doing a full cottons wash cycle.

"I have major things to tell you. Can we do lunch…? So much hot news to share!" She's excited and multiple body parts shake with anticipation. She has a fresh glow and she's wearing her secret smile.

"It's about a man…"

Janey grins and nods. "I'll tell all later."

"Will we sneak to the deli? Get something nice?"

"Deffo. I'll drive us. You're going to be so amazed."

Frankly, after the morning I've had, I need amazing and pepping up big time. So I forage in my desk drawer for my emergency cola, and chocolate bar, family sized. I snap off two lines and gobble them down. Sometimes, only the bad stuff will revive you.

* * * *

"My Pilates friend Rachel got tickets to a charity dance," says Janey. We're sitting in the window seat of Shelley's Deli. "The Rotary Club and the kids' hospital charity and the hospice were beneficiaries of the fundraising night. Rachel runs her own stationery business and she'd donated funds and prizes. She introduced us."

I'm stuffing in my feta, avocado and pepper wrap. It's delicious but the mayo spurts down my chin as I nod. The deli's food is awesomeness on a tray. Janey's falafel wrap sits untouched but I can tell she's so engrossed in the story she doesn't care about food.

"He was sitting beside me. We talked and talked and talked. We totally hit it off. He's so nice. He was presenting an award and I watched him go up on the stage… Oh, Izzy. Can I say, I wanted to totally swoon… He's already texted me today. Five times. He's taking me out for dinner at Papillion!"

"Heck. You'll see Fiona there with Alan Collier as that's where they're going!"

"Maybe I'll send him a text now and get him to book somewhere else," Janey says and in a matter of seconds she's fulfilled the task. I gulp down bites of wrap as I watch her. My stomach isn't placated so I take another bite and talk between crammed mouthfuls.

"Who, Janey, who? You still haven't said."

"Ben Lindhurst."

My jaws cease chewing. It's the kind of news that makes the world's hubbub halt in an instant, that is, your best friend having spent a night falling head over heels for a grade A celebrity footballing icon in world football history.

"Effing hell! As in Ben 'Golden Boots' Lindhurst, Chelsea legend?"

"I can't remember which team, Iz. I was too busy drooling."

"He was their lifeline goal scoring legend for years."

Janey shrugs and takes a small, bird-sized bite of food. "I wasn't listening. But I know he's a famous player and he was top class."

"Ben's a beautiful player. Poetry in motion in his time. He runs a football academy now. Got quite a name."

She covers her mouth with her fingers as she chews. "He's invited me to go see it too."

"Janey. It's in California!"

She shrugs and nibbles some more, totally unfazed. "I know. He's offered me tickets out there and a place to stay. I figure I could do it during the Easter break."

I hold on to my tummy and decide to take the eating thing slower. It's not going down as well as I'd hoped. Maybe it's the camera in class shock thing? Or Janey's sudden huge news?

Perhaps there's too much going on and the side order of pickled onion crisps was a bridge too far? But somehow I have an inkling there's something not right today.

My tummy cramps need calming somehow. I figure lack of food is the cause here. I take a sip of my fizzy water by way of respite. But the bobbing lemon slices don't make me feel better, they turn me off too.

"So you met Ben and you got on like a blazing house of hormones," I prompt.

"We're going out tonight. And tomorrow. He says I can go and visit his house in Harpenden. It's a small country estate."

"Only a small one?"

"He has pot-bellied pigs there. He's a specialist breeder." She shrugs at me, undeterred.

"So what about Mr. Cycle Shorts you fancied from Pilates?"

"Compared to Ben, no contest. And I've always had a thing for adorable piglets," Janey says. "In fact, I honestly think I could be in love. As in proper. Forevers, even."

Janey shoves her phone at me. There's selfie after selfie of the two of them smiling like love's young dream. They do make a red carpet couple. There's a pic of them dancing together, and others of them clinking champagne glasses. Ben's a good-looking bloke and Janey's a total peach of gorgeousness. It's come as a bit of a shock, that's all.

They look totally loved up. I scroll one pic further only to find them mid-enormous, mouth fluid-exchanging snog. She has her fingers in his hair and he's going deeper than a tanzanite miner on a heavy shift.

Janey sees what I've seen and pulls the phone away, her cheeks blazing like she'd fallen asleep in the sun. "Oops. Will Darby must've taken that… He winds Ben up…"

"Darby?"

The wrap stalls in front of my lips. My stomach growls in an ominous way. I can feel waves of nausea that aren't good.

"Ben went to the dance with Will Darby. Will does a lot of work for charity. They're friends and they support Sports for City Kids. I think Ben was staying with Will."

My mouth makes an 'o'. But I can't muster a word to reply. I'm too focused on my stomach and the way I am feeling clammy and hot and bothered. I don't want to swallow what's in my mouth.

"Was Will there with a woman?" I venture with my mouth still full.

"Yes. He had his sister there. She's lovely too, Iz. I told you that before. He and Ben go way back. He joined Tottenham when Ben played there before Chelsea and they hung out. Spent years in France together too — Will has a place there."

The jangly bells above the deli door tinkle and, talk of the devil, Will Darby walks in. He directs a dazzling smile straight at Jane. Then eyes me as if he wants to talk.

"Janey. Good to see you, last night was great." He's so warm in the way he speaks to Janey I'm both glad — because she's my lovely bestie — and miffed that I get only formal fast-freeze hellos. What's with that?

I stand. My legs are unsteady but I need to flee.

"Gotta go!"

My mouth is still full. But my stomach churns. There's no way I can swallow and I don't want to offend the customers. I have to get out into the fresh air. I leave my lunch and push back my chair. The door is still half open with Will in it and he looks at me oddly as I dive past, forcing my way out.

The threat of losing my lunch at rocket launcher speed doesn't allow for small talk. I run to the flower beds beside the car park and I reach them not a moment too soon.

* * * *

I'm throwing my stomach contents up into a car park flower bed and Will Darby is gently rubbing my back, saying soothing things and being ultra-nice. Could things get worse or weirder?

Puking in public is never good.

But doing it beside somebody you make it your mission to hold the upper ground over is just the worst possible kind of karma on a bun with fries supersized. Especially when you'd made inroads at being friends.

Oh, Abject Humiliation, thy name is vomit bug.

"Get it out there," says Will.

"Please. Go. I can do this solo," I say between wretches.

"Get rid of it. You need to."

Like I have a choice. I've been throwing up my insides in a projectile manner for the last ten minutes. If I could stop, believe me I would. My stomach is in the driving seat and I'm accepting the G-force spasms that go with the ride.

"I think she has some virus, she was looking peaky earlier," says Janey.

"Was she out drinking last night?" Will asks.

I go to protest but throw up again.

"She doesn't drink much. Think she was at home."

"My handbag?" I say when I find sufficient breath.

"Got it safe!" says Janey.

"It's okay. I won't steal it. It's not my color," says Will.

"Want to check my hip flask is safe. Being a closet alcoholic," I add. Then I'm sick again.

Gotta hand it to him, he's owed me that crack about the handbag. He no doubt got the photo and what a time to deliver the return parry.

I chuck up again and this time I finally feel like I have enough upper hand to take a breather. I am on my knees but I feel like I want to try rising. I'm panting in Mother Nature's divine clean oxygen, but my legs are wobbly. Will helps me up, then slides a hand around my waist to steady me.

"I wouldn't come too close." God, I am so embarrassed, says the voice in my head. So, so embarrassed.

"S'okay. I'm wearing my washable tracksuit."

"There's a chance you'll be testing it on disinfect cycle."

"Feeling better?"

I nod. My voice hurts, my throat is hoarse. I'd dearly love to drink a gallon of water but I'm scared it'll come right back up. I suspect I looked like the cherry woman in *The Witches of Eastwick*. I will never win a wit battle with Will Darby ever again.

"You're shaking like a leaf," he observes and he's right, I am. "Deffo a vomit bug, I think you should go home."

"You're right," says Janey. "I can take her but I have a class in twenty minutes. I don't want speeding points."

"I'm on a free period. How about I take her home?" Will offers. "They won't mind if I don't go back. Only paperwork awaits."

"Sure you don't mind? I'll notify the school."

"Great," Will replies.

"Are you two in league to make all the decisions?"

"Sick person gets vetoed," says Janey.

"Whoa! I don't want to mess up his posh car. I can't afford Super Valet."

"You won't," says Will. "Shelley in the Deli has lent us a bucket as a precaution."

I have no answers. The nausea has abated. But exhaustion has come into the party and mugged me with a felling punch to the brain. I yawn and try to stay standing up. It takes a lot of effort.

"Let's get you home," says Will. "You need sleep and painkillers and water in due course."

"Thanks, William Nightingale Darby."

"Do you ever take help without comebacks?"

"Do you ever manage comebacks without help?"

Will narrows his eyes at me. Then I look down to notice that I've pebble-dashed my BOGOF shoes during my first sick bout in the flower bed. I never liked them anyway. I step out and plan to dispose of them in a bin somewhere.

Will observes, "It's like a twist on Disney's *Cinderella*. Don't think I want to take those shoes around the kingdom, though. Not without a pressure washer."

"You're no Prince Charming. You're my nemesis."

"Why stop, when I do it so well?"

Janey is writing my address and vague directions on a piece of paper. Frankly, I'm so desperate for a bed to lie down in, I don't care what they do with me. I hang on to my bucket and Will leads me away, carrying my bag. It suits him so well I might gift him it as a reminder of this special day. I plonk my shoes in the trash can as we pass it.

"Your carriage awaits." He picks me up, bucket and all, and lifts me inside. Barefoot, humiliated and sick as a stomach-pumped parrot.

Chapter Seven

I wake up with an iron tummy and a body that feels like it's been slowly squished in a car crusher.

The room is dimmed but I swiftly know it's not mine. It smells different—like an elite hotel with fancy flowers and posh potions. I sit up in bed but every inch of me aches. I can sense I've been Sahara Desert sweating and that has ramifications for the awfulness of my hair. And I have muddled memories of somebody drifting to my aid at regular intervals. A hand holding cool water for me to sip and my head being soothed with a flannel. I'm wearing a white T-shirt—also not mine.

"What the f—?"

"Morning. You're awake, good."

I'd know that voice anywhere. I've heard it on Sky Sports a few times. Damn. Will is at the end of my bed. He looks like an angel—minus wings and halo. He's wearing white track pants and a white shirt and vest beneath. It's a boy band video come to life. He could model for a detergent ad. Even his smile is peroxide polar blast white.

"Welcome to Hangley Grange." He makes it sound like he's a trendy boutique hotel concierge.

I feel as if I've woken up in an alternate universe. And in this one I'm weak, with a sore, strained throat, and a body mugged by a herd of crazed bison.

"Please don't say this is rehab. I barely drink. I've never touched drugs in my life."

"This isn't a clinic."

"It's very white." I take in the details. Sleek, glossy fittings, snowy walls, icecap bedding.

"I live here. I rent Hangley Grange from Paul Bates. You've probably heard of Paul. He's a football Hall of Fame A-lister."

"Most coveted striker at AC Milan Paul Bates? As in one-time England captain?"

Will nods and, from my prostrate position in the bed, I blow a ragged whistle through my teeth. "Bloody hell. You lucked out with your landlord."

"Let's hope he always wanted vomit up his hallway carpet. Thanks to you he's had some refurbishments."

"Shit." I wince and I'm nearly a hedgehog of shame. It hurts me more than I'm ready for. "Double shit."

"I lied. It was in the bathroom. Fortunately it's fully tiled and I'll buy him new linen," he says. "You ready to face the day?"

"I think so."

"You still look pale. So best take it easy. Will you manage a shower on your own?"

"There's no way you're helping me."

Will smiles. "As long as you're sure you'll manage."

"I need space to Band-Aid my pride first." I shrug. Bugger. Why did I admit such frailties out loud to Will?

In my head I berate my weakened state. I prefer a twenty-foot barricade in place when it comes to this guy. Control and composure help me deal with the crazy static he causes for my sanity. And my sex drive.

In truth, I'm feeling weary, embarrassed and slightly ashamed at what damage I've caused while I've been incapacitated. And I've never felt as vulnerable. Lying in a bed he's put me in. Wearing clothes I have no recollection of putting on myself.

I note various tincture bottles and carafes on the bedside table. "If you've brought me here to undertake experiments, the least you could do is tell me what mutations to expect."

"The only experiment I'm planning is to see if you can manage to get up, or have breakfast."

I nod. But I'm not ready to throw back the covers. "How did I get into this T-shirt?"

Will explains, "You pulled it on yourself. I brought you here when there were tail backs and you'd started to feel ill again. Rather than prolong the agony, I figured my home was quicker. Plus I have a ready supply of buckets, most of which you've used. Your bug was twenty-four hours of steady sickness. I'm amazed that a stomach can hold that much…"

"What day is it?"

"Friday. Nearly midday."

"Thank you. For helping me… I don't know what to say…" I keep my eyes on the lump in the bed that is my feet. "I'm sorry I put you to trouble."

"I've had easier and more talkative guests. But I've also had worse."

I feel bad that I've caused him aggravation. And I'm grateful he's done so much. He could've easily run me back to school and left me dying in Jack's basement.

"S'okay. I'll add up your bill shortly. Should tot up nicely."

"Why aren't you at school?"

"Rogerson figured I might have the bug too. He's a raging hypochondriac. But he did give me a job so for that he deserves forgiveness."

It's only at this point, when Will raises both hands, I observe he's wearing yellow rubber gloves. The kind an industrial sanitation company would provide to deal with a toxic incident.

"I've contained the infection so far," he says and sprays all surfaces. It reminds me of the mad cow disease news bulletins. If he starts hosing down wellington boots beside me, I think I may cry.

"Did I make a mess?"

"You've a good bucket aim."

"Thank heavens." But I've spoken too soon.

"Only exception being the bathroom. It's why I got the T-shirt." Will lays a tall pile of ultra-fluffy towels on the bed end with my laundered clothes. "Shower's ready when you are."

Beneath my mortification, I'm utterly aghast at this predicament so I push through it with rubbish jokes. "You brought me here to steal my handbag and see my underwear. Lie and cover all you like."

"It's a technique I use regularly on women. Poison them to sneak a view of their unmentionables. Yours don't even match."

I gasp aloud. He can probably tell from my half-hidden face beneath the covers that this is as painful as the bug. But I realize with relief I have a bra on beneath the covers and T-shirt. He mind-reads my thoughts.

"Sadly your tits were a no-go zone. But getting you to go commando was fun—your knickers are in the washing machine. You forced me to wait outside while you put your pants in a non-see-through bag. You have major control issues. Jump in the shower — we'll talk over breakfast."

I stare through to the en suite wet room with its luxurious stone décor and multidirectional jet palatial shower. But all the time I'm thinking, what knickers did I wear, what knickers? I already know they'd be big ones. I would never wear a thong with no imminent man action. Damn it to hell! And please don't let it be my tartan ones — the ones large enough to shelter a hunting party expedition.

"Can't I get clean and sneak off? Call a cab? I'll never darken your door. And at work I'll never give you a moment's aggro again. Forever after amen."

"I can't let you go, Iz. Your knickers are in my dryer and it's a long walk home without shoes, tights or pants."

"Who needs such trappings? So yesterday."

Will raises his eyebrows. "Stay until your knickers dry. At least I thought they were knickers... I had no idea you had Scottish links." He's trying to hide a massive grin and he's enjoying this more than is fair. "Actually, I lied about you needing to wait for your underwear. I've put new supplies on the chair ready. I'd imagine those tartan things should go to the highland glen in the sky. Or some kind of gaudy kink museum."

"Oh." It's all I can answer.

The door clicks shut. Will leaves me to the sorrow that is my plight. This time there will be no recovery. A Tottenham player nursed me without issue in my time of greatest need. Me, a savage ingrate of an Arsenal supporter who constantly mocks him.

I move my legs from under the covers, knowing I've done Will Darby wrong. When I inspect the bag of supplies it even has toiletries, a robe and a toothbrush. My shame is boundless. I'm going to have to give him respect in future as I have sins to atone for.

Will is the hero of the day. And that's a total shit fest in itself.

* * * *

The shower is sensational and afterward I can't bear to don my dirty bra and so I go naturist commando under the large fluffy robe Will gave me. I head down a Cinderella staircase flooded with so much daylight I almost need shades. This house isn't big—it's a palace among palaces. The front door alone is big enough for a giant and his big-boned girlfriend to fit through.

I follow enticing aromas to a kitchen. When I find the room, it's expansive, high-tech, and could accommodate a battalion while resembling a style mag front page.

"Something smells good."

There's a pause while Will turns and regards me. It's one of those freeze frame looks and I drink him in. His smile, his slightly tousled hair and his feet shoved in loafers with no socks. Pure yummy shot.

But then I'm delusional—I haven't eaten for days. And I've never fancied a sockless man before.

"Good sign—you're hungry." Will continues to do *MasterChef* at the island cooking station. It's TV ad male model lifestyle commercial.

Despite my bravado, I'm barefoot and feeling awkward. I clear something blocking my throat only to realize it's the lump called my tongue. It's drunk on the view.

"Take a seat." He holds out a chair. "You need slippers, Cinders." Will strides from the room. He comes back with a Marks and Spencer bag and places it neatly into my lap.

"Tessa got you these. Forgot to leave these for you earlier."

Shit. Tessa must be his wife. And I'm in here in a dressing gown. I feel like Mata Hari gone unprincipled. Fuck.

I peek into the bag. There's slippers, new shoes and pajamas plus a change of outfit.

"The other items were okay? I should have brought up these too."

He means underwear. I nod. "Please thank Tessa. She's very thoughtful."

"It's her job—she's the maid. Actually she's a super maid. She even has a machine for getting rid of spiders humanely."

"She didn't have a humane Izzy removal machine, however?"

"No. Indeed. But technology makes huge leaps all the time." He smiles and I force my face to pretend to smile. I'm still wondering how he got my size right in knickers.

"I'll reimburse you. How did you know my sizes?"

"Tessa guessed them. I enlisted Janey too—she drove your car from school to your flat. She also brought the underwear—she didn't stay for a visit to limit the virus."

I take out the fluffy slippers and shove my feet inside. They're puppy ear soft and I sigh as I relish their comfort "Thank you. The favors I'm owing are stacking up. Humble pie, here I come."

"Scrambled eggs first, hopefully?" Will piles fluffy egg on a small oval of wholemeal toast. The smell has me salivating. For some inexplicable reason, I want to show him how much I appreciate his kindness. And most of all I want to say sorry.

"Will. I can't begin to thank you."

"Then don't. Eat."

"No, I must tell you. I'm so very sorry about how awful I've been in the past. I'm an arse when I get started."

"It's cool. I quite enjoyed being mean to you back. Please don't say you're going to stop. I'd be gutted if the fun's spoiled. I'd be pissed off."

"It's not cool to needlessly give you the needle for personal entertainment…"

"Izzy, it's the law of the changing room. Never take yourself too seriously. And you're a Gunners girl. Stands to reason you'd get your toys out of the pram about me being at your school. I can take a bit of ribbing. Rhino skin when it comes to ridicule comes as part of the football squad induction."

"In future I'll rein it in."

"Just eat. Get your strength back. I miss the old Iz. Where's she hiding? Tell her to get her arse back into gear, she can't wimp out now!" He pushes the plate closer to me so I'll do as he asks. Then he goes to a cupboard for ketchup. "All bases covered."

I decline Will's offer of fresh orange juice but opt instead for water. My first forkful of egg is bliss on a zipping comet.

"Tasty robe." He nods to my attire.

I know I'm blushing—almost as red as the tomato sauce. "Um no."

"You should wear one to work. I'd vote for it."

Shit. It's a flirty echo of the time he told me he wanted me to *come.*

"I'm waiting for the 'but'. Get it over with," I volunteer as I squeeze some sauce on the edge of my plate.

"I can't see your butt from here. Which is a shame."

"Will. You don't have to flirt with me to make me feel better."

"I suspect this may make you feel a whole lot worse." Will comes around the island and hands me a letter. "It came by courier from school. You weren't fit to read anything—there's a briefing meeting but I told them you're not well enough. I'm going in later so I'll report back."

I rip open the letter, then scan the lines, taking in my biggest shock of the day. The letter's from Tarquin and I've been selected to be an English mentor. My pupils will be a group of second year behaviorally challenging kids, two of whom have had steadily failing grades. One of them is Sophie Charlton. Another is Ellen Davidson. The wildcard third pupil is...Lydia Salter. She's my achiever wildcard in the mix. It's like taking a lamb to the cynical slaughter. Team formulation made in hell.

"I'm a mentor. English class, second years."

"Well, if it helps any, I'm a sports mentor myself. And I'd rather have death by ballet."

But there's more news to follow as I open a second envelope inside the first one. I gulp twice in a row. I'm picked to be mentored in football at the hands of Mr. Will Darby's soccer star school. One of the two teachers who'll be battling each other for supremacy.

"I'm your mentee for Teacher Wars," I whisper. "Did you know?"

"I did. I got a letter too."

"I'm full now, can't face another bite."

And bugger me, but if a gang of big fat tears don't well up behind my eyes and burst forth to make their presence known.

"Oh, fucking hell." I properly start crying. For real, full Monty, a call the water board and find a stopcock situation. And in seconds Will Darby is holding me — in a robe without a lingerie lifebelt. I'm crying and gulping and he's rubbing my back and soothing me by telling me to stop and that it's all going to be okay.

Fuck. Holy commando. I should have left before breakfast when I had the chance. Going home barefoot and knickerless would've been so much easier to bear than this.

At least I've no makeup on or it'd be mascara madness. But my chest is falling and rising in enough of a mess all by itself. Shit. I'm really going for the Out of Order Oscars.

"I never cry. Ever. What the fuck is wrong with me lately?"

"And you an Arsenal season ticket holder. Surely you must cry at least once a month, if not more?"

"Fuck off, Will." I slap him on the chest. His pecs rebound my touch in a fit reminder of how stacked he is with male attributes.

"No. You're wearing my robe and eating my breakfast. I can annoy you as much as I want to."

"Bastard."

And that makes me start crying afresh. Proper boo-hoos of shame. I push my fingers up to my eyes to squelch the tears but I end up with wet fingers and more crying. Will comes close and reaches out to gently touch my arms.

"You're still ill, Iz."

"If I wasn't ill, I'd be going after Rogerson and Endermann with a scalping knife."

"That would make great viewing. I'd get the boys round to watch."

"They're shitbags!" I tell him. "I meant Rogerson and Tarquin. Not your friends."

"It's a TV show. You'll only be doing your job."

"Correction—public humiliation of the very worst kind."

Will stands to full height. And his voice is very commanding—I can see that he'll be a great teacher when he takes firm rein of a class. "I disagree. Reality TV. Just you. Being a teacher. Brazening it out because you're brilliant at your job and they can't scare you that easily."

"How do you know I'm brilliant?" I challenge.

"Because your friends and supporters have told me. Even kids!" Will stares at me with intense eyes.

"How can I learn football tricks? That's major crapola. I can't even hit a ball in rounders. I've two left feet."

Will stares at me and tries to coax a smile. "I promise I'll try to make it painless. You'll be heading the ball and keeping it up on your knee with little effort in only a few weeks' time. I have taught others—I know what I'm doing. And I solemnly swear I can turn you into a passable Pele!"

"Shit. But I don't want to do it."

"Izzy. Take it in your stride," Will tells me. "You get on and don't worry about what the TV show looks like. Do your job. It's a circus. Don't let it affect you. Stay true to you. Annie James from music has been selected to do the soccer skills task with you anyhow."

Judy Jarvie

And the record in my head skids to a screechy end. Shit! There's the day spoiler. Awesome Annie. Netherfield's biggest narcissist nymphomaniac would not be my work buddy of choice.

"Seriously?"

"I had a letter by courier. Read it if you want."

I rub my nose. I suspect it's blotchy and red and hideous. "I'm the least willing teacher in the school for this pile of crap! It's like they know that and enjoy the pain."

"For God's sake, don't cry or I'll have to do something drastic." He takes in a deep breath. Then sighs deeply and his broad chest inflates, as he comes closer still. "I'm in real danger around you. I want to do things..."

"Kill me. Yell at me. Yeah. I get that. Tell me something I don't know."

"Kiss you, you bloody arse-head woman! I've wanted to snog you since I met you!"

I stare at him, so shocked I rise from my seat. "Shut the eff up!"

Will runs his hand through his hair and his jaw is tight as he stares down at me. "I want to kiss you and touch you till we can't see straight. You make my fingers itch. You make me so crazy the only thing I can see is your lips and I have to swear at myself not to try to do something about it." Will says the electrifying words calmly and with ominous portent. Then he bends his dark head down to mine and waits. Patiently, mouths almost touching. "Now do you understand me?"

"Bad idea," I warn.

"All the best ones are."

Seconds later, he swoops. He pushes his lips to mine but I stall. "You should give this thought."

He growls in his throat. "I don't think my body gives a shit about the thinking side of things. Fuck logic, Izzy. I'm not made of stone!"

His lips touch mine. I pull back but the smell of him and the touch of his hands on my arms drives my libido on a swift joyride.

"What about Tessa? Will she walk in?"

"She's at home. With four kids and her fireman husband. Do you only kiss when there's an audience, woman?"

Again his lips are against mine. I gasp in my throat but I don't stop him. I suck in a mini breath and close my eyes. I push my lips into his warm and minty-scented ones. His breath is lovely, his mildly lemony cologne gives me goosebumps. And the feel of him up close has every neuron in me clamoring for more.

So I open my mouth and let him in. His tongue slides ably inside the seam of my lips and it dances against mine as I melt in his arms. He doesn't need a second invitation and I marvel at his kissing skills. He's a stunning striker in *all* ways. His fingers are in my damp, finger-combed hair and he's kissing me as I've never been kissed before. Wow.

Then he's my undoing. Will moans softly at the back of his throat and it's an adorable sound. Especially when his strong, muscular arms encase me and I feel him holding me in gladiator fashion. It's like a spin on a helter-skelter and I've got an unlimited ride ticket.

I let Will kiss me and I kiss him back. It's been a long time and I'm gratified that I don't need a refresher. It's like getting back on a bike and I'm off in third gear and wait a minute—now I'm zooming down the hill of snogging prowess at full speed!

His tongue tantalizes mine. His hand is near my groin, over my robe. I'm gasping for more and I can tell he's pretty fired up too. I find I like it more than a little and I tease him wantonly by pushing closer to him, playing with wildfire. Thank God, I mouthwashed and used the floss in the bathroom.

"Will." I put my hands up and touch his firm jaw line. I look down and the bulge in his white linen trousers can be denied by no man.

"I'd suggest slow. You're still an invalid, remember?"

"And we're making out in Paul Bates' kitchen in clear view of an open panorama kitchen window."

"What of it? We have twenty-feet-high fences round the perimeter."

"I've never snogged while being watched by a gang of Bambis before." I nod to the wildlife through the windowpane. The nature picture should include think bubbles with 'WTF?' written inside. When we both laugh, the deer bolt away.

"See. Problem solved."

We blink at each other, then Will seizes my hand. "Shit, that's it. We can't go frightening the wildlife. I have a plan."

He pulls me off the seat and picks me up like a daisy plucked from a lawn. I gasp as he strides across the kitchen.

"I sense the start of a bad idea."

"Stop being such a ruddy, controlling English teacher for once in your life, woman! Don't you believe in spontaneity?"

His command makes me quiver. And he snogs me again. My nipples peak within their fluffy velvet cocoon, as if reminding me that this is the worst idea ever in the entire world.

"For a bad idea, it feels damn hot to me," he growls.

Big revelation on this one, Tweet it at #*sexonfire* and #*erectnipplesandgaggingforit*—I'm a goner. When I'm in his arms and not facing him off like a shrew, Will's divine. I want him right back. He could rough me up anytime. Any which way.

He kicks open a door on one side of the kitchen and lights switch on automatically. It's a large storeroom that could ably cater to any discerning celebrity chef's outlandish ingredient needs. There are bottles of condiments and ingredients on towering shelves and foods and delicacies piled high.

"Paul's pantry. Is this private enough?"

"Depends what for?" I stare around. "He must have a gold card at the deli. But I fancy those stuffed pimento olives. If we can find a box of crackers to put them on…"

"Fuck!" he shouts at me. "No crackers. No Bambi eyes. No disturbances! No denials that this isn't what it is and necessary for us both! And, finally, no evading me." He slips me onto a nearby high-backed chair beside a large cook's prep area.

From the way he's already caressing my body through fabric, he clearly knows where all the turn-on knobs are located. And I don't mean on the cooker. Said knobs are singing siren songs for his speedy attention.

"I don't like cooking much."

He glares at me. "I only intend to be tasting you." His eyes darken and my womb goes on turbo boost. Which is perplexing, given my lack of underwear.

I lift my chin to whisper. "What about you going in to school?"

Will's growl is sexy as hell by my earlobe and causes a delicious lick of thrill. "Sod work when the party's started in your bathrobe and I've got a VIP backstage pass. If you're up for this — we might be a hot killer combo taste sensation. Let's put it to the test."

Chapter Eight

"Iz."

"Yeah."

"The robe is affecting me in good ways."

"I always said the black silk and red lace gig was overrated. No contest compared to plush microfiber by the meter."

"I'd shag you wearing a sack." As if to prove it, he squeezes my breast gently and kisses my neck.

"Your charm school etiquette needs a refresher, Darby."

"I meant I'm all over you like a rash in a good way." Will nips my neck to silence me. I think I drive him crazy. God help me. "Fuck, Izzy. I'm totally hot for you." Will tugs my robe collar and presses his lips to mine. The kiss is molten and leaves me panting. He pulls me close.

"I can tell." He knows exactly what I'm referring to. How could he not.

"I'm turned on because you're torture with talons."

"But I have short nails."

"I mean I want you so bad it's bittersweet. I need to take time to feel connection with you but when I'm with you, I can barely hold back. Can you handle that? If I want more from you than I can give back?"

Will stares down at my now gaping robe. There's plenty of ripe cleavage on display.

"What do you mean, Will?"

"I want to ravish you. But I might want to do it the slow route."

"I still don't follow. You want us to take things slow? Now?" I say.

"I want you fast. But when it comes to me, I may need patience and time. For a while I may be a one-sided lover."

"Meaning?"

"I want to give you orgasms. Lots of them. But I might not want to go there myself for now."

Oh. Wow. That's a bolt of a bombshell.

"Don't you like me to touch you?"

"It's just... Well. I need time. Can you handle an affair with me on those terms?"

I pout for effect. "Multiple orgasms. No expectation of reciprocal pleasure? Will, you ask a lot. As sick as it is, I'll take it."

"This is the cliff edge. Do we jump? I can't guarantee it'll be a smooth ride. But I sense you and me together will blow both our worlds."

Fuck. I'm still processing what he's asked of me. I want to ask why but something holds me back. He must have his reasons. And he's told me it's not me, it's him. Do I believe and proceed?

I watch Will, considering my reply. He's come clean and admitted attraction. In truth he's every lyric from all the Pointer Sisters songs come to life. Do I smart crack and stand off? Or for once in my life do I grab this situation by the lapels and wrap my legs around it? I vote Pointer Sisters all the way.

I level completely. "Will, inside this normal, boring disguise, I read erotica and dream wild dreams. I have unexplored sex fantasies. I crave excitement like a starved fox pacing the perimeter of a chicken farm. And you're opening a charcoal grill of sensual thrill with no expectation? Fuck sensible. It's time to snatch the platter and savor."

Will offers an approving nod and his eyes dilate as, inside me, something melts more. He touches my cheek, strokes behind my ear. Then he kisses me and I reel in wonder at the oblivion rush that is Will Darby, sex god. He spins me into orbit with the merest touch, and this isn't about fulfilling my forfeit—this is beyond meager requirements. Will makes my pulse thrum with need. I'm completely certain that sex together will shatter all else and replace it with parameters that will redefine lovemaking in my future.

"I want to give you pleasure, Izzy. I want to turn your life into sensual nirvana. And I love your kisses."

"I'm something of a fan of yours." I feel his smile as he kisses around my jaw line. For some reason *Creole Lady Marmalade* plays in my head but it totally fits. This is the closest I've ever got to wild. I smile and Will stops kissing.

"What?"

"You make me all hump-ready hot bordello hostess and I don't even have a corset in my closet." I kiss Will with urgency. He makes me want to be bad and ramp up the heat. Maybe it's because he's given me boundaries and limits? My skin is prickling in a good way and I yearn to kiss him, touch him and explore his body. I reach for him but he catches my wrists.

"Let me be good to you, baby."

My robe falls open when I move back and Will lets out a hiss.

He parts the fabric farther with his fingers. "Nice view."

I kiss him deeply and tempt him with my tongue. Then I nibble at his ears, his neck. When he pulls me back, I revel in the thrill of the way our tongues meet and that his breathing makes my own breath catch. There's deep longing that's been lurking inside me, like a storm that's brewed overlong in muggy weather. It's building to cause serious structure damage and possibly a power cut.

Since I've begun to read and write erotica and feel its calling, I've needed this. An illicit, spontaneous affair. I tease Will with my tongue and get a reaction like a swiftly rolling boil from him. My hand goes down to the bulge that's straining in his pants but a strong hand stops me.

He's as turned on as I am. Why the prohibition rules?

"No touching. For now. I'll tell you when that changes."

Will lays me back in the seat. I'm all but falling out of my robe. I push it aside, hardly caring that he's no more the gentleman and suddenly fast and eager. Will sweeps it off me and I'm naked in the pantry.

"Wow — that was fast."

"I can be when the moves count." He removes his top and, in seconds, he's shirtless. His chest is a hymn to worked-out, glossy skin and a sexy dusting of dark hair leads the eye lower than Will permits. His ramped breathing makes me horny.

"I want you, but I want to kiss you everywhere. Do you approve?"

I nod and he lowers his mouth to my ear.

"I can't hear."

"Yes."

Already there's a deep ache between my legs. As if sensing my thoughts and feelings, he instructs, "Let me touch you below."

As his hand meets my mound, my head is whooping for joy and trying not to listen to the screeches of trepidation in my head that tell me this is uncharted terrain. I do as he says. Sir Darby must be obeyed, surely? Will puts his fingers to my core and flicks deftly. He rubs and I know that I'm hot and totally damp.

"I have plans." The next thing I know, my wrists are held together tightly. At this point my brain and my womb go on crazy turned-on synch. Will's tying something. It's the robe belt. He must've kept it? "You like to be tied?"

"Never tried."

"You want to?"

"Uh-huh."

"Good answer, Miss Tennant."

I'm tied with my hands behind the back of the chair. At his mercy and arched for exploration.

Again his mouth comes close and his breath tickles the skin of my neck. He dips lower and takes my nipple between his teeth, then laves it with his tongue.

"You like?"

"Uh-huh. Oh yep."

He gently sucks as, with his hand, he does serious kneading and teasing to my other breast that sends my privates Def Con One. "I will kiss you all over. And then I'm going to make you come with my hand and my mouth. Deal?"

"Definitely." He's made me horny as hell saying the words. Already he's stroking the flesh of my breasts in soothing, smoothing strokes and I'm finding it rather stimulating. Each sweep of my flesh is like a whole body caress. My neurons and nerve endings are in a jangle but it's a good mess. A hot one.

"Would you like a blindfold?"

"Thought you'd never ask."

I love his low throaty chuckle. It's as if he'd read my favorite bits of Silver Tie Guy and thrown them together for maximum heat in minimum time. He's my Heaven-Sent Mr. Horny. He stands and fetches something from the rail. I suspect it's an apron. It gets a whole new use in Will's hands.

"Was that a yes?"

"Yes, blindfold. It's a goer."

"That would be, 'Yes, Sir'."

"Yes, Sir." I lick my lips to wet my parched mouth. Suddenly, I'm shaking and everything is heightened as if I'm on top of the highest Christmas tree in the world and just as lit up.

Will is doing exactly as promised — touching my skin. He swirls with palms and fingers and kisses me. My breasts, then my thighs, calves. My feet. My ankles. My décolletage. Who knew such places could be this erotic? He licks my collarbone too, as if savoring a meal. Then he comes back to my pussy.

"Relax, Izzy. This is a taster for us both."

I say nothing. His finger is on me. Then in me. Then on again. He's at my folds and I'm wet for him and up for whatever he wants to do — I'm unable to stop myself grinding his hand and pushing into those fingers. It feels so good, it's better than a continental chocolates buffet.

"You like that. Me too." His words are pure provocative mantras.

His fingers slide over my clit tip and he strokes, then slides. The restraint heightens the sensation. The blindfold has me feeling more turned on than ever. My senses are on overdrive, I'm shaking and I'm panting. He's barely touched me but I'm close to the edge and could scream. The rest of my body urges him on as I get off on his hand. My heart drums, breathing's ragged.

Then it's his mouth that claims me and I'm shaken, stirred and wired to the max.

With enthusiastic licks of his tongue, he masters my clitoris. I shudder with need at the impact of his every touch. His finger teases my breast and my nipple thrums to an aching peak. I moan for more and his mouth responds to my call. His hand is on the folds of my molten pussy and I can't breathe or hold in the noises.

I'm thrashing on the chair and all I can do is enjoy every stroke. And now I'm losing it and about to go over without him. I sense it's a whopper like I've never had before. The deft flicks and pressure are perfect for purpose.

"Oh hell. Will, fuck! Don't stop!"

"Thought you were lost for words, baby. Who needs to talk?"

His hand's back on my clit this time in earnest and he knows the moves that prolong my excitement. I'm shouting my appreciation and it echoes around the pantry — wow. The smell of citrusy hygiene wash will now forever remind me of spinning into erotic orbit on a chair, under Will's expert hand. Hands tied, blindfolded and blissfully overcome.

That caressing hand claims my clitoris fully and my body can't get enough as it explodes in waves of pleasure and I'm pushing myself up and into his hand and away with force and pumping movements. Unsure if it's for relief or to heighten this amazing sensation even further.

If this is desire, I want a lifetime subscription. He's barely touched me—I haven't touched him at all. But I'm screaming and wild as Will takes me to heaven—without a season ticket or a view of the goals. But plenty of appreciation of performance.

* * * *

I'm in the cocoon of Will's arms. His smell is divine but the spell breaks like a shop window in a night riot when he removes my ties and blindfold and pushes me to standing, then slaps my behind.

"You. Are. Bad."

Shit. Did that just happen? He made me come and now he's hurting my backside? If I wasn't a hard-core erotica fan I'd probably be having serious worries right now. Mr. Wonderful turned into Mr. Buttock Whip Crack in a blink.

"Why did you just slap my behind?"

I'm rather excited by this. Yeah, yeah, I know some women would be grabbing their bonnet and calling the plods. But I'm a seasoned erotica girl and this is a whole new side to Will that has me doing jiggery-pokery.

"You just slapped my arse."

"I did and I wanted to and I want to do it again. Izzy the Inflammatory. I find you make me itch to take revenge."

He didn't hurt me. I can tell it's in semi-jest, though it was a decided slap. And it was rather nice. I don't imagine I'll have a welted bum to show for it. But still, it was a surprise.

"I'll do it again unless you apologize."

"For what?"

"Handbag pic. Say 'sorry, Sir'." His tone suggests he's either pissed off or good at pretending he is. He sits on the seat where he made me orgasm and looks dark and tousled and even his nipples are gorgeous. He pulls my spanked arse down to sit on his knee. The erection is back to say hi.

"And what if I want you to spank me?"

"Good. We'll both be happy. I want to spank you and I want you to like it and loathe it."

In a jiffy he's propelled me onto his knee and he's spanking me like a good-un. And no, this is no *Guy with the Silver Tie* tame spanking for senior citizens showcase. This is full-on slapping my behind and each time gets harder. Trouble is, I'm laughing hard and squealing and turned on all at the same time. Wowzer — who knew?

"A photo from the web hardly deserves extreme vibrato smacking on the behind."

"Don't play with fire, Izzy Tennant. From now on overstepping warrants penalties. You will be disciplined. Especially since I'm your mentor. And especially since I know you like some hanky spanky."

I turn and grin over my shoulder. "More please."

But instead he caresses my buttocks and he teases me with his fingers – dipping back to the place he licked so very well.

"You like this more."

Oh God. I can feel my heightened state already and all he's done is touch me once. But even that touch of fingers over my folds, forward, back, in slightly and out has me ready for a full-on straddle and mount.

"Will…"

"Yes, darling. But you should call me Sir, remember? Don't slip up or there will be repercussions."

Shit, did he call me darling?

"Sir. Don't play with fire. When my backside gets it, I turn decidedly frisky."

"Oh. But frisky fire is exactly what I like."

He stops that tormenting finger as abruptly as the spanking had started.

"Let's leave you panting for more, shall we? I find that has greatest impact and I'm all for raising the stakes. I want to leave you feeling like you've been hit by a train. In the nicest way."

I'm peeved. My clitoris has woken up again and now he's asking me to cancel the party and force her feather boa back in its box. No way!

"No, Sir. I promise to do better." Wow. He made that sound as if this could be a regular gig. And now that my vagina's ready to do the lambada, it's having a minor strop in the corner that he's stopped. Will that be it? Or will this be a regular tryst arrangement? How do I feel about that? Um… Going by the way my body feels, I'd love it!

"I want you down there again…" I admit. Hell, my cheeks are flaming – both bottom and top – and I don't care. I'd rather be honest and blunt than left moist and panting.

"Good. Glad to hear it. But time isn't on our side... I need a shower too. Keep your desire warm and willing for me. I'll make it worth your while when I get back."

Now back to the pronounced shaft that's pressing against my upper thigh as I sit on him. "How do I say this...but...I'd quite like to make you feel good too? And there's something here that says it's not ready to take no for an answer."

"I meant what I said about limits." His gaze is firm and there's a glint of threat. "As gorgeous as you are, I do have to go to school now."

"With a hard-on? That could involve a night in the cells later."

"I'll take care of it. Work comes first."

"Work certainly comes before Will. Which makes Will a very dull boy in my book."

He replies, "We could revisit if you promise to stay the night?"

I don't answer. I'm pretty shocked at this little turn-up for the books. "You want me to stay?"

"Oh, I want you all right. Tip...of...the...ruddy...iceberg, Tennant. Bet your life on it! I want you every which way I can get you."

I watch Will pull on his shirt, then he takes me by the hand and leads me out of our pantry of passion.

This man who's so ably turned our brief acquaintance into private lessons in sex has turned my world on its head yet acts like it's all so easy, breezy business as usual.

"I'll report back after calling into school. You'll be here when I get back, won't you?" Will asks. "We'll go to bed. Then I'll cook dinner tonight. For now I must go change." He bends and kisses me softly on the forehead.

He disappears and I'm left to scan the palatial abode that is his home. But when Will returns in a fresh change of tracksuit and running shoes, he blows me sideways.

"Don't leave. Or do anything exciting without me," he warns. "Don't answer the door. Or the phone. But stay here and wait for me to come back and pamper you! And most of all…"

"What?"

"Don't you dare shave your bush. I like it that way. I suspect you'll go all coy and manic with the shaving gel and razor. I like it the way it is. In fact… I love it. It's perfect."

Fuck.

And how did he read my mind? I'd never have dreamed of getting the jiggy on without a full body depilation session. But it seems he likes me warm and fuzzy.

"Can't I shave my legs?"

"Only legs. That delight between your legs is all mine. And I like it perfectly formed the way I found it."

F.U.C.K.

I do want to stay. And I want my private terrain between my legs to be his. And what the fuck have I turned into? I nod and wink at him.

"Consider it pass code protected in the name of Will."

He laughs loudly and my womb tremors in delight at that. "You are the woman of my most scandalized dreams." He blows me a kiss then departs. The door clicks and he's gone. Damn, that man is good!

"I can't believe I am doing this!" I say softly to myself. I think I might have slipped into somebody else's life by mistake—but hell, fuck, bugger, I don't intend ever giving it back when it feels this good.

* * * *

I stand at the hallway window, watching the deer on the outskirts of the grounds of Hangley Grange. I know how they feel—skittish, afraid, bewildered.

How will we hide our thing? Do we even have a thing? What's with his 'don't touch me yet' shit? I haven't even felt his thing. Oh, so many thing issues. Can we keep such a big secret?

I still can't believe I've let rash lust and hormones have free rein. The sublime echoes of Will linger on me like a favorite scent. But it's a scary, dark *parfum* with an imperative secret under note.

In two days my world has been hijacked. By a man who's intent on making me come and hiding his own stash of goods. But the sex is fantastic!

I mosey round the rooms and end up in the lounge. The cinema TV screen's so wide and there's a load of newspapers across the sofa. I pick up a couple to take them back to bed and something I see stalls me like a ghost sighting.

It's Janey. On the cover of a tabloid daily newspaper. *Fuck.*

She's with Ben Lindhurst but the words aren't as flattering as her picture. "Football Ace's Knockout Lady Has a Shady Sexy Secret," reads the headline.

My pulse shoots off at knots and I know I have to do something. I'd call her but I don't even know where my phone or handbag are. And the former is likely out of charge. Nor do I know how to lock the door. But I'm at the landline phone and I'm calling Mo because I have her shop phone number memorized. We'll work the lock out later. Janey needs us.

I have to go. My friend's in jeopardy. As much as I don't want to walk out on what's happened with Will, my friends' needs come first.

Chapter Nine

Mo answers my summons without delay or comment. It's only when I'd called her that I'd realized I don't know where Hangley Grange is. I left it to Mo and Google Maps to find out and she arrived twenty minutes later. She's shouting swearwords into the security entry phone by the time I work out how to open it.

"You took your time answering! Effin' hell, Iz. Just look at this gaff," she says, slamming her car door.

I know it's grand. But I'm only appreciating a tiny inch of how palatial it is myself given that I've spent most of my time here in bed, in one way or another. But I'm not telling Mo that.

"How did you end up 'ere?"

"I was ill and a shining knight helped me."

"Rich bloody knight. It's like an effin' safari park. Has he got a woman? Is he lookin' for applicants?"

"I'll ask when I see him."

"Tell him I'd give him free chocolate for life."

Admittedly her tiny, battered Fiat 500 looks humorous in the driveway fit for a palatial Dorne set from *Game of Thrones*. But this is no time for comparisons. "Give me your phone. Mine's kaput and this call's urgent."

"I need to leave," I say to Will, on the number he'd left in the kitchen, as soon as I'm through. "How do I set the locks and shut the door? Must go. My pal Mo's here and she's going to drive me."

"Sure you're well enough?"

"Yes. This is a big problem. It needs sorting."

"Let it lock on double bolt. I'll get the property maintenance company to set the alarm. If you don't mind hanging on for twenty minutes, they'll sort it before you leave." Will's voice is all serious school master, so I can tell he's occupied with people waiting for him to put the phone down. I'd smile if I wasn't stressed.

"Tell them it's your mad wife. I've escaped from the attic and I'm boiling the pot-bellied pigs."

Come to think of it, he'd make a wonderful Mr. Rochester. He's that kind of magical mix of dark and changeful grumpy bastard and super stud hunk. He also has strange secrets about nobody touching or getting access to his member. Shit. Why do I keep coming back to that?

"Thank you for your suggestion." I can almost hear his teeth grinding and the image of that flexed jaw is so worth it.

"Later then, Mr. Stroppy." With that, our conversation's over.

No 'Hi, how are you?' No chitchat in the aftermath of his orgasm mastery. No friendly, brief banter. Just terse instructions. But right now Janey needs me more.

"Do we have to go?" Mo whines at me. "I'd give both my legs for a tour. It's effin' amazeballs."

"Be sensible, Morag!" She hates it when I call her that.

Mo pulls a face. "You can't call me here then not let me see. I want to look. I want to do cartwheels over the lawns and snoop through cupboards!"

"You have thirty minutes. Knock yourself out."

As we leave, I put the offending newspaper article into Mo's hands. "Take me to Janey's. That needs fixing."

Mo reads, "'Teacher Janey by day. Pole dancing vamp by night. For demure-looking special needs teacher Janey Woodside sidelines as a pole dancing pro. Her sexy tricks are some of her many charms. And it's her asset-showing moves that have Ben Lindhurst hooked! Close friends say Ben's talking long-term futures.' Effin' hell on a fire-spitting Harley!"

I urge Mo to stop talking and get driving.

The action squad are on the case. From wrist-bound sex to S.O.S. Today I'm covering it all.

* * * *

"You look better than when I last saw you," Janey tells me as we hug. She's remarkably chipper for somebody whose life's been tabloid-marauded. No sign of tears and she's acting like her usual happy self.

"Thanks for sending me stuff. You're a rock."

"Ben, meet Izzy and Mo, my friends," Janey says and we all shake hands and exchange 'pleased to meet yous' with the global football icon that is Ben Lindhurst. He's handsome. And he has a nice vibe, as far as it's possible to know.

"Didn't you go to work?" I ask, fearing Janey's hiding from the world now that she's tabloid fodder.

"I had a dentist appointment this afternoon and Ben took me. Ben's staying over. He's cooking dinner tonight. Why?"

Janey's golden, light-filled sunroom is decorated like a cream-themed film set fit for a princess to preside in. Bronzed, virile and dressed in neutral loungewear, Ben is the latest accessory to complement her perfectly executed tableau.

But while Mo and I are hyped and stressed about things, we've walked into serenity corner. Scented candles flicker, lilies stand in a gleaming vase. Tinkly spa music drifts on repeat. Ben's outfit goes with Janey's cream linen shirt and palazzo pants. It's as if they've walked out of a catalog shoot. Um, where's the drama? WTF? Why isn't Janey in floods of tears?

I hold up the newspaper. "Have you seen this?"

We watch as they smile and blow tiny kisses to each other. If I hadn't been so ill, this act may well have challenged my stomach's fortitude.

I reach over and hand Janey the article, guilt stabbing me for shattering this little nook of Namaste.

She dismisses it with a hand wave. "We've heard about it from Ben's agent."

"It's kinda bad," I say.

"It's toxic, Izzy. By absorbing the story, I'll be contaminating my mind."

"She's right, ladies. Tomorrow it'll be another headline. Another story. We must rise above the frequency of drama," Ben advises.

I'm pausing here. This isn't the Janey I know. She has been known to like Pilates and occasional yoga classes. She enjoys a trip into a hippie shop for the odd CD. She usually likes a good random wallow in the fountain of drama like the rest of us, however. Usually.

Am I wrong in thinking she's somehow swum a good stretch farther into the New Age lake of mystical mellowness than we've realized? I'm thinking Ben's big when it comes to vibes.

"So you don't care?"

"No."

I watch him with a pinch of worried wary. "It's patently untrue. But Rogerson might get concerned when he sees it. Did you talk to him about it yet?"

"I have. It's cool."

"So he knows the story is lies? How did they get a pic of you coming out of a pole dancing club anyway?"

Janey stares at Ben. Ben stares calmly back.

Their serenity reminds me of the big Buddha statue on a lotus flower at the local museum. "I am a pole dancer. I don't perform—I teach. Rogerson was shocked. But it's not a problem. He won't sack me. I've agreed to help with the BBC filming project."

Mo and I are staring, our jaws dropped lower than low. "You pole dance? You've never told us." Mo asks.

I'm glad. I need it repeated too. In triplicate.

"I've done it for years."

"Shit."

"It's very good for body and mind. I don't tell anyone. I don't go to Pilates. I only tried it briefly. I consider it a white lie. Pole dancing is my passion and I go three times a week. But not in the seedy way you imagine."

"So how did they know?"

"No idea. Somebody must've told newspapers or seen me with Ben and followed me. I taught a class on Wednesday. A photographer must've followed."

"Holy Mariachi bands and jumping jalapeños!" Mo loves her Batman exclamation speak. Each one's a creative event in itself.

"Wow. Janey. This is news," I marvel.

"Actually, ladies," Ben clarifies, "it's only the start of Janey's new future, taking pole dancing to the masses. We're not doing drama, are we, Janey? You're facing things and making your mark."

Janey looks at us all in turn—so serene she could give the Mona Lisa a run for her money. "I welcome the opportunity. I'm an athlete and I'm creative in choreography. I am Janey and I pole dance—now the world's going to know the truth."

Um, it already does love, says the cynical voice in my head. *And I have a hunch you're going to be in the papers for a long, long time to come.*

* * * *

I'm back at home, lying on my sofa, pushing Janey's random, raunchy secret surprise from my mind.

I'm feeling better but as soon as I got in, I showered and donned my PJs. I'm planning on a solo chow mein takeaway from Wongkee Garden tonight and, hopefully, a chapter or two of my current erotica read.

The doorbell rings as I've pulled my coziest throw over my legs. I swear then get up to answer. I'm pretty sure from the male silhouette through the door glass that it's Will. Or a pretty damn good doppelganger.

"Will Darby."

"You didn't stay. I might consider that warrants a penalty?"

Shit. I'd forgotten about his arse-slapping preferences until now.

"Did you find your crazy escaped wife?" I ask him.

"Just have. She's at home in her bunny pajamas. She's lookin' pretty hot too!"

My, but something inside me swells and thrums — ah, that's it. Estrogen and the impact he has when he fantasizes about me as his wife. Fuck. *What. Is. Wrong. With. Me?*

"Hi, Temptress Tennant." He raises an eyebrow. He's debonair. He virile. He's hot. Even in a shirt without tie, and chinos, he rocks. My womb is purring like a vixen escaped from foxy town.

"I knew those rabbit pajamas would be a hit."

"Hardly." I narrow my eyes. "Why are you here? Is it because I forgot to pay for them? Can I write a check?"

Will says, "Invite me in?"

"Isn't that what vampires say?"

Will scowls. So I step aside, let him in and close the door. "I'm here because I wanted to check on the patient. And Jack was all for coming over and doing this job for me. I figured you might rather have me. Who would you rather give you a tuck in and a kiss?"

I sigh. "So Jack wasn't available." I suck in my urge to laugh. I welcome in the man who excites my loins like no other.

"Did you sort out your problem?"

"I'd tell you but it's all so bizarre I can't even begin. I'm feeling tired and emotional. Think it's caught up on me." I put my wrist to my head in a pure drama meets weary pose.

"Go lie down again. Have you eaten yet?" Will has a bag. It's marked with the Italian deli's logo. Crazy, given all the ingredients in his pantry, but I let it pass.

"I've nothing in — haven't shopped. I planned takeaway."

Will shows me the goodies. "I'm cooking. I said I would. Mario at the deli has gone a bit overboard. So…let's get to it!"

I point him to the kitchen. "You'll make somebody a lovely wife."

"Lie on the couch, woman. We'll eat, then I'll put you to bed. Then I'll leave you to recover."

I lie down and pull up my throw to my starting position. "Um. Will?" I'm feeling naughty.

From my follicles to my toes, it's zizzing inside me like live voltage.

"Yeah." He's already out of his jacket and rolling up sleeves, chopping things up with my big chopper. I knew he'd be a big chopper man. Knew it sure as eggs are eggs.

"I am feeling tired. But I'm kinda not sure I want you to leave me all alone tonight yet…" I bat my lashes on super speed.

He smiles. "No touching still applies."

"I can handle that." *Oh, believe me, babe. I can handle all you can give me.*

"I'm so very pleased you said that," he tells me.

My womb is happy dancing and hitting a *piñata* till it's pulverized.

* * * *

I resist the urge to give a blissful moan at how good the food is. Pasta salads with a light dressing and something amazing made from roasted sweet potatoes. Who knew this would rock my world?

"I spoke to Rogerson regarding your wariness about me mentoring you in football."

"You did?"

"For some reason I think Rogerson reacts well to me, no idea why."

I tell him with my mouth full. "Tottenham fan. Why bloody else?"

"Anyway, I told him and he says if you don't want to do it, then that's fine. But the English teaching element is his main 'must do'."

I chomp as I mull this over. "Wow — you did that for me?"

"I did. Call it my softie side."

"Do you mind if I leave you to the perils of Musical Annie? She's a nympho by the way."

"I know. She's my idea of hell on heels." Will shakes his head. "I want you to be happy, Iz. Though, for what it's worth, I think you'd be great. If you gave yourself the chance to try, you could master a few football tricks and that's honestly all that's being asked here."

I push in another delicious, sublime forkful. "I'll think about it. But I'm pretty sure if I have a get-out clause, I'm going to take it."

"Shame. I was looking forward to a bit of rough and tumble on the pitch with you." Will places his fork on his empty plate and pushes it aside. He crosses the space between us like a green-eyed, sleek panther intent on a kill. He takes the fork from between my fingers and pushes the morsel between my lips. "Let me feed you..."

I moan as I bite down on the fork. "You're bad for me."

"You're hungry. Let me satisfy you. There's dessert so keep room for something indulgent..."

"Tiramisu?" I bat my lashes.

"Don't spoil the surprises. I said I'd make your night tonight and I still intend to," Will tells me and pushes his mouth to mine.

It's going to be a long evening. And, for the first time ever, I'm jubilant I got so ill. It's brought such amazing fringe benefits.

* * * *

I'm raw molten heat inside as Will stares at me across my bed. My bedroom was recently styled in muted shades of taupe in an effort to keep it minimalist and trendy. I now realize that Will is the only ornamentation this room has been yelling for. And now I have him I don't intend to waste the opportunity.

"Strip for me," he commands.

I'm wearing PJs so it's an easy enough feat. Three seconds and I'm bare. And every pore is goosebumping—for him. I know I'm blushing.

"Don't be coy, lie down. Wait for me. I don't have to prove how much I want you." He's right—there's plenty of evidence tenting out his trousers.

I grin up at him as I lie back. I feel like a model in a painting by one of the Old Masters—voluptuous and come hither and uninhibited, all at once. It feels damn good. He kisses me and in a matter of moments his mouth is on my thighs. I'm not complaining, it's blissful and I find I have a particular preference for his own unique brand of five o'clock shadow against my sensitive, intimate skin.

But already it's back to Will's mouth on me. I daren't complain when he's as good as he is, but I'm sensing a pattern.

"You taste so good, I have to savor."

I lie back and welcome him like donning a favorite outfit. We fit so well. And when his tongue meets my clitoris and circles my folds, I'm utterly at his mercy again. Will manages to induce orgasm in record speed. I'm weak and quaking at his touch as he licks me into a stellar orgasm that pulses on and on so deep I wonder how he and I can breathe.

"Wow. You do that so well you must've taken classes!" The sheen of perspiration makes me feel like I'm marathon woman.

Will sits back and grins. "Let's say I've an inspiring subject."

"Please tell me we're going to do it," I say, staring at his proud member to relay my true meaning. It's tenting his trousers as if trying to capture our attentions. It certainly has mine.

"Maybe not in the way you think."

Damn. This man is all confusions and contradictions. Why doesn't he peel down his pants and let me welcome him home to mamma? Okay, I'm not Mrs. Experienced. I've never been ultra-wild but I'm certainly keen and I know enough from my reading to give this a stellar attempt at enticing the man. Whether it be a blow job or a happy hand of heavenly pleasure, I'll give it my best. If reverse cowgirl would stir his stallion, I'd happily get to it.

I want to touch, to taste and to explore. I'm definitely picking up severe constraints and reticence issues in this department and it bothers me more than a touch.

"Will. I want to see you naked." Turn-on makes me bolder. I thrust my chest out a bit for emphasis and he hisses between his teeth. He's shucked off his pants and his shirt's flown across the room pretty sharpish as if it's outside Dorothy's shack in Kansas during the tornado. All that's between us and another very good time are clingy sports boxers. "Come to Iz, I promise I'll be kind," I urge, as if they're the magic red ballet shoes and I'm about to seize the upper hand.

But reticence lingers heavily like the smell of party poppers after the New Year's bells.

"I'm going to be specific. I'll make you come with my mouth, my hand. And if this goes further, in lots of other varied ways. I'll do it so well and so fast your head won't be on straight for days. That's a promise, Iz. But when it comes to touching me, there are rules."

An ice wash trickles through my bloodstream and my cells go on sensitivity wary mode. "Um... Will. What's up here?"

"Can't you go with me on my needs? Can't you follow orders?" His tone's changed. "It's not a lot to ask."

Hell, the whole vibe in the room's changed. From tones of neutral to shades of scarlet and dark-striped Will-who-must-be-obeyed. He has a firm expression I don't want to cross, and a tone that's pure RSC lead hero part at Stratford-upon-Avon during a pathos scene.

"I care for you, Izzy. But when it comes to sex, we have to do it my way or no way."

"Why so strict, Sir? Surely a little fun might cheer you up?" I'm gulping down more reservations than a box set of *Bonanza*. But simply because I don't know what's up or how this dynamic has changed. I realized he wanted a slow lead-up but a little more info would help here.

I want him—but I want to know the score. I sit up. I hug my knees. And I pull for my robe from the end of the bed.

"I can sense you find my preferences difficult."

"It's not your preferences. It's the mystery and cloak and dagger shit. Why don't you tell me what's going on here?"

Will stares at me, then simply shrugs. "I can't be what you want me to be."

"But all I want is to turn you on."

He sits beside me and his hand is on my thigh, rubbing lightly. "It's something you'll have to get used to. And it's not up for discussion."

"Will. I want you. I think we share a connection. But if this is going anywhere, you have to tell me what this is all about."

Will stares at me. He's looking down at his feet, but then I notice the problem is staring me in the face. It's in his lap. His hard-on is gone.

"Are you getting my signal?" he asks. "I can't promise the earth will move. Sometimes it will. Sometimes…not."

I gulp as realization dawns on fast flow. "Shit, Will. I'm sorry."

"Don't be. This is the very reason I didn't want to tell you. Apologies are even shitter than the obvious disappointment."

Will's eyebrows furrow so hard he must've had input from a plow and oxen. He sits on the bed, like a man defeated after battle, and every pore of me wants to take back my words and hug him close.

"Will. I… I don't know how to…"

He gets up swiftly and I can tell he's brimming with fire, rage and humiliation. A mix that, if it were to go on a Guy Fawkes bonfire, would combust in a deadly fashion.

"Ironic. I'm the striker who can't score in the goal mouth. Now you know. Satisfied? Or should we make that decidedly unsatisfied in a very important way."

"Will, that's not even funny. But... How did it happen?"

He stares at the now flaccid wreck of his earlier erection. He turns to face me. He pulls me close to gently kiss my cheek then my forehead. I kiss him back and the gesture's tender and arousing — I notice, from the feel of him at my groin area, that his pants are telling me that he's finding it that way too. We're back in business.

A big part of me lets out a sigh of relief. So...he's not exactly impotent because he clearly gets excited, like now. It's not me being the biggest turn-off ever in the history of the world. But there's still something else...

Will rises and retrieves his shirt. He dons it and does up the buttons with his back to me. "Don't say anything. You don't need to. I like you, Izzy. And nothing you've done or said is wrong. I need space."

He walks to the door, his expression darker than his hair. But he's stooping some and that leaves a dent of pain in my heart.

"Don't go, Will! Please? I'm so sorry I brought this up."

"No, you're right. You need explanations. But I'm not ready to give them. I need time. I'm sorry. This won't work."

Will walks out of my room. I hear his heavy footfall on the stairs then the door slam. And he's gone.

Chapter Ten

I have a whole weekend to fester and wonder. About Will and how everything blew apart. And yes, there's a whispering shroud of guilt that jabs me at regular intervals to make me uncomfortable about how things turned so wrong so fast.

What a bitch you were, the shroud reminds me. For a shroud it's got an annoying voice and it's quick to judge.

The man has a problem but you didn't need to force him to confront it immediately. I pause for thought on this because it's true — erectile problems go hand in hand with questions about male identity and virility. *Why were you such an aggressive harpy about it?*

I have no answers except yes, I was wrong and too fast to force things. Will Darby's gone. He nursed me back to health, hand-orchestrated my biggest ever orgasms most splendidly — twice. Then took off like the proverbial bat from the abyss because I had the audacity to question his most private privates.

As scenarios in life go, nobody could have guessed at this one. Now we'll work in the same building while trying to avoid contact. I'll have to see him at meetings. Face my nemesis with him as a mentor. Shit karma or what?

I have, in my defense, tried to text him. Twice. I kept them brief and light but there has been no answer or reply. So I've stayed home. Read two books cover to Kindle cover. Almost considered going over there to speak with him then totally talked myself down. Then I've done what I needed to do most. I've written erotic sex scenes.

Just like I've experienced with Will. And a few more that are purely from my fantasy erotic imagination and yes, he's the starring hero. My keyboard's been smoking and I hasten to admit I've been in a pretty high state of thrill through fiction alone. And all the while my guilty conscience smarts and snaps like a poorly put out campfire with the latent potential to take out an eye. Or at least maim me irreparably in the groin region for life.

I pay homage to his skills as a lover by writing about them on my laptop. I write about sex with Will because it has changed me. I never expected what I could become.

* * * *

Next day I'm gobsmacked to find out we've a new addition in the Netherfield car park. It's a small gaggle of photographers bedecked with lenses and cameras and flasks of coffee. They're waiting by the car park gates with menacing portent.

As I'm wracking my brains on why—well, I have been off for a few days and a lot can happen in a short time—I realize the answer and it bugs me to swearing point. *Janey. Shit. Kill the fuckers.*

They're here to catch the pole dancing diva. As I lock the car, I'm about to go and give them a mouthful until Jack shows up with one other burly junior janitor called Phil. I assume they're going to tell them to get off school property sharpish—they'll likely use data protection to cover a myriad of ills.

I can't see Janey's car in the car park. I'm thinking she's not in yet—either that or maybe Ben's dropped her off? Good job.

And as I'm walking through the car park searching for Janey, I spy Dibian in her car. Now, call it my Spidey Sense but something's not right. She's eating doughnuts. One in each hand. Something jars. I reverse walk to stand beside her Volvo and tap on the window. She rolls it down. I see the mascara tracks telling a story all of their own.

"Bollocks, Dibs."

"Don't be nice to me, I'll only cry more." Her voice is a tired squeak.

"Let me the fuck in. What the hell's up?" She may be my boss but we know each other well enough by this length of time working together. We've weathered sufficient Christmas parties and private bitching sessions to ably know gritty reality's swearword-infested tundra.

She may be a crap head of department but her heart's in the right place. "You don't want to know, darling." She's sniffing—it isn't hay fever season.

"Course I want to know. Fess up."

"I can't bear it."

"I won't budge until you do." I give her my death glare. "And I don't care if I'm late for class or if we sit here all morning and I lose my job but you're going to confide."

"Oh, fucking all right but it's totally dire. I'd rather not go there. Online arsing dating, that's what! I've been duped by a charlatan and he's ripped me off big time. Taken my money, promised me a Christmas wedding and now he's left with half my heirloom jewels." And now her tears and her nose are running afresh and she looks like a makeup counter car crash, straight through the decency central reservation.

Dibian pulls a hanky from the top pocket of her ruby tweed suit and blows her nose with sufficient gusto for a cruise liner blast. "Met him months ago. Marios. Thought I'd met The One. Of course I believed his sweet lines and didn't for a minute question why somebody as gorgeous and young as him wanted an old boiler with bingo wings like me. He had the cutest arse in the galaxy, darling, and I don't even want to talk about how well hung he was. Anyway, that's history. He's dumped me, nicked my money. He's not even called Marios at all."

"The bastard!" I interject, but she's still going strong.

"He's a ruddy Ronald and there's another six women he's scammed. The police came last night. He's made off with my building society savings and two credit cards. I haven't slept a wink. The bugger even adopted an elephant in my name—I'm thinking it was a cruel joke. It's virtually all I'm left with. A virtual elephant called Whopper." She howls. Proper gusto.

I feel like a plumber who dared to press the bowed ceiling and got the whole deluge of flood—rafters and all—upon his sorry head. But Dibian is golden-hearted and doesn't deserve this sorry situation.

"Shit, Dibs!" I pull her for the hug she needs. It proves to be a sticky hug. She's eaten a heck of a lot of therapeutic doughnuts. Most of them double glazed and supersized.

"Don't dare tell a soul."

"As if. But you're going home," I tell her.

"I can't. Work is all I have!" Another wail escapes her peony lips, one that's so bad I need ear defenders to withstand it.

"I'll see Rogerson. I'll tell him you're ill with the bug and I'll come and see you later. Can you drive?"

I look at her. It's a rhetorical question. She could drive but I might have a pile-up and a roundabout multi-catastrophe news bulletin on my conscience. "I'll get Jack. He'll drive you. That bastard Marios…"

"Ronald! Ronald Brown! Rhymes with clown," she corrects. "I'll never face a drive-through McDonald's again!"

"Whoever the hell he is—as God is my witness, he will pay. Because Ronald's a rogue. But for now, you're going to watch the Comedy Channel, eat ice cream and think about booking a cheap holiday online to somewhere hot very soon."

I dial Jack's number. What would I do without my superhero, situation savior janitor? Answer? I'd be in a lot more shit more regularly than I could cope with.

He answers my call, and Jack can't contain a long sentence about how he and Will Darby have been getting to know each other and went out for a coffee, but I have to stall him. I don't even go there with the tiny needle stab of pain in my heart when he mentions Will's name. I block it out.

"I'm so sorry, Jack, now's not the time. We'll talk later. Dibian's unwell and needs a lift, can you oblige? We're in her car in the car park. Come pronto."

"Mistress Hicks taken poorly? Of course — on my way."

"And if Rogerson asks, she's green and you had to stop in lay-bys."

"Copy that. Over and out."

He's with us in less than a minute, willing to oblige, and the relief in Dibian's tear-stained face is ample reward. Now I'll have a speedy, impromptu meeting with Rogerson. There are several things I need to handle. My own mentoring slot being the most pressing.

* * * *

I catch the esteemed headmaster of Netherfield Secondary School at his desk, thumbing through a copy of *Candle Making Weekly*. Who knew? I think he may even have gone up in my estimations.

"Izzy, what can I help with?" He hides the magazine in the desk drawer before I'm fully through the door.

"Dibian's ill. I took the liberty of sending her home. After last week I have a good eye for the signs and she's definitely got my bug."

"Diligently spotted." Rogerson sits as far back in his chair as possible as if remembering I recently had a deadly plague. "Are you quite well? Sure you should be back? I heard stories, a pretty grim affair."

I'm taken aback. Mostly because he makes it sound like I'd turned half zombie and I'm eyeing his limbs as a snack. It was nothing that a rest and a bucket of bleach didn't put right.

"I'm well. And Dibian's classes need covering. I've two free periods later so I'll gladly step in."

"Very good." Francis steeples his fingers. "Anything else?" He's gagging to get back to that candle how-to—he was probably in the middle of *Wick Trimming for Dummies* and I'm detaining him.

"I also want to talk about football skills. Will Darby mentioned you may be amenable to me taking a leave of absence?"

Francis gives away nothing. I wonder for a flicker of a moment if Will's made it up. "We had a conversation. But things have moved apace. You will have seen Janey's predicament in the newspapers?"

"Yes—crazy business. I came by to say I will do the football skills mentor participation. I've thought long and hard and I realize part of the point of the exercise is for people to face demons. Playing football is mine. I love the beautiful game and I hate the fact that I can't do it justice. But I should try. I think appreciating Will's skill on the pitch will do me good."

"A very wise move." Francis dons his predatory feline smile. "Just as well as I can't spare you. I need you in the slot and Tarquin agreed."

"Oh." I'd thought I was being magnanimous. I thought this would help me put things right with Will.

Turns out he wouldn't have let me leave anyway. Am I annoyed or am I perturbed? And either way, does anybody care? So much for Will's assurances. I'm more piqued than a very piqued person. I have held a grudge with Rogerson since he set me up with Tarquin the Terrible's ominous campaign of reality TV humiliation in the first place. I'd make an impassioned plea but I sense it's pointless.

"You like candle-making, Francis?"

"I do indeed. It's something of a fascination."

I nod. "I can imagine. In fact I have experience."

Francis looks up and over the top of his half-rim specs. "You do?"

"Yes, and you'd make an exceptional chandler. My nana used to make candles so I picked up a lot of tips."

His radiance glows in response. "Why thank you, Isabella. Perhaps you could help me out with a project or two?"

"Perhaps you could tell Will Darby to be lenient on me and cut the football footage time?"

"I'll certainly have a word."

"And perhaps you could ask Tarquin to tone down the football mentoring slot and then I'd have more time for private tuition in Nana's candle secrets? I'll show you how my gran's famous magic wish candles are created."

He smiles. "A phenomenal suggestion — I'll speak to Tarquin. I'll make sure it's agreed."

I keep quiet on my real opinions on why candle-making suits him. Mostly because he gets right on everybody's wick and we'd happily watch him burn. Preferably slowly.

Taking on private lessons will be okay if I have Rogerson on my side. And if I have to use my candle-making craft ken to lure a good deal, I'm willing to go there. Sometimes you have to set light to the only taper you've got.

* * * *

I plan to seek Will out at lunch break. It's time to confront our deadlock. But when I venture to the PE department—and, shit, this is becoming a far too regular habit—he's not there.

Due to the fact that I still haven't got my appetite back, I didn't bring any lunch. So I detour via the canteen. I'd been thinking salad roll or healthy pitta but when I walk in, the fatty fug of freshly made French fries hits me like a welcome but waistline-damaging wave. The simmering pot of slutty temptress baked beans in their steel serving dish winks and hypnotizes me into submission.

"Beans and chips please. Double portion, Rita."

Dinner belle Rita scoops but doesn't comment—she knows when to keep the lips zipped.

My stomach growls like Bigfoot in the wilderness. Or at the very least Chewbacca grizzling at Han Solo. I'm carrying my fries-and-beans-laden plate to the checkout when I see Will and my stomach freefalls.

He's sitting at a table, looking stellar, relaxed, gorgeous. Way more sexy than Han Solo ever could, and he was damn fine. But he's opposite a glammed-up, eyelids batting, blonde hair swishing empire threat of the very worst kind. Nympho Annie from music and it looks like she's practicing her prelude to praying mantis. My inner Jedi is mortally wounded and I stagger back to regroup.

Then I scream inside my head—*fuck, fuck. No.* Something twists within my ribcage and my deepest emotions crash and commit GBH on my heart. It's beating crazy fast. I think the string basket that holds my coronary organ snapped under the weight of what happened this weekend.

It's carnage. My pulse is staging a mutiny that's telling my brain to march over and take action. But I ignore the bloodstream rush. If she wants him and he wants her—I have to live with that. The dark forces will overcome and I'll hand my lightsaber in for confiscation.

Even though my insides are staging a protest that the man I'm kinda attached to is sitting with another woman and my body wants to revolt, I cannot take action. I made him walk away.

They're laughing, smiling. Eating pesto pasta salad together as if they're on a Tuscan veranda, having made thunder love in a pink-walled villa.

I can't smile through it. I try but I have to put down my tray and plate because my hands are shaking.

Even Doreen behind the tills is looking at me oddly and repeating, "One pound twenty, love," over again at me as if I'm dense. I scrabble for the money and drop it on my tray.

"You all right, duck?"

"Fine."

"'Eard you were ill, love. You still don't look right if you ask me. Peaky," she tells me. "'Eard Darby the hunk saved ya. Lovely chap. Such nice manners and soft hands. Sexy eyes too!" She winks.

"I'll put in a word for you."

She cackles and blushes like a girl. "Please do. I'd trade in my Stan for that new model any day! And those fingers can hold my hand anytime—amongst other things."

I have to stifle a gasp. Even Doreen's noticed my personal hidden fave thing about Will. His hands. And he'll never touch me again.

I splutter out a gasp and I can tell from her face that she's worried I'm going to puke.

"Are you all right?" she asks over and over and over like an echoey dream.

I'm not right. I may never be again. I'm in love with Will Darby. Or at least my heart is. And how the hell am I ever going to live with that or put that right in a month of Sundays? I may as well put my chips and beans in the bin. It's not the sick bug, it's being heart sore and it hurts.

I walk from the canteen and I have to stop the tears. How ruddy ridiculous am I? Crying over a boy. And he's not even an Arsenal supporter. He's the enemy. Tottenham Darth Vader.

* * * *

When the home time bell rings, I almost sing in relief and thanks. It's been a very long day.

As the kids pour out, I bid them goodbye and stand on a chair to close the top windows I'd opened when it got too muggy.

"Hey, Izzy."

I almost fall off the chair when I see Will. "Hi." I get down, hoping I don't land in a heap.

"How are you?"

"Good. You?"

"Likewise. Actually… That's a lie. I'm shit."

I shrug. "Me too. Kinda."

"Rogerson tells me that they're downplaying football in *Class Wars*. Thought you should know. He tells me you told him you wanted to go ahead." His eyes are solemn when he holds my gaze.

"I did. You made me realize that facing things can be a good thing." I shrug. "I have to open up, quit opposing, and move on."

Will stalks to me and, in a matter of seconds, he grabs my hands. "Yes. I get the point."

"What point?"

"Facing things. You made your unspoken point fully heard. I need to change. I shouldn't preach to you when I hide and evade myself."

Shit! I hadn't even meant to do that but if it works and we're talking and he's smiling—which he is now—and holding my hand then I'm all for it.

"I was wrong to bring things to a head...um... I mean... Sorry. I was wrong to press the point. Shite! Kinda hard not to use double entendres."

He smiles and my heart wobbles. "You weren't wrong. I shouldn't have walked out. But it has forced me to think and examine my beliefs. I needed to do that and had avoided it. I know I need more time with you."

Inside me, the bouncy balls are going crazy and it's good. It could knock me off my feet but it's definitely good. I smile at the man I now know I'm extremely fond of. Who am I kidding? I hang on his every word. "So we're good?"

Will leans in to kiss me gently on the lips. In my class. On a school day. Fucking hell, it's great! "We're way more than good. Can you come to mine later?"

"School night?"

"If I promise a curfew?"

"Do you hafta?"

He grins. "Can you meet me at the pagoda?"

"Um. What?"

"Paul's fancy oriental garden building. It's lovely inside—a house in its own right. Can you come via the back lane in Waggon Way and meet me there? I have visitors I'll need to evade. Come say nine?"

I nod. "Okay."

"Good." He kisses me again and, wow. I'm in a fog of total lust and happiness. I brush his cheek with my hand and stare into his eyes.

"I am sorry."

"Don't be. Save it for after. Laters."

Chapter Eleven

Dibian's house is a hymn to theater set meets Willy Wonka's world. While I've picked her up from outside her home a few times, I've never been inside, and now that I am, I'm somewhat taken aback.

There are neon paintings, vibrant silk hangings and Venetian masks. An enormous piece of wall art features an otherworldly peacock feather design with a fake peacock's head sticking out—every inch living art. A chaise longue in purple with golden stars and a small tent in the corner sports orange and reds and indigos. There's even a grand piano that's been painted in a Mexican *Dios de la Muerte* candy skulls design. Elton John, if he saw the flat, would want to move in immediately. Her living room's a paint factory explosion and an optical challenge in one. Her batik silk kaftan in rainbow hues I haven't even covered...

"Did this guy take a lot from you, Dibs?"

"All told, fifteen grand."

My pause hangs heavy as a bowling ball in a clutch bag. I would normally swear and exclaim but I don't want her to feel any worse. It's much more money than I expected. Bastard!

"Plus a bit more," she admits and I long to whistle between my teeth but diplomacy overrides the instinct.

"Dibs. Are the police following it up?"

"I don't know if I can face pressing charges. Could be the worst part."

"And let him get away with it? He's a shit and he should be brought to account."

"My nephew's a sergeant. If my sister finds out, she'll make me feel worse than I already do. And, believe me, I feel bad enough. I guess I'll have to mark this one down to naivety, stupidity and desperation. And I'm glad he didn't persuade me to sign over half the house to him. He was hinting."

"Dibs. Don't be so hard on yourself."

"Who else is to blame?" She fiddles with the corners of her gauzy, glittery pashmina and her gypsy earrings dangle like crazy. Even when pissed off, she has a flair for garish fantasy fashion gone wild. And wrong.

"But lots of women fall prey to these mercenary guys out for a green card or money or whatever drives them most. It happens to lots of women, probably thousands. Why wouldn't you believe him?"

"I should've considered. Why would a young, handsome, suave man fancy an old duffer like me?"

I reach forward and hug her hard. She has a keen sense of humor. She laughs in such an endearing, self-deprecating way when she does. She has shimmering, clear blue eyes and fine, amazing skin.

"Because you're you. Kind. Intelligent. Funny, warm, compassionate. I'm not writing the list but you're you and you've the kind of warm heart that arse wipes like Mr. Gold Digger hone in on. You're a victim, Dibian, not a fool. And you need to realize that. You're wonderful and you deserve the man who will one day treasure you as you deserve!"

Her blue eyes fill. "Thank you, Izzy."

"Don't cry. It's time to forgive yourself and move on."

"I knew I employed you for a reason all those years ago," she smiles as she hanky dabs her eyes. "Underneath all your attitude and bluster and the swearing, you're a wonderful woman. If only you didn't like football so much."

I grin. At least a glimpse of real Dibian is back. Albeit three tubs of luxury clotted cream ice cream have died a fast, messy death to get to this point. And I suspect there'll be a lot of luridly colored retail therapy to help get her better.

"Football is to me what color is to you. *Chaque a son gout!*" I tell her that the key to moving on after a bad situation is to pull on big girl pants and party. "So you're coming to Will Darby's party on Friday night."

She grimaces. "So not in the mood."

"You're coming. Will wants you there."

Dibian shakes her head. "I don't have party mood in me."

"You will. Even if it means me coming here and us getting dolled up together. In fact, why don't I bring my girlies over? Or even you come and get ready at mine?"

"Okay. But get your pals to come here. Let's give this place some nice memories beyond Mr. Bastard the Gigolo, who I still see everywhere I look. At the moment, every time I sit here, I think of him feeding me grapes and I want to cry!"

It's a tad too much info. But I get her point. "It's a date."

"Okay, and one more thing. Since when did you start calling our new Mr. Darby by his first name? Or start getting a smile and a twinkle when you talk about him?"

Fuck. Shit and bugger with its tits out.

"You're imagining things. I'm being mentored by him. I have to call him Will."

Dibian nods. But her eyes have gone all Cleopatra on me.

"Dibian. Stop!"

"I know what I know. I will be listening and watching carefully. At least one of us has action on the horizon."

"He's a guy. And when I'm finished with you, the guys will be queuing around that grand piano!"

Dibian has her color back. And fuck, but I think it's unearthing some of my truths that has helped her most. But Dibian is the last person I want to know about my private affair. She won't mean to but, if she gets wind, she'll blab about me and Will without realizing.

"I heard Will stepped in when you were sick. Somebody told me he took you home." Dibian pushes.

"Yes. His maid was there more than he was."

"Do you know that over the years I've become pretty good at working out when I'm being served fiction?"

"I'm concentrating on climbing the career ladder and taking your job, so you'd better treat me right." I pick up empty ice cream cartons and take them to the bin. "I don't need a man. And most of them have no interest in me. Unless they need football scores. I always have that info."

"Oh, Izzy. You protest way too much."

"I don't do relationships, Dibs. Too much shit." I've fudged and tried my best. But I know my lines stink like Stilton left in the midday sun. And Dibian wouldn't believe me, even if I'd brought them out on a wooden board complete with grapes and crackers.

My secret's out and I know it. And so, most sadly of all, does she.

* * * *

Hangley Grange is four miles away from Netherfield in Totteridge, one of North London's ultra-wealthy, mock countryside super suburbs. Given how brief my first stay here was, I decide to take more notice on this visit.

I park on Waggon Way and walk up an overgrown pathway with a bin store. There, a twenty-foot-high security wall and an army of anti-intruder camera sentinels are dotted like buzz-off bling.

It's a lot less scenic than the front way in. I feel like a lowly tradesman, pushing back overhanging bushes to find the single door entrance. I use an entry code Will gave me and the door clicks open.

A meadow-style pathway leads me to an open expanse of rolling lawn. Fuck, this place is huge. No wonder Mo was impressed.

There are lights for dramatic floodlighting and modern sculpture strategically placed. A fountain graces the expansive lake, and when I round a cave-style stone garden worthy of Capability Brown at Chatsworth, there's an ornate secret Japanese pagoda.

"Nice one, Will. Rockin' it."

I have to remind myself that Will isn't the owner. These magical details are the brainchild of Paul Bates, one-time England squad captain and most coveted striker at AC Milan. Who could've guessed a soccer star could be so garden landscapes and horticulture attuned?

"Well, Paul, it's not too shabby," I tell Paul Bates, wherever he now may be. After all, beauty should always be appreciated.

Then, through the trees, I spot the main house and I have to stand and take it in. There's twenty bedrooms — that's upstairs. It's the McMansion. So why exactly am I meeting Will in the pagoda when there's plenty of conference facility indoors?

I'm about to send him a snarky text but I hear the snap of twigs underfoot and I want to jump a mile in the air. Instead I freeze and a cold evening breeze blows past me and makes me shiver.

"You!" A hand goes over my mouth to silence the scream that's in my throat. "Now I've got you."

It's Will. I'd know his smell anywhere. But why's he looking like a bloody black-hooded ninja? Is he ready to give me a Bruce Lee lesson? He loosens his hand on my mouth.

"You bastard," I tell him and, on instinct, I slap him.

"I told you to be discreet." His eyes narrow and he barks his disapproval. "Why the fuck are you standing sightseeing the house like an OCD estate agent?"

"Shut up. Aren't I allowed any perks of my position as your sex slave?"

"Suppose. When you put it that way." He grins. "Anyway I wanted to gauge your self-defense reactions. No time to lose, let's get into hiding."

"Hiding?" Now I'm confused.

"Shh. Keep it quiet. You're here and shouldn't be. There are guests in the house I couldn't evade. Let me take you to my hidden haven. And get ready for some fast sex action, babe—we haven't got long tonight."

Charm and seduction, thy name is William Darby.

* * * *

I'd expected a draughty garden structure slash spider playground. The pagoda is as far from my image as could be.

Inside it has white walls and shining ebony wood like a serene Japanese tea house from films. I recall a Sean Connery Bond movie with a room like this. Only this one has a screen wall ahead of me and, through it, I can see a black sheet-bedecked double bed with tall orchids in white pots on each simple wooden bedside table. Simple. Perfect for purpose.

"Paul's into martial arts. He uses this as a practice pad."

"And the bed?"

"Who knows? He's faithful to his wife—I know that much. Maybe he comes here to escape her? She's quite a woman! He'll need the rest. But that's another story." He smiles.

"It's a proverbial dojo of delights. But why am I here?"

"My mother's over there. She's using the sauna and having a pampering massage for a few hours. And Ben and Janey came over to use the gym earlier. I figured we'd stay under the radar!"

"Shit." I'm shocked at the revelation. But now I approve of the tactics.

I've barely put down my bag and taken off my jacket before Will has me in his strong, addiction-forming embrace.

"Izzy, I need to explain why I'm taking things slow. I lived at a retreat in France after I was ill."

"You're okay?" I blurt.

"Yes. But it was serious. And I've had to adjust. I've never tested out the equipment, if you'll pardon the pun. I'm not sure I can... Not sure I'm as able as I once was."

"Is that all that's up?" I ask.

"Well, it's more often about being not up that's the problem. And it's big to me."

I itch to know more, but he's told me enough. He's trusted me enough for this window and maybe in time there'll be more. For now I'm on the page. And we can do this. He can do this.

I pull Will to me and kiss him as I've never kissed him before. Putting my heart on the line and my emotions behind the gesture, kissing him slowly and gently and with the kindness and love I'd love to be kissed with. Like he's my window on treasure and I'm grasping my chance of taking a cut.

"Love me, Will. And let me love you like I want to. Don't worry about if it works, if it doesn't or about the next second. Just go with the flow and love me. Did none of your past managers ever correct you for overthinking things way too hard?"

I slip off my blouse and underneath is something more suitable and sexy. I'd guessed that tonight was about getting out the big guns—and I don't mean chicken fillet bra enhancers. Because things are at stake here—this fabulous male has had an ego machete slice to his manhood. He needs to know he's a man again and having that responsibility is a rare privilege.

I also want to apologize for our prior encounter in my bedroom gone bad.

They don't call me Bulldog Izzy at school for nothing. I like to seize a challenge and get results. Will deserves the best I can give.

I've taken my armor from my knicker drawer—a negligée teddy thing made out of lace. It's sheer, ultra-high cut and a French knicker style with peekaboo texture where it counts most. It's everything I'm not, it's positively wanton, but tonight feels like the night it should come out to play.

I stand before Will and remove the black ribbon from my pocket. I sweep my hair up into an untidy updo and I'm ready. I undo my trousers, let them fall and step out of them. I've even remembered to spritz with NachtGarten parfum and I'm done. Or should that be undone?

"Will I do?"

I hear Will's breathing hard against me and I guess the new guise works. "Fuck, you know how to tempt a man to distraction, you crazy woman."

"You like?"

"More than like."

"You want?"

"How could any man not?" He's already tracing my nipples through the sheer fabric. I tip my head back and moan.

"Wanna test the goods? See if you fancy more?" We kiss deeply. "No pressure from me. You set the pace," I tell him. "Ready when you are."

Will strips before me and my tongue is redundant in my mouth again. He's naked and erect and so damn gorgeous that my insides are on hot, deep, internal massage mode. I walk to the bed with Will's hand in mine and I lie back on it, my legs placed for maximum allure.

"Your rules," I say, and pull the ribbon undone at the front of my sheerest of sheer lingerie so my breasts fall free. He's on me and I feel his lips roam all over me. One minute he's at my mouth, the next he's covering my neck, my décolletage, my nipples. He particularly likes those and he laves them with a tongue so skilled he prompts extreme sounds of arousal. I'm glad we're deep in the darkest corner of the grounds. He nips the peaks of my nipples and I writhe on the bed as he caresses my breasts in a manner they've never hitherto witnessed. *Wowzer.*

Will's eyes burn into mine. "You have been sent to slay my willpower."

"What next?" I ask. "You're the boss. Secret Sir. You control the pace."

"Touch me." He's kneeling on the bed, inviting me to go there. So I do, I dip my hand to hold his long, swollen shaft and a raw gasp escapes him. His face is flexed as if pained.

"I won't hurt you, you're sure?"

He doesn't answer but shakes his head. So I take his engorged penis in my hand. It's long and throbbing and ready with a moist tip. I've no idea what's happened to him but it all looks orderly down below with no obvious impediments. Maybe he'll tell me soon?

A sharp hiss bolts from between his lips when I dip my fingers over and around the head. I sit back, afraid to do more.

"Would you suck me? I might not last?" His face is drawn and dark. He looks so pained admitting this to me that I sigh and want to cuddle him like a child.

"Will. I don't give a damn about longevity. But I do want to give you pleasure. May I at least try?"

He nods. "I think so. I want you to try."

"Lie back and relax. You're coiled and this should be pleasure," I instruct and I get up to kneel at the side of the bed for easiest access. "Relax. This is nothing to do with scoring points or achieving anything. Trust me on this. I'm right." I taste him and relish it. He is sweeter and more seductive than I anticipated. His fingers grip the bed sheets like his life depends on it and I wish I could drain the stress from this fabulous man.

"Put your hands on me," I encourage him. "C'mon. Loosen the hold."

Will's hands rest at the back of my head. He threads his fingers into my mussed hair and gently kneads.

I decide now is the time. I lick from the bottom of his shaft up and over to the head. Then I take him in tentatively again. Just the head. And his gasp tells me he likes it.

A noise comes from so low in his throat I can feel Will brace himself. I lick the tip again. Slowly, evenly. With gentle but steady pressure. Completely attuned to avoiding sensation overload, I blow him fully, smoothly and with steady speed.

Will moans at my mouth's touch. I curl my fingers around him and thrill speeds a circuit through me as his voice meets my ears.

"That's it, baby. You've got it."

I'm smiling with new confidence, swirling with my mouth and tongue. I draw deeper and farther — not too much. I've had 'blow-job confessions' with friends and gained from their tips. I may not have a ton of experience but I do know the drill. Now is my time to try it out.

I pay careful attention to slow and steady with my fingers at the base and I sense he's near his summit.

Will's hips move in an erotic dance that has me wet and thrilled.

"Hell, Iz." One arm shoots across his eyes as he braces his weight, trembles too. "Almost ready," he tells me on a breathy whisper.

I smile as I finally slide my control knob to max. If Will is coming, I want to guarantee a mind bender. I suck, leaving no doubt that, when it comes to mouth love, I'm the woman for his needs.

I sense he's coming soon, so I take him deep and Will pulls my hair—the sensation thrills me more. With bucking hips, Will loses his last vestige of control and I keep up the motion until he softens with spent energy as he closes his own pleasure. He's done better than good and I'm heady with delight. Breathing hard, he tugs me close. "Not so bad."

"Not so very bad at all."

I grin and revel in the feeling of our embrace. "There's more where that came from. I'm a great teacher—it's practical I excel at. I don't expect flawless performance, I just want application."

Will smiles and I find all that coiled, manly potential. I sense my actions have eased his worry.

"And after that taster, this student doesn't mind the ride. We're going to rub along well together," he answers.

He deserves recompense for whatever he's been through, causing his celibacy's scars. Full therapy— and I think I may have rocked his world.

* * * *

An hour later, Will sits up in bed and checks his watch. "Shit. Gotta go. Mother will wonder where I'm hiding and send a search party out."

I grin at this image. But it's an abrupt ending to our passion pagoda's exquisite lovemaking. He's made me come in three different ways, each more impressive than the last. I'm enjoying learning to be a tongue temptress too.

"Didn't have you down as a mummy's boy." I giggle. "Sir has a big secret fear, then."

"She scrutinizes my business. If she thought there was a woman, she'd rag me senseless." After pulling on his trousers, he leans in for a languorous kiss. "I'm keeping you well out of harm and interrogation's way."

It's different from any sex I've ever experienced before. Not because the orgasms have been plentiful and stellar. But because—it's not wham, bam, boom. I've touched Will and made him come. But he hasn't come inside me yet. I know why. I can give him time. I have faith that the right care can help him.

"Your mum staying for a while?"

"No. It's an enforced visit I didn't foresee. She'll be gone by the party."

I nearly swear. Shit, I'd forgotten about that. "Ah. Party. Yep."

"You are coming Friday?" he says, narrowing his eyes.

"Of course."

"You got the news that fancy dress costumes are the dress code of choice?"

I shake my head. "Nobody told me. But I have been busy."

"I figured it might help people loosen up. But you can come as you want. Stay over after?" He tries to seal the deal by kissing around my décolletage to make me weak and wanton.

"We'll see. If you're good."

"Drop by my office soon. I won't stand waiting till Friday for an Izzy fix."

I get out of bed and pull on my clothes, much slower than it took to remove them. We stand on the threshold in an embrace, both dressed and ready to return to life outside our clandestine sexy bubble.

"Pop by tomorrow."

"Okay. But no kisses in the corridor at work or it'll be *sayonara* discretion."

He smiles and I do too. "Top secret. Strict terms."

"Our dark secrets will stay that way. Count on it."

"Stay at mine Thursday?" he asks finally. "Give me something to look forward to."

"Is that wise, school night?"

He claims my mouth in a kiss that sweeps me into the atmosphere on a wave of blissed-out buoyant magic. "You like this?" he says and his hand stakes a claim on my ass.

"Thursday. I'll bring my flannel pajamas. The ones you like."

"Bring the black bits. I like them best."

My Secret Sir. He's real. And I'm loving it. Loving him — gulp, no, too much too soon, must step back.

And tonight — I must write it all down. Every touch, every blush. Every erect and pulsing inch. This is the research that I've yearned for and now I intend to make it work. Bestseller — Kindle cloud rocket — here I come.

Chapter Twelve

Next day as I drive to work my phone goes into an email frenzy, bleeping the R2D2 email alert tone from my handbag.

When I check it as I walk into Netherfield, I see that it's the book club members reacting to my emailed book chapters. They've caused a storm. My erotica mystery about the mysterious Sir P—who invents exotic places for sex with his mistress Zizi and she has to work out location from clues—now has full-on steamy, erotic lovemaking scenes. I'm pretty darn pleased with the results.

Already there's been a pantry, a pagoda. And from the look of the emails, the girls highly approve—the titles include *WTF, Give Me More Now!* And *Izzy, You're Heading for the Bestsellers List!*

They all clamor for an emergency book club meeting at Fiona's place. Given that I'd planned on writing tonight, Arsenal tomorrow with Jack and Will Thursday, then the party Friday, I'm struggling to fit life in. Thank God I don't have lots of backed-up teaching prep. I send a group mail to invite them to Dibian's place to get ready before Friday's party and I tell them we'll squeeze in a book discussion. Dibs will have to be included and sworn to secrecy. Given her problems of late, the book club will probably do her the world of good.

I'm smiling unashamedly as I tuck my phone back in my bag and walk right into Annie James. She doesn't nix my smile but she does dim its wattage some. "Izzy. Got a sec?"

"Hi." Annie the Nympho has a predatory gleam. I check my watch to hatch an escape strategy. "Ten minutes till bell. If you don't mind talking and walking? I have to get resources set up before class."

"No problemo." She falls in with my step, even though she's on seven-inch platforms.

It might be unfair to call Annie a nympho. Man eater would be more accurate. She plays the alto saxophone like she's making love, and I'd guess it's with herself — sometimes our school recitals verge on the porn periphery. She's a fourth form pin-up for all the worst reasons.

"Good to know you're my soccer skills buddy. I'm hoping to slay you with my killer headers." She says it as if she's eyeing up the competition and can't find anything to recommend me.

"You can try, *buddy*. But I tackle like greased lightning on a slippery, stormy night." My tone is ultra-cool and I'm lying through my arse. 'Buddy'? More like arch enemy. I know darn well she downright hates me. I see revulsion waiting to pounce behind her slanted sapphire eyes.

"Great to know we're both skeptical but game for the challenge."

"This is a hundred percent career move for me—it'll be viewed by millions and probably watched by my next boss."

"Planning on moving on?"

She bites her lip. "Nothing lined up yet. But after this, we may be headhunted. Our virtues may go viral. And my eyes are on a prize of another nature."

I keep to myself that the only thing likely to go viral about Annie is her pneumatic chest and ample cleavage. I hang a death U-turn from the truth. "You like football?" I ask. It's a low blow—all she knows is that it's played on a pitch using a ball.

"Love it. Nothing like watching players swapping shirts! Phwoar!" Her giggle could strip decade-old paint. She probably thinks the purpose of the entire game is to show off chest hair. I serenely evade the chance to chainsaw her spindly wisdom tree.

"You play much?"

"Beach volleyball's my thing." She flicks me a 'take that, sucker' look. "Went to California—did an exchange. Dated a movie director. Great times! My ex made Dutch movies of a physical nature. I was even in a few." She flicks her hair in a move that's pure Mattel's most famous doll. I wish she was die-cast so I could stick big pins in painful places. She tongue-wets her much-glossed mouth.

Ah, now I get it—she's fame crazy. She barges the conversation up a cocky cul-de-sac. "Cutting to the chase—it's about Will. I'm totally interested. I think he is too. So you won't mind giving us a bit of space and leeway during the mentoring stint. Do it for the sisterhood and all that." She says it with some tiny nods — does she have a tic? She also stands hands firmly on my desk, bracing her weight, boobs jutting out in a provocative threat gesture she probably used in her ex's movie.

There's an estrogen war in the offing and I sense she's firing FF canons on my D-cup boats. Fucker. If only I had a poison-loaded blow pipe in my hand instead of a pencil. Nothing annoys me more than somebody putting their mucky paws on my desk. Or my man.

"It's football classes, Annie, not speed dating with balls and a TV crew."

"But if he asks us out for drinks after play, I want you to do the decent thing and decline. I'm moving in on him, stealthily, and I *always* get what I'm after."

"Annie Gets Her Man. Should be a musical. With a big ratty cougar in it."

She fake smiles. "He'll obviously fancy me. But if he shows any interest — bear in mind I saw him first and I'm staking a claim. Do we have an understanding?"

I want to do cock eyes and blow her a raspberry, but more than that, I want to be Sarah Jessica Parker and pin her hand to my desk with a stiletto heel. Then hear her squeal like a pig. Sadly I'm wearing low wedges.

"Want me to save time and put in a word with Will?" I ask her.

She grins as she sashays over to my door and wraps herself around it like Madonna on a tour dancer. "D'you think you have anything that Will would take any notice of?"

It's at times like these you wish you'd filmed your recent sexual encounters for the purpose of action replay to piss her off.

"I'm barely on his radar as a woman. But I think he might play for the other team anyway."

Her face pales. "No way. Will's not gay."

I open my desk drawer, take out the extra print with the handbag and the tuxedo, and I hold it up for her to view. Sometimes the coolest lines are the silent ones where you only raise eyebrows. Well, that's how it makes me feel anyway — especially when I see her eyes widen and her jaw clench.

"Fuck, that's unexpected," she answers. "But I'm still game to give it a try in case he swings in both directions. At least he has good taste in bags."

* * * *

At the end of that day, I'm in for a shocking surprise when I go down to Fiona's science lab in search of working magic markers, only to find her room empty. I decide to take the marker hunt into my own hands — Fiona won't mind as we regularly pillage each other's supplies.

I'm rummaging in the pot on her desk when I hear noises. Noises that make me stop and freeze. Noises that make my neck hairs prickle, then the pens fall from my fingers as I take a swallow. I'm scared to hear more in case the noises turn out to be what I think they could be.

Shit-o-la! I fear it may be noises of passion.

It starts subtly. A light, woman's murmur. Then a bump, was that a chair moving across the floor tiles? Then a moan. A grunt. A deep moan of exclamation is the climax. I wish I could beam up and Star Trek outta there.

I hear Fiona's soft, soothing words through the wall from the science cupboard where the action is taking place. "Poor boy. Let me make it better, my tiger lover! My squash lob macho man." Her voice is a sultry purr.

I feel ready to lose my lunch. Especially when I consider how many tanks of stinky mealworms are in there with them while they do the deed.

"Aaaaagh!" comes a male moan that's so loud it makes me jump. Holy fuck—it's like waking up in an acid bath and I feel the searing, jolting need to evacuate and shed my skin. And clean out my ears with a carbolic soap and bleach mix.

But I cannot, as it's still going on. There's another breathy, deep moan and I know, right away, I've walked into voyeuristic hell. I love my friend dearly, but witnessing her sex fest isn't part of the BFF code.

There's a man's low voice that's making the kind of noise only some strange wild man from the deepest depths of the Amazonian wilderness could make—or is it Chewbacca's primal mating calls?

It's deep, guttural. And it goes on for about five seconds. Half howl, half anguished ecstasy. This isn't any kind of sex noise I've ever known. I wonder if I should call in the Bigfoot team or medical help?

Shit. I walk away from the desk. Forgetting the marker hunt and vowing forever after never to use a marker again, I carefully tiptoe past the desk and toward the door. Which would've been fine. Nobody need have known a thing. Except my phone trills into life loudly—with ZZ Top playing *Sharp Dressed Man*, the song heralds my identity completely like a marching band coming to commemorate the event.

Double shit. I try to walk past the science cupboard door on fast speed and purposefully avoid the oblong of window pane, lest my eyes see a glimpse of Alan and Fi in the act of the 'at its'. I'm mortified to hear the door open right beside me as the outer doorknob is tantalizingly in my grasp.

"Iz! It is you!"

Oh heck. I keep my head down and my fingers are turning the doorknob anyway, such is my longing for escape.

"Izzy, don't go!" Fiona's right behind me and, while my body wants to keep going and pretend I don't know, I realize I can't. The cover's blown and eye contact, however awkward, will now have to be made. "Izzy. Just the woman. Can you come in and see this?" Fiona says beside me.

"Um."

"Come and see Alan. It's rather important that you do. We need a second opinion."

Hell, I didn't see those words coming! I look up tentatively. She's wearing her clothes. Her hair's in perfect place—not in mid-intercourse disarray. And she's also wearing her eye protectors and her lab coat. She even has on protective latex gloves.

What the bloody hell were they doing in there, and how big is Alan in the trousers department that she needs to make sure he won't take an eye out?

"Come and see Alan. Do you think he should have it seen to by a chiropractor? Frankly I've never encountered anything like it. It's a golf ball lump and the poor baby can't take the pain. He says something like this happened before after he lost control of his toboggan. This time, it was playing squash."

I walk into the room as my thoughts are still jiving, unable to formulate reality.

Alan Collier is lying flat out on Fiona's science bench. His bare back is dusted with a fair smattering of dark Bigfoot-esque hair and his trousers are turned back at the waistband. Fortunately I cannot identify his butt crack or that would have had me run, arms flailing, from the room.

"He twisted something. Now there's a definite lump and he's struggling to walk. He can drive but he's walking like he's wearing a wet nappy. It's agony. I've been trying to work it out but I think it's best with a professional. Do you have any experience of backs?"

I shake my head, hugely relieved that they weren't in the throes. My God — my heart is beating and I can feel sweat run down my back and it's the perspiration of mortification. I wonder it's not given me a few gray hairs.

"I can give you a good number," I tell her, then I fire up my identity-betraying mobile phone. "My neighbor's son runs a place. Say you know me and he'll fit you in. Alternatively we could call them right now…"

Alan tries to turn and look at me then starts 'ouching' and moaning again, which attests to the acute level of his pain. I take this as an urge to make the appointment soonest.

"You're a doll, Izzy. You might be useless at squash but I'm seeing you have hidden depths." Alan's still face down. The man looks like he's having a nightmare.

"Al, you're boyfriend to one of my best friends now. You get the VIP treatment. But if you're mean to her, I'll do your kneecaps with your squash racquet. *Comprende?*"

"Roger that."

I call the chiropractor and, when I get through, I secure an urgent appointment.

"Thanks, Iz. This is a bitch of a thing," Alan says weakly.

"Alan. Language," says Fiona. She's stroking his back.

We help him up and he assures us he'll be okay to drive. I stay while Fiona finishes and prepares to leave, debating if I should confess my imagined incident or not.

"You like each other, don't you?" I eventually opt for.

"Definitely." She gives me a sly, pleased-with-herself grin as she plops test tubes in their holders and fiddles with the mealwormery beside her.

"That wasn't a squash injury, was it?" I say biting my lip.

Fi's cheeks turn bright red in an instant but, fair play to her, she stands her ground and meets my eye. "Sex on the kitchen table. It was rather athletic, perhaps a bit over-enthusiastic. But let's say it was worth it—it had been a long time waiting for that one and it proved a sensation." She stares at me. "I know what you're thinking... He may look like a stuffed-shirt prig and at times he has the most God-awful laugh but I'm training him to be better. He's got a great body underneath the bad clothes. Plus he's got a kind heart, Iz. And he worships me. I don't think he's ever had sex as good, either—to him I'm the full package. And I'm touching forty, Iz. I need a man and this one's interested. He even has a holiday cottage in the Cotswolds with a garden that's to die for and, once you get over his tendency to always win at squash, he's not all bad! He's hung like a donkey and pretty agile in the bedroom department! The hairy back thing aside."

TMI. But if he's treating my friend well, I figure I may have been wrong to judge so swiftly. He's keen and so is she. Good luck to them.

"I'm glad to see you've got your sparkle back. I don't care who's giving you it!" I tell her.

But thank God I haven't heard them shagging.

"I'm glad you're happy, Fi. Just maybe encourage him to consider a back wax?"

"Back, sac and crack booked for next Wednesday." She winks at me. "I'm not totally stupid, you know. He has buns of steel. I intend to groom him up nicely!"

I'm grinning so hard at Fiona it's positively a whole face hug. "Poor guy won't know what's hit him." We lock up her classroom door. "And if he's that noisy having his bumps rubbed, I dread to think what happens when you touch his boy part."

"It's something to behold, Iz. Something to behold!"

* * * *

Two days later I'm feeling somewhat frazzled with my schedule as a career teacher, a football fan, book club organizer, erotic author and a vamp. But I'm still hanging in there and tonight's my tryst with Will.

"I'm still coming but I might be late," I tell him, softly and swiftly, at the end of lunch break by popping by his office. I have to do this with more discretion than a secrecy convention that's gone underground and changed its name.

When I arrive at the PE department, I check first that nobody's within earshot. If anybody asks, I'm discussing my mentoring schedule. Having a cover helps with subterfuge. How clandestine has my life become in only a few days? Darby has become my guilty secret. And my guilty pleasure.

The last few nights have been spent writing about our exploits again so I've more chapters to pass on to the book club on Friday. I know I've given my book *oomph* — it gets me hot and bothered skim reading.

"Mr. Darby, I've come to ask you about my timetable for filming," I say in a loud voice, with a wink.

"Good idea, Miss Tennant."

I close the door and we're in each other's arms in an instant. I'm kissing him as if he's a petrol canister and I'm a spitting barbecue. We cling breathlessly in the aftermath of our vigorous snog onslaught.

Next, he grabs my hand and hauls me like a crazy wild bear on a lust bender. Two tugs and I'm through the cupboard door, off his office. I'm thoroughly kissed again and I've no time to take in how truly vile it smells in here. Blame whiffy basketballs and too many sweaty youths.

"What are you doing? Don't!" My protests are futile. The rubber smell hits me like a Mutiny Bay wave. "Wow. What a stink!"

"Personally I find it earthy. A musky turn-on!" He tugs me close for proof.

Oh my word. For a guy with sporadic erectile issues, you'd never know by what he's showing me in terms of regard right now.

"In school too!" I admonish. "Sackable offense, or is that a ruler in your pocket, Sir!"

"I'd rule your world if you let me."

"I worry about you, Darby." He's kissing my neck. It's more than a little fantastic. His lips have talents only genies could have taught via a mystical workshop. "Uh. Don't. How can I possibly go back and teach grammar after this?"

"I love it when you talk English lesson shop," he says in that voice that sends my womb to lust mush.

"I came to tell you I may be late tonight. I need to go shopping for something to wear to the party."

"Come the way I want you — in your birthday suit." Seconds later, he's pulled up my work skirt. Today, there's a thong present and, unfortunately, he finds this helpful because he slaps my arse with a strong hand. I yelp, but remember to keep it sotto voce.

"Fuck, Will. What was that for?"

"You've been keeping secrets."

Shit. Does he know about the chapters I've written? Did he leave a spy cam in my room?"

"You took another man to football. You didn't clear dates with other men." He's glaring but I can tell it's a joke.

"Jack? Jack and me have been going to watch Arsenal for almost a decade. He buys the coffee and I bring two pasties. Get real."

Another arse slap makes me turn and hide my backside from him. "I mean it. Stop that!"

"And I hear you're having private assignations with Rogerson. What are you trying to do to me, woman?"

"We're ruddy candle-making. I wanted to get him onside. If you want, you can come along too. Bring your own wick and wax and I'm sure we'll all have a ball together."

He pulls me close and he kisses me again. I prod Will in the ribs. A waft of his cologne makes me want him badly. He's surprisingly hard in his abs and I long to let my hand explore again, but now's not the time. Years of gym work have given him a body that gladiators would do the cha-cha-cha in a morph suit for. He's holding me, wearing a smirk that would put Wile E. Coyote back to drama school.

"I want to leave my imprint. It's a taster for tonight," he says, and pulls me closer still. "Countin' down the minutes, babe."

I pull away and straighten my clothes. And I sound like Yoda to my own ears when I answer. "A patient boy my Sir must be. A very patient boy!"

* * * *

By the time Friday comes I'm cream-crackered and ready to drop.

Last night I stayed over at Will's and there was rather a lot more adventure going on than sleep—mostly in the games room at Hangley Grange. Orgasm central, in fact, and I was playing the starring role. He's still not comfortable about penetration—but I live in hope. Given that I had to trawl Brent Cross's delights for a party outfit prior to getting there, it's been full-on, like a social life Zumba-thon without breathing breaks.

But now that Friday's finally here and we're at Dibian's with a drink in our hands, the good news is my friends are completely hooked on my book. They're raving about it and they're completely in love with Sir Pablo P, my hero.

I'm somewhat staggered but I'm also very grateful and humbled by the impact my writing's had. Also my book is finally finished. I've written all the wild sex scenes I needed—so, minus a last extensive polish, I am now the proud writer of *Secrets with Sir P.* I hand out CDs of the full book in draft to all of my friends.

"Your input will help me get it right," I tell them. "Criticisms and pointers welcome."

"It's simple, this has to be published. You could try and get an agent, or send it to some publishers yourself? But basically I think you should do it now," Fiona tells me.

Mo adds, "Iz. It's totally hot. We want things to move fast on this! You deserve success."

"I love your hints about his tortured past. I sense that he has problems in the trouser department, am I right? The man is so hot and that killer, deep secret wound breaks my heart," Janey tells me.

"You'll have to read on and find out."

They all cheer and congratulate me, and we clink glasses in a toast to the book's success.

"Why not self-publish?" Janey asks. "I've a friend who did that and made lots of money."

"I'm not sure." I've been so focused on the writing that I haven't considered what next. I've barely had time to kick back, and in fact it's hindered my sleep as I've been getting up in the middle of the night to write more.

Fiona, however, has done a lot more thinking about all of this than me. "Are you going to use a pseudonym? You need to think up a name then get a website. Presence on social media too."

Dibian is flicking through my chapters printout. "Izzy, you've surprised me, but I must say I'm very impressed by the passionate hero and the intensity of this story. I have an idea. Can I take this with me? I have a friend who may be able to help you."

A tiny trickle of wariness skitters down my spine. Maybe I should be a bit more prudent here — but then I remind myself, it's Dibian. She's my trusted boss and friend. Surely she understands to keep things under wraps.

"Top secret at this stage, though, Dibs," I tell her.

"It's a friend. A publishing friend."

"And I don't write because I want fuss or fame or anything like that—I love to write. I just want to create the kind of characters I feel deeply about."

"Well said," says Dibian. "This book could be big, Izzy. There's something about the hero… But you need to work out exactly how you want this managed. And one more thing… I'm dying to know the inspiration?" There's a wicked gleam in Dibian's eye. I gulp and avert my gaze when I see it. Then, when I look back, she winks at me so swiftly the others miss it.

"Nobody in particular. Just my fantasy guy. He's not real."

"I'd dearly love to meet such a man."

"A man like Pablo Pascal could never exist. Sir P's nothing but a fantasy, I'm afraid."

Dibian purrs, "Well, whoever he is, he's a man a lot of women will want to read about in future."

Shit. Maybe this wasn't such a good plan… I didn't bank on Dibian being pushy or joining up dots. Shit. And maybe the hero's Achilles heel being an erection issue wasn't a good move either.

I sense I may have given away a bit too much too soon.

* * * *

The girls are *oohing* and *ahhing* over our outfits as we make ready prior to the party. There's a gasp of astonishment when I unveil mine.

"Shit, Iz! What the hell's got into you?" Fiona gasps.

"Miss Whiplash strikes again," says Mo.

Dibian merely comes over and rubs her hand over my leather-clad form while Janey has a fit of giggles and doubles up on the sofa.

"I figured that since I'm now the erotica author gone public, I should go a bit all out tonight." I shrug my leather-clad shoulders and stick out my bum in my shiny leather butt-clinger pants.

The lace-up leather boots and biker jacket are ones I owned already. The spray-on leather jeans and black corset beneath are new. As is the leather choker. And my new add-on long ponytail that reaches past my waist.

"I fancy you myself," Fiona says, and squeezes my arse.

"Hands off! Pretty hot for a teacher, huh?"

My friends break out in a fit of applause. I laugh. I know it's ridiculous and so far removed from my usual style but this is about fun. Fancy dress is allowed — so why not fantasy dress? I can't wait to see Will's face — he's the inspiration.

And anyway Mo's dressed up as a sexy army cadet with khaki fatigues and war paint while Dibian sports a vibrant Carmen Miranda outfit so I'm hardly the most OTT of the pack.

We're going to an A-list mansion house party for food, drink and frolics. And I've got a secret man with surprising benefits while only Dibian has a clue.

I grin at them all and wink my jewel-bedecked faux lashes. "Tonight, my friends, we're wild women with all the moves that count."

Chapter Thirteen

Gaggles of handsome young men in football strips guide guests to parking spaces in the grounds of Hangley Grange tonight. Our taxi driver takes us up to the main door and my friends are flattered and impressed to have these sporty helpers assist them like suave, gallant hotel parking attendants.

"Isn't this wonderful?" gushes Dibian, holding on to her pineapple and bananas for dear life. Her cleavage in that outfit is something to behold. Clearly it has not escaped the attention of her footballer attendant who's staring at her as if hypnotized.

I suspect this kind of male attention will do her the world of good after her Ronald dating disaster, so I can't find it in me to be irked by her. She's had a bad time and she deserves to have a ball tonight.

"You can say what you like about our new sports head but he knows how to crowd-please," I tell her, then bite my tongue. Why am I dropping myself in it? Why am I openly talking about Will when I should keep him ultra-hush-hush to avoid suspicion? Especially with Dibian.

Fortunately, she's too engrossed in the moment to interrogate me or notice my Will fluff. And anyway, he has gone to town for his party. The driveway is bedecked with glowing Chinese lanterns and burning color-changing lights twinkle from the rose beds while sculptures and features are floodlit for impact.

"Wow. What a place!" says Fiona, looking around her like Alice perusing Wonderland's wild delights. Her blue gingham dress showcases curves a lab coat conceals. She's carrying a basket with a cuddly stuffed Toto inside. Her ruby slippers nearly didn't arrive from Omazod and it was touch and go whether she'd end up with a green face, hooked nose and witch's hat instead.

"Not often we get to hang out at the McMansion, is it? Enjoy it while we can," I tell her.

"You picked a great place to recuperate, Iz. This house is stellar! Would Will let you show me around later?"

I have to stay mindful that my friends don't know the truth about Will yet. I find deception super hard.

"Hopefully. Wait till you see inside." I hug my many fab, sexy memories to myself. My friends have no idea how attached I am to this place. It's the location for my dirty secret sensual trysts with the man I'm crazy about and only we know the sordid details. Too bad Dibian suspects, but having my special secret is delicious.

Moments later Alan Collier approaches us, to present a corsage to Fiona with a flourish. From the way he's walking, the chiropractor must have worked magic. Fi gasps in surprised pleasure and it warms my heart to see them kiss. She bends her leg at the knee like in the movies as he snogs her full on. The woman's clearly got it bad and while Alan may be a tool, he's cock-a-hoop for her and the cocker spaniels have taken a back seat. Thanks be for small mercies. Tonight he's dressed in a tux, and fortunately he's left his sandals at home. I think he possibly consulted with Daniel Craig beforehand to check the dress code.

"Alan, you're a charmer." She takes his arm. It's very sweet even for a dyed-in-the-wool cynic like me.

"Maybe I should call you Dorothy. You're certainly my rainbow's end tonight," Alan tells her, before kissing her thoroughly again. I'm not the only one smitten, it seems.

I feel a need to sing *Ding Dong, You're Loud in Bed* but I suspect Fiona would take massive offense so I keep it zipped.

Ben Lindhurst arrives smiling at our party. We all laugh when we see his nod to fancy dress is a Greek god's toga and laurel wreath. If anybody had the body for it Ben does. And it fits perfectly with Janey's Grecian goddess costume. It's like watching Brangelina on the set of *Troy*.

"Don't they fit like a hand in a kid glove!" Dibian simpers. "Delicious duo."

Janey's eyes flick to mine and they're sparkling with delight. "Ben. What are you like? How did you know my costume?"

"Got one of your friends to snitch," he tells her. "Told you we are perfect for each other. Had to buy a lot of chocolate to get the info, though." Ben winks at Mo.

"You promised not to tell," Mo says, scowling behind her army camouflage makeup, flexing her knuckles and tossing her ponytail, while using her miffed voice.

"'S'okay. Glad you told, Morag! I get the best view of his legs this way." Janey winks. "Win, win!"

They walk toward the house and I grab Dibian's arm in mine. She's here to have a good time—not be reminded of coupledom. I beckon Mo to take my other arm and force my jolly smile. Kinda innocuous accompanying my leather-clad Lady Whiplash Vixen Hellraiser costume.

"Come on, Carmen. Let's whip them into shape on the dance floor! How about you, Army Mo—gonna be a ball-buster drill sergeant and find yourself a man for Mission Mo?"

"Sod men. Let's dance and get hammered!" she answers. "Where there's wine, there's a way."

We follow the pulsing *Moves Like Jagger* riffs. It's going to be a long night of funky frolics. Yee-ha!

* * * *

When I see Will, my womb takes a high dive into a hot tub from a hundred-foot drop and the descent is more than good when our eyes make explosive contact.

"Holy jalapeños!"

He's Batman. I know this because he's wearing a badge that says BatWill.

And fuck me, but this Batman gives Christian Bale a good seeing to in the sexy stakes. He's dark. Dressed like that, and with muscles molded, he's brick-wall-hard-as-nails meets sexy danger. Maybe even the sexiest man ever to walk the planet?

His eye mask has me mewling in my throat for personal time in the bat cave. It's yummy! The spray-on black fabric suits him way too well and does everything to anesthetize my tongue to the point where I can't talk straight. In fact, my tongue is probably lolling lifeless out of the side of my mouth. It'll be clashing badly with my sexy black Goth girl lipstick.

Fortunately I'm flanked by Dibian and Mo, who do the talking for me.

"Look at the abs on that!" says Mo.

"Don't forget the arse!" says Dibian.

"That man is fit as a butcher's dog on a treadmill!"

"You picked a goodun there, Iz."

Mo asks. "You fancy him? You told Dibian and you didn't tell me?"

I would tell her to 'shh' and be quiet but as I said, my tongue's flat-lined and incompetent. I wonder if anyone has spark plugs for a recharge.

Mo lets out a whistle that makes the whole room look up and Batman smiles right at me. My heart does a pitty-pat in response. He walks in, a symphony of muscles on parade. Wow. Pinch me, I'm drunk on a testosterone-filled barrel of sexual high.

"Whiplash." I nod. I nearly curtseyed. "Carmen. And Sexy Army Girl Mo. The party's started now the hottest girls in town are here!"

He knows how to be smooth. I could kiss him for being so kind to my single pals. And that's why he slays me — he says the best things. Dibian's flapping her eyelashes at Will and acting like a big gooey girl. Mo's grinning at me from behind her warpaint, bush-clustered army helmet and camouflage outfit.

"Miss Whiplash. You leave me shaken. And stirred."

"Different movie. Wrong hero. Does Batguy have a line?"

As the girls head off to look at the nearby bar, Will slides right in beside me and I feel his warm hand caress my leather-clad hip. Wow.

"How's 'let's shag now' for a line?"

"Not doable in all this leather."

"I'm not so easily dissuaded. How about 'let's go fuck in the Batmobile'?"

"I've seen the back of your Bat wagon before. Roomy. But some of us prefer vertical to legs akimbo landscape." I stifle my chuckles and opt for seriously sexy siren. I've never been one before but tonight I figure I can step up to the mark. "Batmobile does sound uncomfortable. Wouldn't you rather ditch the costumes and get naked anywhere closer?"

"To the Bat Cave. With that whip. Now!" he commands, and inside I swoon and go a little giddy-crazy with the giggles.

"Sorry. I've butts to whip," I tell him. "Most specifically Rogerson and Tarquin. They here yet?" I flick out my whip and make a meal of showing him the crop that's tucked into a neat pocket in my boots.

"One's come as Daddy Warbucks. It's seriously worrying," Will tells me. "Look for the shiny bald head. The other's come... No, I won't spoil the surprise. Let's see if you can spot Tarquin for yourself."

"Spoilsport. I suppose you think that's a challenge I can't meet."

Will fixes me with his dark, serious stare. "I have no doubt you could achieve anything you put your mind to, my dominatrix English teacher. I want you all to myself—later. It's the only thing that's keeping me going. Lots of slow, hard sex with you."

"Shh. Somebody will out us."

"I'd like to say I give a shit, but I don't. Seeing you in that outfit's fired me to the point of kick it to hell."

I raise a brow. "Good. Because that was the point of wearing it, Batboy."

I feel his sly bat hand travel round and rest on my butt cheek proper. I narrow my eyes at him but it has little impact. These superheroes are pretty hard to keep within the party decency boundaries. Another sharp look sees the hand squeeze then slip away. From behind Will's eye mask, I watch those green sparklers dancing an Irish groove.

"Have you spotted those two idiots yet? You aren't trying to find them?" Clearly Rogerson and Endermann have surpassed themselves and Will's enjoying it.

My eyes scan the assembled crowd and pretty quickly I do pick out Rogerson's famous philanthropist father. Tarquin is still nowhere I can find, though currently there's a busy dance floor packed with people gyrating to *Gangnam Style*.

Mo and Dibian return beside us and I'm grateful that Batman's hand is no longer resting possessively on my arse. "You want some punch, Iz?" asks Mo. "The buffet here is fab. Can't wait to try some."

"Grrr," I find myself saying and sounding like a she-wolf.

"What's up?" Will asks.

"That!"

It's Nympho Annie. She's dressed up as Kylie Minogue in gold hotpants with expansive cleavage on full parade. How predictable. She's also ogling Will and pushing out those boobs in time to the music. It's a flesh market in a thong.

Will and I don't say a word for some seconds but he senses my disdain. "Shall I lock her in the pagoda? You can flay her alive later," he asks.

"Too good for her. We need a dungeon where we can chain her to the wall."

"Be careful what you wish for," Will answers darkly and I'm unsure what he means. If he wants me to be contrite about my Annie phobia, he'll have a long wait.

I thought it was a good line but Will hasn't laughed. He merely sighs deeply then asks about my evening.

I burst out laughing because I've seen Jack at the bar. He's wearing his full Arsenal football gear, complete with a giant Arsenal top hat. I wave at him and he waves back and mimics heading a ball to me. I kick the imaginary goal winner back with my pointy, high-heeled boots. Dibian throws herself at Jack for a cuddle—maybe she should show restraint with the punchbowl—and one of her bananas knocks him in the nose. She makes a great fuss of nursing him better.

I'm laughing aloud when I feel Will's hand slide over my rear again. It's definitely squeezing hard and insistently now.

"Careful, Mr. Darby. We have company."

"More's the pity. How about we escape for a short while?"

I'm about to answer but that's when I see Tarquin and the penny drops. "Bloody hell. He hasn't!"

Will replies softly under his breath. "Oh yes, he has."

Tarquin Endermann is wielding an imaginary lasso in the center of the room. Because he's leading the *Gangnam Style* horse jockey-style dancing. He's wearing a white tuxedo and shades and he's doing every move as if he's watched nothing else on YouTube for a month solid without stopping for sleep. He even has the jet-black, jeweled quiff hairdo and I'm trying to work out if it's a wig or an entire plastic stick on head. Whatever he employed to get the look, he's pretty impressive as Mr. Gangnam Style.

"I've been itching to put the track on all night. Shall we speed it up and play it backwards next?" Will asks.

"I love your wicked side. Do it. Then we'll scarper."

Will goes over to the sound system and presses for *Gangnam Style* to be repeated. This time, the tempo is faster and I don't know how he did it but it makes everyone go crazy and I can't help but laugh. I almost put a hand over my eyes to avoid the horror.

Endermann's horse jockey grooving like a crazy *X Factor* reject to his favorite tune and nodding at me to join him.

Will returns to my side then adds, "Apparently, his first choice was to come as Lady Gaga. All that man in too much PVC. Shudders guaranteed."

"Sexy lady, come join the fun!" Tarquin shouts at me. I itch to wrap my whip around his neck.

"I'd rather watch."

"Shame," says a voice near to my ear. "Can't take my eyes off you. I had to come over and force you to dance."

I turn to find Andy Regis beside me. I hardly recognized him without his camera and usual grungy geek rock clothes—he's dressed up as a cowboy tonight, chaps and all. It has to be said he looks pretty hot too. If you're into that sort of thing. Or should I say, if you're not into men with wild dark hair, green eyes and pointy bat ears.

Will is back beside the sound system and I can't get his attention. Ben has appeared beside Will and they are wetting themselves laughing at something, probably Tarquin and Annie competing for dance supremacy.

"Let's dance," says Andy, taking my hand firmly in his. "You're so hot in that costume. It's a shame not to show it to better advantage. You know how to make a man drool, Izzy Tennant."

"It's so not my kind of tune…"

"C'mon. One little groove won't hurt. Where's your fun side got to? I know it's in there…c'mon."

He tugs my hand harder and I'm forced to lurch after him. He pulls me toward the dance floor. In these heels it's not so easy. I feel like a pole dancer made to do ballet moves on stilts.

Dibian is nearby and, unclear about my motives, she pushes me closer and Mo, unaware that my interest is otherwise engaged, forces me army style into his arms with shouts of 'Woo, Izzy, go!'

Andy's doing grinding moves next to me, way too close for comfort. Shit. I can feel Andy's hot breath against my cheek. And his eyes are glittering in a way that tells me he's aroused and assuming his luck's in.

He's a nice enough guy but when you put him and Will together and do a comparison, there's no contest. Will's raging vermillion to Andy's mild beige.

"I've been watching you carefully since I first saw you," Andy confides. "You're quite a woman, Izzy. And I'm into you. I think we could be good together. Don't waste your time on that Bat bloke."

A slow, icy wash of self-questioning drenches me and my thoughts unravel in past recrimination. In being relaxed enough to enjoy Will's company and attentions, have I put us at risk of detection?

"What d'you mean?"

"That I watch you. And every time he's glued to your side. Gets boring when there's a guy here who wants to keep your attention fixed."

"Will's mentoring me. He's giving me advance tips— I like to win." I'm hoping my jocular brush-off will work but I'll have to keep a close internal eye on our actions in future. I kinda itch to shove my whip in his mouth to shut his guff up. I don't want to hear any of what he has to say. Note to self—you're not interested. React to the memo.

"You're a hot woman," Andy says, seizing his ghastly chance to tell me his feelings. "And tonight is the night I intend to impress you that I'm a guy who's interested. *Very* interested. How about we go outside and spend some time one on one?"

"I'm not sure we'd work."

"Don't knock what you haven't tried," he tells me. And I feel another arse squeeze. This one doesn't cause womb meltdown like Will's did. This one makes me feel icky. I don't want this.

Gangnam Style Tarquin appears beside us. He's smiling and dancing and making it impossible for me to give Andy the firm brush-off.

So I am forced to endure Gangnam Styling with a second-rate cowboy who has the misplaced hots. And it would be a car crash enough—if I hadn't seen Will glare at me. Eyes cool and dark and hard, and accusingly direct.

I shake my head.

He stares at me with firm, tense body language and turns away.

And Andy Regis chooses that moment to sweep his arm around my waist and push his groin against mine in a flagrant lambada-type dance. Now it's hell squared.

Will looks back and his dark glare is cold. I sense his aggravation as much as I feel my own cheeks flame.

"C'mon, Izzy," Andy encourages. "You know you want me."

Nympho Annie doesn't need to be asked twice to get into the spotlight and she chooses that moment to pounce on Will. She's doing the moves with a good dash of porn queen.

"Good old Annie. She's probably been watching for this very chance."

I vow to damn and dump Andy and finally take my chance to extricate myself from his amorous dance grasp.

"I don't like this song and my heels are killing me. Excuse me, Andy. I need to get a drink. Don't follow me — we're not on the same page."

I stride off. The sight of Annie pawing my man, and watching him reluctantly walk onto the dance floor with her are too much to bear, so I strop off, wishing I'd had a few cups of punch to make me bolder. Or less fragile. I walk up to the bar and grab a pint glass and start ladling punch into it, including big chunks of fruit even though I've no idea what the hell's in this mystery lethal brew. I drink it down in long gulps and feel it fire my bloodstream. Which means that, most probably, by tomorrow I'll have a head like the Tibetan singing bowl choir gone loco with pneumatic drill accompaniment. Right now I'm too pissed off to care.

When I get to the bar, Ben joins me. I'm all too aware, from his awkward manner, that he can read my mind and has watched my reactions.

"She's no competition, Iz," he tells me. "Don't get your fur in a bunch."

"You reckon?"

"I know. He rates you highly."

"And blokes talk of these things?"

"We do. And take this from a man who knows — Will doesn't fall easily."

My inner vixen has scaled the hencoop's perimeter and pounced on the chick nest at that last revelation but I don't let it show. C'mon. Give me some credit for guile.

"I have something to ask you, Ben." I continue to swig down the lurid, orangey-red mixture and feel it steadily burn a path down my throat. With everything I've got, I hope Andy Regis will have taken the message and won't start chasing me around this party all night long. "I need a favor."

Ben raises dark debonair brows worthy of Bond. And I don't mean Basildon.

"What would you say if I asked for some very confidential help in training me up for this football mentoring stint at school? I'd pay you hourly. I can't give you much but all I want is not to make a total arse of myself when I'm being watched by the nation."

Ben swigs his drink and mulls over my proposition. I'm prepared for him to decline. He is, after all, a much sought after Premier League player with obligations and a busy schedule.

"I won't charge. But I will expect commitment. How about every other night straight from school. Come to my gym in St. Albans."

"Really? You'd help me?"

Ben closes in and whispers softly, "Will's my best friend. You're my girlfriend's bestie. Yes. I will. See you tomorrow. Quarter to five sharp."

Then there's another voice behind me. "What are you doing? Don't you dare think about escaping me. And stop chatting up my best mate if you know what's good for him." The voice nearby is shortly followed by a large hand that grabs my arm and tugs hard. *Shit. Not again!* I throw a last weak smile of apology at Ben as I'm dragged away.

"Move it. Don't stall. Just walk. If that walking cock touches you one more time, he's a bat snack that won't see the light of day tomorrow."

I look up to see Will's eyes staring into mine. He's taken off his mask. Or perhaps Nympho Annie has sucked it off mid-snog. "How masterful you sound. Tired of dancing with your sex-crazed nutter? Is that the kind of woman that fires your bat bits?"

"Whiplash! You know how I roll." Will pulls me by the hand and strides out of the party with his cape fanning out behind him. It's a wondrous sight to behold. "Bat Cave. Now. Ever had sex in a dark space that echoes before? We might even try it upside down!"

"Could be tricky in these suits."

"Nothing too hard for this Caped Crusader."

"What Batman does at the party, stays at the party," I answer. He is, after all, the guardian of Gotham City. And right now I've never wanted him more.

"My hand is itching to get inside that suit and give you twenty of the best spanks of your life for your cheek, woman. And for bloody well dancing with that dipshit. What the fuck is with Woody the dancing cowboy anyway?"

I smile at how I've riled Will. It feels good to be so fully wanted by this fulsome man. "I tried to attract your help but you were too busy with BFF Ben and the Nympho Stalker."

"You could've said no."

I pull out of his grasp and stand my ground. "Where are we going? Can't we find a cupboard? It's clear you only want me for sex and Fiona tells me it's fun that way."

Will stops. Right up close, nose to nose. And stares me down and doesn't say a word. It makes me gulp back trepidation.

"My place. My way!" His voice is hard but smooth as rain-washed gravel chips. Our eyes meet and hold. "I don't *want* you for sex, Izzy. You move me like no woman. I *totally desire and crave and need* you for sex — it's my every waking thought. And right now you've given me a raging hard-on. I wish you hadn't pissed me off so much in the process, woman!"

"I love surprises at parties," I answer with a droll voice. "You should've said earlier, Sir. Houston, we have lift off, let's go!"

Chapter Fourteen

Will leads me down a long dark corridor with gleaming mahogany flooring and the potent aroma of wood wax. A winding iron staircase descends to the basement where a dimmed corridor features three dark doors and low-level lighting.

"Where are we going?" I ask.

"Guaranteed privacy."

I struggle on my overly high heels as I follow his brisk but long bat-strides. "Hate to spoil your plans but isn't this your party?"

"As the host, I'm entitled to set the itinerary."

"Being host kinda involves schmoozing—they'll notice you've gone. They'll come looking. I know Dibian will, for sure."

Will shrugs his broad Batman-caped shoulders. "I've left Ben in charge—we won't be disturbed. Did you wear the leather skin suit for me? I'm interested in finding out if there are underclothes or if it's, as I suspect, the way I like it, bush commando."

I raise my eyebrows in shock. "It could take five shoe horns and a winch to remove this gear."

Will's hair is a delightful mess from the mask but neither of us cares. His midnight velvet voice spellbinds my senses, and hairs respond on my arms. "Don't bet on it. I assure you I'm game to give it a try."

He turns me to face him in the dim basement and kisses me. But kiss is way too tame a descriptor. More like he devours my mouth and leaves me without breath and a boneless husk being supported in his arms. I'd blame these skyscraper heels, but I'd be lying. It's Will's assault of heady testosterone.

Wow, what a guy. I go back for more. We're snogging in the hallway and it's all very sixth-form disco. I have to remind myself—he's Batman and I'm Whiplash. We're both thirty-something teachers having a raunchy, real-life sex affair, gagging for naked thrills and pushing each other's boundaries. How bizarre my life has become since Will Darby waltzed into my school...

Who cares, when the payoffs are this exciting?

"As much as I love your kisses, I'm not risking getting caught down here," I tell him between panted tongue tangles. My hands are wrapped around his head and threaded through his hair, which kinda belies my claims for caution.

"Like I care," he growls. "I'm Batman. Nobody's gonna cross me and win. I want my woman. My way."

"And if Rogerson creeps up on us? Teacher fraternization isn't encouraged, Mister Bat Ears. You won't get a pay rise."

"Only one rise I'm interested in...and Rog is too busy downing Christal bubbles to care about us having orgasms below stairs. It's cool."

When Will is kissing a delicious line from my décolletage to my earlobe and licking the bulge of my corset-clad breasts, it's pretty hard to object. "Find somewhere with a door that locks. We're in danger of getting a reputation." I look down pointedly at the massive, straining bulge in his skin-tight suit.

"Iz. You're so hot. Can you blame a guy for getting excited?"

"Come on, Darby. Leash the beast for two minutes."

"I can't keep my hands off you! See what you do to me?"

He steps back, licks his snog-stung lips then produces a key from some hidden Lycra pocket. And this will prove to be a moment I will never forget.

He *does* have a Bat Cave. Only this one's a massive, shocking game changer.

The key turns in the lock, but the door stays shut as Will's eyes meet mine. He moves over a few steps and enters a code, using the buttons in the wall panel. With a rasping sound, the bolts slide to release.

Will grasps my hands. His eyes are solemn. "You must enter here without judgment. This place isn't mine."

I raise my eyebrows but say nothing. Mostly because I've no idea what he's on about.

"No questions, no answers. Understood? We go in here and nothing more is discussed. I made a promise I won't break and this is not my room. On that you must be assured."

"Okay… I think."

Frankly, he couldn't bamboozle me more. But there's something about a mystery that gets your interest and cuffs it to the radiator with panting nosiness. Consider mine duly chained up and gagging to get to the skinny.

"Come on, Will. No need to be so cloak and dagger."

"I think there's every need. You'll understand soon."

The room is in darkness even though I crane to see. "What's in there—your jewel stash? The wine cellar? Bloody expensive wine if it needs Fort Knox locks. Don't tell me, it's the gold bullion you stole in a train robbery!" I think of another joke and can't hold it in. "Damn. It's your cross-dressing wardrobe. Why didn't I guess?"

"Why is everything a joke with you? This is serious." Will shakes his head, his jaw clenches and the look on his face makes my innards flip. It's grimmer than Stephen King storytelling in a graveyard.

"What is it, Will?"

"It's not wine. It's for something stronger."

Something in his tense stance makes me falter. I've never seen him so earnest—it could almost be his middle name, and that would be wrong. Why is this room so private?

"Less wine cellar, more dungeon." Will's face takes on a grim cast.

The door opens wider and he hits a switch, causing lights to come on in slow but steady succession. Their muted red glow throws a spooky hue. He pulls me to him and we're inside the room, then he firmly closes the door behind us. It has the ominous deep click of bolts that mean business—I find myself hoping I won't regret coming in here in the first place.

I look around me and my breath catches fast in my chest. "Holy shit, Will. What…the…fuck!"

The windows are shuttered—the room's contents breathtaking, and not in any way that could ever be imagined. I'm still turning round to peruse it all as my eyes meet shock after shock. "Holy shit. Who built this? Torture Chambers Are Us?"

"No judgments remember."

"No judgments but plenty of Oh My Bloody Gods, Will."

"Strictly confidential. It's not my secret. But it is somewhere I know we can escape to without being disturbed tonight. If I haven't shot the moment to hell by shocking you."

I let out a slow, low whistle. "It's a bloody dungeon and if this is what you do in your spare time—I'm starting to think you're way more whiplash than I'm ready for!" I gulp and swallow on the hard bulk of my dry, shocked throat.

"If you want, you can still leave."

My emotions have taken a rocket trip to full-blown toxic shock as I stand immobile and absorb what faces me.

Will is explaining but I'm barely listening, "Paul Bates' wife Shana built the room. He gave me the entry code but I told him I'd never need their 'playroom'. If the truth comes out—can you imagine the headlines?"

I feel his heart drumming and my mouth dries as the need to retreat takes hold. But a weird part of me wants to know more. Here lies a spacious room where shuttered windows have created a dimmed lair. There's dark wood flooring, dark walls and the heady notes of exotic, sensual flowers and spices scent the air. A vast, square bed is sheathed in black silk sheets. A ceiling mirror reflects the heady opulence. Tiny bottled oils grace the lacquered table nearby.

Panels of deep claret silk are festooned from the ceiling and along the walls. Long leather ropes with elaborate brass cuffs are fixed to the bed. A nearby ebony table also features chained cuffs and manacles. If it's for massage, these treatments aren't for chillax or muscle tension relief.

I fail to summon any response. While delving into Will's landlord's sex secrets isn't my business, part of me can't not have questions answered.

Ebony glossy cabinets stand against each wall and a large rack is lined with whips, canes and other threatening implements that don't bear close scrutiny.

I circle to absorb this revelation. "Holy crap. This is some kinky side."

"They're props. Paul says it's consensual. Now you'll see why I was trying hard to keep eyes out. But, for tonight, it means we can be alone."

Will runs his finger over a layer of dust that's built up on the table beside him. "Paul told me Shana's sex slave phase is over. Been a while since it's been in use. We've got the privacy. Still up for this?"

I blow out a breath. Man, these are some surroundings. A girl would be forgiven for feeling overawed. For backing up with a mighty 'ewww'.

Then again, I'm with the man I'm into like no other. The implements around me are strangely thrilling and remember, I'm a dyed-in-the-wool erotica fan who's read and dreamed about fantasies like this. Shana Bates may well be a woman after my own heart.

I'm in a room straight out of my fave erotic book. Am I about to say no thanks and do a U-turn?

"Guess I'll have to stay here solo," he says coquettishly. I can tell he's only seeking a reaction.

Will pulls at his Batsuit and it peels away from his taut body. My eyes widen as I watch and I'm minded of a strip show I went to once where the male dancers' trousers flew off as if by magic.

"We don't have to do kinky shit if you don't want to," says Will.

Fuck! As bloody if! "You saying I'm a wuss, Darby?" I pull my ponytail over my shoulder and slip out of my leather jacket. Then I place my curled whip down on the gleaming table, unconcerned by the manacles and shackles.

"I wouldn't dare."

His eyes darken as I stand before him in my tight leather jeans and black lace corset. I run my black gel nails up the side of my own neck to get him even more hot and bothered.

"I'm feeling hot." I close my eyes and gulp. "What should I take off first?"

My words work, because he rushes at me like a blood-starved urban commando vampire and I'm grinning as he snogs me full and hard.

I hold my finger up between kisses and point it at his chest. I pause for effect. "I'm up for kinky shit. But we've not got much time tonight. Kinky takes time and deliberation."

"There'll be other nights...now that we know it's here waiting. How about hard and fast and crazy?"

"My favorite kind. Dim the lights if you prefer? Being a creature of the night..."

He growls low in his throat. "I want to see everything." Will smiles wide before he grabs me. I think I'm rocking it like a sexed-up Beyoncé and Batman's a very happy boy.

We're naked. Delightfully, deliciously naked. I can see some of the hairs on his arms stand to attention — mimicking the actions of that most important part of him.

Will has peeled my leather layers away and his Bat skin Lycra lies like a giant black condom on the floor.

I giggle and that fires him more.

"Enough, Whiplash!"

And, wow, but Will is turned on. He's erect and wet. Strong and sleek. His muscles are something that should be celebrated in art. His man parts are resplendent.

And so am I—wet, that is. My breasts are heavy with desire, and when Will pulls me to him, I melt into those sensual kisses that spin me into infinity. He cups my breasts, he teases and molds me. And, as he kneads my nipples, I mewl in the back of my throat, wanting more, always more. His mouth dips to trail kisses down to where his fingers have worked their magic. And man, but that is a sinful mouth—I know from personal experience.

He takes my nipples fully in his mouth and I gasp aloud. His teeth scrape me lightly. Then his tongue ravishes the spot he tortured. One minute my nipples are hard and peaked. The next I'm heavy and aching for everything he can give.

"You're going straight for consensual straight vanilla, Will Darby."

"Can't wait, madam. You shouldn't play such a high-octane fantasy dress foreplay game."

"Oh. But my. It was worth it." I giggle.

He sucks my nipples then plays them with his tongue. To think there's a straddle bar in here, manacles, handcuffs, whips, crops, restraints aplenty. And all I want is Will. Kissing me, sucking me. Promising the delights of his cock.

All I want is him. Us. Like this.

"You didn't shave. Ah. I like that."

"Would I dare to defy my Sir?"

He slides his hand into my hairs and he hisses between his teeth when he feels my naked, wet heat. I'm positively molten.

"I love it when you're like this."

"And I think I love it back."

We're against the wall and Will pulls me to him. He puts on a condom in record time and I raise my leg. He eases into me, and his weight presses so temptingly against my clit, I cry out at the sensation. It's painful but sweet, heady pain as I widen and stretch.

"More..."

"Sure?"

"Give me all you have."

I feel myself get wetter and wider. I encourage him with a wide-eyed stare and he smiles as he screws me tighter and I want it more than oxygen.

"Ah. Hidden depths," I purr.

"I want you."

"I want that cock to stay at the party. Shall we? Sir?"

His cock presses deep between my moist, hot folds and I have him fully to the hilt and harder than he's ever been. It's the biggest head buzz ever. I moan at the sensation of widening as far as I can to accept him and I close my eyes, relishing having him in the deepest part of me. I'm the hottest and most turned on I've ever been in my life. My gaze sweeps the room and takes in all the instruments of kink. Seeing it all turns me on and takes me higher.

I gasp and moan out in my ecstasy as Will drills me with his powerful thrusts.

"Good, baby?"

I can't answer in words — only moans.

I rise on my toes as he stays deep in slow, steady fulfillment. Is it too much to hope that tonight we might conquer my burning ambition of satisfying him? Full-on penetrative sex and orgasms for us both in a manner that lasts long enough to blow his world.

He pulls out then jams straight home and I shout his name.

He does it again and again, moving in a slow deliberate pace that makes me pant and moan over and over.

"Wow," I whimper. "More. Harder. Take me."

"This is all I've wanted…"

He grasps my butt as he claims me, to raise me up, and I take him as deeply as I can. I'm fully engaged and accommodating him now and it's rocking both our worlds. He's inside me—joined as I squeeze him with my legs. I want to stay like this forever. And yet…

"I love this."

Wow the *L* word. Fuck.

"One glance at you tonight. I knew. You've done this."

He rams into me again, again, again, again. We're both making noises that tell me it's crazy time. But the sex is stellar and this is what we both wanted and knew we'd have. Fucking magic.

The sex explosion of my life.

As if to emphasize his words, he thrusts into me, presses and stays as his mouth finds my neck and he kisses me meltingly. Then he slams again so forcibly that I yelp. It's a good yelp but a loud yelp and I don't even care as he's drilling into me and we're noisier than the school orchestra on a good day. It's pleasure, it's desire and a need for more.

"Fuck me, Will. I want it. I want you."

I'm urging more as he fills me full and deep as delight bubbles through my veins. My clitoris is responding to his magic as my excitement starts to peak. I relish each moment he thrusts into me, taking me higher. I cry out his name against his ear as he claims me against the wall, pinioning me to Paul Bates' passion room as if I'm an autumn leaf on a nature wall chart. He makes me feel at one with nature. Synergy — a whole human being because of his organic, electrifying touch.

I think I'm in love. Body, soul. The works.

"Oh God, Izzy."

I can tell Will is near the pleasure pinnacle, as every muscle and sinew are tensed to the brink. His pace builds to frenetic mayhem and, even though it's rough, I welcome the rush. Being pounded this way is life-affirming and I relish the way I gasp as he crashes into me and my clitoris absorbs each thrust. The power of our orgasm is like a tsunami of need that's swept us into oblivion. Will thrusts, moans and growls with his desire and he judders against me as he comes deep inside my pounding pussy.

"Baby. Yes. Baby."

He clings to me, spent. His pace, once frenetic, swiftly calms as we cling drowning in the moment as waves of steady pleasure continue.

The climb was a mounting buzz. The aftermath is bliss meets nirvana.

My inner vixen is buoyed beyond words that he's succeeded here. I know the battles and scars he bears.

"Thank you. I love you," he says against my ear. "Next time. Kinky shit. Guaranteed."

Um. Wow. Love?

My heart is thundering and not just from the sex. But I'm not quite sure how to voice my surprise.

"You okay?" he checks.

"More than okay. I knew we'd be good."

"I want to stay down here forever. I want this again."

"I'd love to. But there's a house full of guests. Hold that thought for later."

And I think I am, I'm totally in love. And more scared than I've ever been before. Love, fuck. Love.

This has gone to a new level—one that's scarier than I'm ready for and I fear I'm over the threshold and into the no exit zone without knowing I've taken this route.

Will's my danger zone. He's a man who scares me because I suspect he has the power to deeply scar me. I hide my true wounds well. So well nobody realizes I'm fragile beneath the surface. I lost the center of my world—then I lost trust in myself. It's a place I never revisit.

I staunchly cover these innermost weaknesses. Yet they are hanging together at heart by a thread. How do I cope with opening such secrets? Can I resurrect my defenses? Can I risk my heart against all odds?

* * * *

We're leaving our lair when we run into a search party of one. It's Annie James, hotpants and all. Of all the people to come find us... Why am I not surprised? Just when I think I can't hate her more—whoops, I managed to ramp up the loathing.

She pouts cherry-glossed lips that I swear must be no strangers to Botox. "Will, I've been looking for you for ages. What're you doing down here?" She puts her fists firmly on her hips. "What have you been up to? Don't tell me Izzy's commandeering you yet again!"

"Headache pills," Will segues and I push my hand to my temples and wince without prompting.

"Migraine. Must've been brought on by the punch. It's got plenty of thump behind it."

There's one person here I'd like to punch. And it's not the male in our midst.

Annie narrows her eyes. "I wouldn't know, I've been too busy dancing. And we didn't finish what we started, Will."

I find myself wondering if she's noticed that my corset laces have snapped in the middle due to the eager fingers of my beau or that my previously sleek ponytail's been ravaged by Sir's firm attentions.

"I have host duties, I'm afraid," says Will.

"Then Izzy shouldn't be hogging your attentions with her headaches. That getup does look a bit tight, Izzy. Not surprised your head hurts. You've probably caused nerve damage," Annie snarls at me.

"Like your hotpants. Vintage is very you, though. Nice to see a woman showing her age."

Basically this woman needs a good bitch-slap and I'm wondering if now may be the time. My, but that woman is a spiteful cougar into the bargain.

Annie's eyes narrow but she runs on, "Will, there's been unpleasantness in the grounds. And as one of Izzy's friends is involved, it would be best if you come without her. She's, after all, a biased party. It's been a fight. And I understand the police are on their way."

"Who?" I ask immediately.

"Joe... No. What was her name? Mo? I can't remember. She's dressed up like a guerrilla and frankly it's a huge tip-off to her character. Highly appropriate given her violent tendencies. She claims she caught some prowler in the bushes, though I struggle to believe it. And she foolishly took things into her own hands. Your security boys have intervened but I think we need police involved. She kicked the man in the privates."

"But is she okay? Before you play judge and jury and get it all wrong."

"Yes. Though I think she gave as good as she got. The police have been called because I told them to get right on to it," Annie says.

It's the last thing that Will needs. To have cops and prying eyes crawling into his private life. Especially given what I now know about what lies below stairs. He may have a point.

"Let's go see what the fuss is about," Will tells her, but his eyes are on me.

As we head for the stairs, he whispers near to my ear, "Play it cool. You're great in a crisis. Help me sort it out, please?"

And I will. "Of course."

Because he's my hero. In more ways than his costume and his playroom moves.

Chapter Fifteen

There's garbled shouting going on outside the main doors of Hangley Grange, and I don't need proximity to recognize Mo by the language flying like nunchuks. As I get closer, I can see a flashing blue light outside the gate. Shit.

You leave a party for some hush-hush sex and all hell lets loose, complete with the boys in blue.

I feel like I've walked into a *No Sex Please, We're British* production.

I pull Will aside quickly. "I'll talk to the police. Let me do the schmoozing, okay? It'll be fine. Nothing untoward — you're entitled to have a house party even in a mansion."

Will nods and we split up to each fulfill our roles in diplomacy.

I reach Mo and, as I do, her shouting turns to floods of tears. Which is going to play havoc with her warpaint let alone her mascara. It's only then that I notice she has a torn top and the massive shiner of a black eye is not face camouflage gone wrong.

"Mo! What the hell happened here? Who did that to you?" I'm incensed. When I first heard Annie's claims, I thought it was probably bluster, but seeing a black eye on your best friend fires you up for repercussions.

"Photographer. Filthy scum. And he denies everything," says Mo.

"Bastard!"

"Bastard's too good for him. He even tried to do a runner. Though my tae kwon do worked wonders. He took a right doof in the nads!"

The man in question is sprawled on the grass. I can hear his moans and see his abject pain. Two of Will's car parking attendants are keeping him down. He does, indeed, have cameras—a bag full, in fact. They're now lying beside him. He looks less than pleased and I wonder what the hell he was after? Shit—why are we having papping stalkers here?

I hug Mo to me and I let her have the cry she needs.

"And her!" Mo says with volatility, pointing at Annie. "She was a chocolate teapot in a crisis. Bloody nutso woman tried to fight me off him and jumped on my back. I saw him skulking by the cars so I followed him and he tried to jemmy open the back cellar door round the back. Found him when I nipped out for a fag with Jack. He was looking a bit peaky."

"Who was peaky, Jack?"

Mo nods and I realize I haven't seen him. He's kinda hard to miss in his massive Arsenal top hat.

"He okay?"

"He's inside with Dibs. He had a sore chest and he was breathing bad."

Shit, not again. Both gates have opened and there's an ambulance with paramedics and a police car coming up the drive. The evening keeps dishing out surprises of the nasty kind.

This is proving to be quite a party. And not in the way I'd have thought. There have been incredible highs. I suspect this dip isn't one of them. And suddenly I feel the need to run and find Jack.

* * * *

The policeman, as it turns out, is related to one of Dibian's neighbors and she recognizes him straight away His name is Rod O'Leary and he also used to be a prefect when Dibian was a trainee teacher. I'm pretty sure Rod the Plod is a nickname he doesn't care to have reiterated, so I don't use it. I keep it all under lock and key in my head.

As policemen go, we got a good one and his partner in crime is a doppelganger for Samwell Tarney of *Game of Thrones* fame, whose frame suggests he's more accustomed to pen pushing and doughnuts than baddie chasing. And while he looks like he's the jolly, amiable one, maybe he has a surprising, vicious side when it comes to questioning suspects.

Mo is in the vast dining room with Rod, making a statement. Her tears have turned to pert interest and I think it's due to seeing Rod in his shirtsleeves — he has gym-honed arms and rigid pecs. Rod's quite something to behold in a uniform and Mo is so very easy, it's almost a sin. She smiles as I enter to offer moral support and raises her eyebrows in a silent 'Wow, he's lush! I've got a good one here!'

"So we have attempted break-in. Assault. Car damage in order to steal goods," I can hear Rod saying as he scribbles in his pad.

"And he swore at me. Called me a dumb army bitch and to eff off to Afghanistan."

"I merely wish to record your version of events at this stage. We will investigate fully," Rod says with the tight lips of the mother superior at the convent-of-our-lady-of-the-perpetually-strained-patie nce. He gives her a sly wink, which I'm pretty sure isn't in the policeman's protocols manual.

"You'd better be interviewing him too? Secret snapper camera-toting scumbag that he is. He was up to no good, whatever he says! Find out what he stole from Tarquin's car!" Mo says.

"Mr. Endermann and the perpetrator are also being questioned in the lounge down the hall. Rest assured, madam, we want to get the train of events recorded. Do you want another cup of tea to calm the nerves?"

"No. I'd kill for a double Jack Daniel's and a plate of vol-au-vents, though. Did I tell you I'm a chocolatier by trade—I'll make sure you're fully reimbursed for your troubles in chocolate ganache truffles."

Again, Rod flashes her a proper pert grin. I think he's interested. Though it could be Mo's double F boobs in a clingy army vest that's the cause.

"Perhaps once the questioning has been completed." He watches her as if he's veering toward the selvage edge of his patience's pinafore fabric.

"I'll get tea for you both," I interject. "And biscuits. Tea and biscuits always help steady the nerves! Especially Wagon Wheels," I say and I take this as my cue to go and find out what's happened with Jack.

Unfortunately, if the photographer assault surprise is bearable, Jack's situation is the biggest downer of the night.

* * * *

Jack is lying on a couch in a bedroom on the ground floor. He has an oxygen mask on his face and his complexion is ashen. His eyes are shut and Dibian is holding his hand as paramedics simultaneously talk reassuringly, but also give instructions.

It's clear, within only a few moments that he's on his way to hospital.

"I'll go with him," says Dibian, nodding on fast speed. "You stay here and sort out the rabble. Do I need to let any relatives know?"

I shake my head. Jack has nobody I'm aware of who'll need to know right now. He does have a sister in Southend but I don't know her address or contacts.

I notice Dibian's headdress is gone, her gaudy Carmen outfit now covered up by someone's gray cardigan. I can see when she looks around and her eyes meet mine that she's had a shock and there are telltale mascara tracks. I go to her side.

"What are they saying?" I ask simply.

"Not a heart attack, but definitely a heart problem." Her eyes probe mine in silent communication that it's serious. Being managed but serious nonetheless.

"Are you sure you want to go? I'll go."

"As much as you mean well, my darling, you'd scare the natives. I wouldn't live with myself if I didn't. I'll handle it, darling."

"You're a fantastic woman, Dibs." Shit. I feel it come on me. I'm crying. And I never cry. Well, that's a lie, isn't it? I cried when I was ill. It seems in moments of true weakness and big life problems I do crack.

"Shall I come and keep you company too?" I ask. "I don't give a shit if I look weird. I can borrow clothes from Will."

She looks at me and nods.

"Go and get changed. I'll ask them if you can come in the ambulance."

"You go in the ambulance. I'll get a cab. Text me where you are."

We hug.

I long to hug Jack but he's so still. So quiet. There's lots of tubes and things stuck to him.

I'm suddenly very scared. Like an icy tap's deathly drip down my spine, and some horror instinct that I don't even want to face yet that's telling me — you have to go, he may not rally. Go or you'll regret it.

Fuck.

"I'm going to get dressed and sort a taxi now," I tell her, wiping stray tears away with nothing but my fingers. "I'll be there every step of the way."

Sometimes, as I know too well from experience, you don't get a second chance in life. Some moments are drama, pathos, tragedy and you have to go with it and take it and stoically step up to the parapet. I'm so very afraid that this could be such a time.

Like it was with my dad. Like it was with me.

Jack. Please. Don't die tonight. Please.

Fuck.

* * * *

When I get there an hour on, wearing a pair of Will's combats and a T-shirt and sweater, the hospital is what hospitals usually are.

Me and Dibian sitting, huddled for warmth, waiting for news that doesn't come. The hospital is new and, like every recently furbished hospital up and down the country, it's clean, crisp but uniformly nondescript. They may as well have a sign that says 'Warm Welcomes and Reassurances Left at Home'. This is a land where a vending machine is your only highlight. But I guess hospitals aren't there for our entertainment, are they?

So far all we know is Jack has some kind of heart condition. He hasn't suffered a heart attack. But definitely some kind of coronary episode—Dibian related that the doctors are most worried about a possible problem with his arteries. Apparently, his legs were starting to turn a dark shade. It doesn't look too good. And that revelation leaves us both feeling more than a little grave.

"Poor Jack. He'll hate this," I say.

"You're close to him, aren't you, Izzy? I didn't realize quite how much until Jack talked of your friendship earlier."

"A friendship partly forged out of the mutual football thing. But he's a great guy. I've known him on a personal level for many years."

Dibian's once bright magenta lipstick has paled to a pastel pink. Her eyes are dark and black rimmed. "He talks of you like one would do of a daughter. You make him proud."

"Me? Don't be daft." I huddle deeper inside Will's sweatshirt.

"He's fonder of you than you think."

"Don't!" I say softly. "He's the dad I haven't had — mine passed away when I was four. Mum brought me up solo, after he died in an accident walking into work as a Billingsgate fish marketman. Early morning accident, poor visibility and a careless driver. Uncle Cyril passed on Dad's love of Arsenal. Meeting Jack forged an instant bond — sometimes I swear we read each other's minds." I gulp out a final sob. The tears are running fast and free. "I'm so cross with him because he had a turn and he told me he'd gone to the doctors. I suspect now he was giving me a line."

Shit. Now I'm crying. Now do you see why I don't go on memory lane trails? I like being stoic Izzy, the non-crying, sensible pragmatist. Emotional Izzy, the weeping train wreck isn't a version of me I encourage.

Dibian's arm sneaks around me and provides surprising comfort and calm.

"There, there. I know why he picked you. And vice versa. I find myself becoming ever so fond of you both."

"Dibs. I'm not good with crying," I say, my voice dry and strained.

"Who is? But it's better out than in."

She's right and I let the tears roll.

"Do you think he'll be okay?"

"I hope so, darling. I do hope so. And he's in one of the best places to make that happen. Let's give him all the positive vibes we've got, eh, sweetie? Vibes, positive energies. And hope. Let's feel a firm conviction that he's a lot more Arsenal matches ahead of him."

* * * *

Jack is doing better. It's a huge relief — there are question marks over the handling of his future health condition, but it's been positive that he's improving. He remains in hospital — still under observation, but we've been reassured that our vigil in the waiting room won't help.

We've left him to the medical experts and returned home to restore and replenish. Dibian's going back for afternoon visiting and I've agreed to pop back soon.

Back at my flat, I look like a total troll tonight. Possibly the result of too much crying and sitting around without sleep in hospital. Even Flo shut up in shock at my appearance, and that speaks volumes.

It's partly because, with backed-up laundry, I had to get down and dirty with the U-bend, due to a problem with the washing machine. I'm no stranger to jubilee clips or fitting a new washing machine seal, so I did my bit. But, alas, I got spewed on by the outlet pipe in the process. My hair's a bloody disgrace and I fear I smell like a ruddy bog monster. And when I've smeared something up my face while removing my rubber gloves, the doorbell rings.

I'm fully suspecting it'll be Will.

After all, isn't this when you want the man of your loins to find you? He's dreaming of lace and lingerie and I'm smelling of stagnant water and rancid sinks. This view will certainly challenge our relationship.

But it's not Will.

It's Tessa, Will's maid. I can't even cover my shock.

"Oh, hi," I say as my mind reels on why she could possibly be here.

I slap my forehead with my palm. "Shit. I forgot. I need to reimburse you for the pajamas and things...

Come in! I apologize that it slipped my mind. That was so bad of me… Life's been a bit crazy."

A tiny semi-smile tugs at the very corner of her lip but it, as swiftly, vanishes like the briefest slash of golden sun during an overcast, gray, leaden picnic. "No. I'm not here for money. But I want to talk."

I've only ever seen Tessa from a distance. She's model-caliber good-looking — thin, long ultra-blonde hair, impressive boobs and a Cupid's bow you'd kill for. There's an accent to her voice I can't place. Her manner's more than a little off-putting. Maybe she's had a bad day — clearing up after Will's party, that's hardly a surprise.

"Nothing wrong is there?" I ask and motion her toward a chair in the lounge, pulling stray throws and strewn hoodie tops off it, in order to clear the way. "Must've been a right mess to tidy up after the party. Hope nobody threw up in the Jacuzzi." I rummage in my bag to retrieve my purse and, after a lot of fruitless searching, I'm delighted when I find it at the bottom of the bag — like a forager finding a truffle in the forest.

Tessa sits tentatively on the very edge of my sofa seat, as if she thinks it's going to bite her bum and gnaw a bit off. She closes her eyes briefly then stares hard into mine. "I don't clean. I'm a services maid, not a cleaner. There's a team at the house getting it ready now. I don't deal with such menial basics."

Wow. Talk about touchy. I feel like I've stood on a status landmine or something. So I backpedal. I can't undetonate the faux pas but I can wrap it up in apologetic gift wrap.

"Sorry. I figured you managed the team or something. Anyway…how can I help you? Will okay? Nothing's happened, has it?"

She stares me down. "Everything's happened. Since you came. You do realize you're one in a line."

I stand, staring back at her, nonplussed. My brain is fighting off the rabid ninja instinct to grab her by the neck, even at the inference of what I think she means. But my ninja's had the day off booked for a while. Maybe he doesn't want to come to the party when I look and smell so bad from my behind washing machine and under sink activities. So today I'm on my own in terms of fending Tessa off.

"I'm sorry. You'll have to be clearer and explain what you mean."

Man, what a wuss. Ninja get the fuck out here now and help me.

"You're his latest thing. It'll pass. Don't get ideas you're special."

"Will?"

"Who else do you think I'd be talking about or interested in?"

"And why are you telling me this?"

"To give you the message to back off."

"Why? Tired of changing bed sheets?"

I inwardly salute my tenacity. I can see a glimmer — he may not have totally departed the building. That last one cut a slash and I can see from her face that she's displeased.

Her blue eyes are ice shards, meeting my gaze head on with piercing threat. "I've slept with him. Many times. You're his latest thrill. You were there at a disadvantage and, heaven knows why, but he got interested. But don't bank on it lasting beyond a few weeks. It never does."

"And you'd know this because you're his...what? Relative? Employee? Micromanaging maid? Or scary stalker? Take your pick. I'm kinda thinking all four would fit the bill."

Tessa makes a pit bull face and spits out her words. For a pretty woman, she's damn ugly when riled. "I knew you were a bitch when I first saw you. You and your ridiculous tartan knickers. What kind of man could ever fancy that?"

My purse, in my hand from when I rummaged to get it to reimburse her, is still there clutched in my fingers. I unzip it and yank out forty pounds — leaving me with only a couple of quid to my name but hell, who cares? I toss the money in her face.

"Take your money and get out, you slag."

"I don't want your money. I want to warn you. Back off. Leave him alone or you'll regret it. I will make sure you regret it."

"What are you going to do? Beat me to death with a duster? Spray Captain StreaksAway in my eyes? Ouch. Watch me tremble. Me and my tartan knickers are quaking with fear!"

"Fuck off. You're an easy lay. You can't possibly keep him interested. He'll be back, knocking on my door, before you know it."

"He said you have a husband and kids. Nice *Mary Poppins* image you're presenting here?"

"And who are you to criticize me? My husband knows I have needs on the side."

"Tessa. I don't think I want to talk to you anymore. I might catch something."

She rises from her seat. It's only then I notice her higher-than-high leopard-skin stiletto shoes. And the tiny anklet that glimmers with diamonds around her ankle. She's a leopard all right — but I'm no fusty, fat old cat and I can give her a good old feline fight if pushed.

"Fuck off. Don't dare to speak to me again. And keep your dirty bed-changing, rubber-gloved desperate hands away from Will. He's with me now. You weren't his thing. Deal with it." I almost can't believe I've used her profession against her, it's so against my principles but sometimes only the lowest jab will do.

I'm right behind her, forcing her back up my hall and out of the door with my words. It would have made me feel powerful if she hadn't tossed her waist-length, much-highlighted hair in my face as she turned on the door threshold. The over-sweet smell of her bubblegum shampoo tickles my gag reflex.

"Better go and buy some new underwear if you stand any chance of turning those words into action."

She turns, walks down my path, gets into a sleek, scarlet-starlet sports car and slams its door as I let rip with mine. But, as I'm standing behind the closed door, my hands shake.

I've been bitch-slapped. But hell, so has she.

And what the fuck do I think of this little episode? I'm so confused.

I dive for the phone and ring the only person I can.

Dibian.

And that's something my friends would never have bet on in a month of ruddy Sundays. Fuck, how weird has my life got.

* * * *

Dibian proves to be exactly the right choice for reassurance — mostly because she was the one who first knew about me and Will. She's practical and would make a brilliant agony aunt.

"Nasty little fucker," she says.

I love Dibian. Couldn't have put it better myself.

"And do you believe her?"

"Well. That's it. I'd love to think not. That she's just a deranged, jealous bunny boiler. But I haven't known Will that long. As much as I'm enamored, he could be faking and playing me a line? What if she's right and she is telling the truth?" And much as I hate to think it, I'm risking a tightrope of taut, treacherous doubt by casting all my hopes into Will's, as yet, unknown waters.

There's a long pause while Dibian ruminates.

"Do you plan to tell and ask him?"

I bite my lips. "I don't know. We've not had things going on that long. A big part of me doesn't want to sully the fragility. Or dampen the thrill or the excitement."

"Then don't."

"Really? But what if I'm wrong? What if she's right?"

"Leave it with me. I have means of finding things out." Dibian's tone doesn't brook questioning or doubts.

Then again, I've never been one to back down without answers. "What do you mean?" She's always so full of mystery. What on earth can she be planning? Is she going to read our tea leaves or something? Does she have a spy-cam up and running in the school or a bug on his phone?

"I mean that. Leave it with me. You try your level best to be as you were with Will. Forget Stalker Girl ever dropped by. I'll use my contacts to get to the truth."

Easy for Dibs to say — but she isn't the one who'll be seeing suicide blonde streaks and acid-bath eyes staring out of the dark at night. The woman would kill me in a blink. She loathes me and my knickers with an insidious hatred I can only liken to my fear of oral tests in French.

I pipe up yet again. Forever a voice with misgivings. "But isn't shrugging shoulders and pretending like she doesn't exist going to be more than a bit tricky?"

"Depends how you deal with it. Trust me, Izzy. Leave this to me to do some digging about Psycho Maid. And put it out of your mind. In fact—set up a tryst for amour. You can use that time with Will to ask him some gentle questions, safe in the knowledge that I'll get to the bottom of things for you. And you'll have more great memories to treasure with your man. Trust me—we'll find out and then you can make an informed choice. And I'm pretty sure she's trouble-making—I have a great instinct for these things."

If only the same could be said for her 'instinct' for the many crimes of her paramour, Ronald.

"I'm not sure. Kinda smacks of denial."

"Oh. No. You're dealing with it cleverly. And skillfully. Trust me."

"But how on earth are you going to do this? I don't get it."

"Best you don't, my love. But trust me. Where there's a will, there's a way. No pun intended. I'll get your answers. And you can help me in return."

"How?"

"Let me go and visit Jack tonight?"

"You sure?" I'm quite shocked at her directness. Then the penny drops and I realize she's got a crush on my pal. "You into Jack?"

"Course. I'm outside the hospital now for afternoon visiting. Cutting to the chase, I'm keen on him. I do want to see him. If you don't mind. I'll tell him you'll drop in tomorrow? I wanted a second chance to drop in today."

"Of course." I smile. Impressed and slightly pleased that Dibian has a crush on my best buddy Jack. She clearly has good taste. And I'm so very glad that Ronald the Pilfering Rogue is second billing. She couldn't find a nicer guy to get over bad stuff with.

Will Jack be up for it?

We'll have to wait and see.

"Go for it, girlfriend," I tell her.

"Just putting on my lippy now." I hear her lips smack together on cue. "I wholly intend to, darling. Jack's a keeper and I know when I've hit solid gold. Wish me luck, Izzy. I've never prayed for it more."

My phone pings with a text seconds later. I wonder what I'm going to say to Will, if it's him, but I needn't have worried.

"Can you come by the gym earlier tonight? Say half four?" It's Ben and we've a coaching session planned. Shit, I'd forgotten about it entirely.

"No probs. Cancel if you like?"

"No way—you don't avoid it that easily. You can't default on me, Lazybones." His answer's on the money. "Tonight Janey and I are doing something special. Very special. Stay tuned."

I intend to grill him at my lesson. For something inside me tells me this might be a bigger deal than he's revealing.

Chapter Sixteen

Ben refuses to put me out of my misery about what he and Janey are doing tonight, though he wears a rather enigmatic smile. Not quite Mona Lisa but a mysterious celeb-footballer looking pretty pleased with his private thoughts expression was in evidence.

Of course, I've never been any good at taking advice, however well intentioned. Call me Izzy the Idiot. And now, after my football session, and because my visit to the hospital has been canceled, and my brain is playing paranoia solitaire with itself, on insanity mode, I'm in a dangerous mood.

I'm girlfriend with a gremlin on her shoulder, telling her to take things into her own hands and enact exacting measures... Never a good idea. I should simply go to the pub and get hammered. But I don't.

The gremlin suggests going over to Will's unannounced to see if he's getting the jiggy on with Temptress Tessa and, before I know it, I'm behind the wheel, chain-eating caramel chocolate drops while doing thirty miles an hour toward Totteridge.

Some would say I'm crazy. The psychotic among us would say—right on, Izzy. Great plan. Let's go, and gun the gas while you're at it!

All the way over, I'm telling myself one minute I'm quite right to turn up on the doorstep at Hangley Grange. After all, he's maybe there schmoozing Tessa? She's probably in a French maid's pinny, see-through French knickers and no bra with stellar tits—way better than mine could ever be. At heart, I do have a thing that one nipple is slightly higher than my other, but I've never admitted it to a soul. In my paranoid fantasy, the Psycho Strumpet is straddling Will in the whirlpool, and feeding him Parisian absinthe macaroons…

Does he even like macaroons? The other voice berates the very thought and shoves my hair shirt on my self-flagellating guilty shoulders. End result is I'm getting angrier and more perplexed by the minute, and if I'd known how crazy this was going to get me, I'd have stayed at home to do class prep. Instead, I'm here because I don't know when to back down. Sodding bugger.

In the end, I pick up the phone and dial Dibian from a lay-by somewhere near Arkley. Dibs should run her own agony hotline franchise called Dial-a-Dibian, or something.

"It's me. I'm heading over there. I need answers."

"Whoa. Darling. This isn't a good time. I'm indisposed and breathless as a mating seal on a midsummer's night."

Ick. "Are you with Jack now?"

"Yes, darling. Things are intense."

"In hospital?"

"Believe me. He's very much better. Dibian knows how to medicate a love-starved man."

"Oh. Dibs." Shit, why did I ring her? She knows how to put limited time to good use and I dread to think what they're up to behind the ditsy hospital curtains.

"Don't you dare go," she says but it's too late.

I press the red button. I'm not finishing the conversation. Ten minutes later I pull into Will's long and affluent avenue and soon have my finger on the security gate's entry buzzer.

"Hi. Will. It's Izzy. You free?"

"Izzy?" I hear Will's voice and the question in it, but I'm not in the mood for roadside explanations. Or further recriminations. I can hear my phone trilling in the back seat where I threw it. It's Dibian. There's no way I'm being talked down from the parapet now. Believe me. I'm wearing my crazy circus tutu of angst and my tightrope ballet pumps are primed for dance.

"Yep. It's me. Just passing. Thought I heard something dodgy from my car engine so wondered if I could check?"

I bite my lip. Shit, as excuses come that one's as lame as a limping clog dancer. And oh, what a hussy of the multifarious untruths am I?

"Sure. Come through. Great timing! We'll have a look under the bonnet." He sounds so homey and regular guy-like and honest—and that fires me to a hornet's nest of inner tornado mad.

Would a man caught in the middle of a blow job by his maid use that particular welcome and be so keen to dabble in mechanics? I'm about to find out.

Shit. Shit. Shit.

But already I'm sensing I'm guilty of overdramatized fantasy gone demented. Yes. I should have sat at home. I should have resisted.

But too late. I'm here and I can't very well scarper back up the drive and pretend I never came, can I?

Or can I?

I'm considering it but the door opens and Will walks out, looking like a demi-god in a vest and track pants low on his hips.

Bollocks. No surrender. Live the lie and work it like Gaga in a rib-eye steak dress. "Hey, babe. I was beginning to worry," says Will. He motions for me to click open the bonnet of the car. I oblige and hope he can't smell my bullshit when he's under there.

"What kinda noise?"

"A faint knocking. Sounded dull… Clanky."

Will purses his lips and braces his hands on the car. I lose him for a good four minutes as he bashes and clatters things.

"Turn her over," he says and motions for me to start the car.

I do and of course it starts first time, then purrs like a nursing mother cat who's been given a box of stray kitties.

"Anyway, why were you worried? You said you were worried," I ask.

"Hadn't heard from you since last night. Texted and called—no answer. Wondered if you'd given me the brush-off."

"I did have brushes off. The brushes of a broken washing machine. He wouldn't listen to reason so I took his innards apart." Nor would I, I'm thinking.

"Shoulda called me. I'm great with my hands." He grins at his own sultry wit.

"Wearing Batsuits and saving the world. Fixing cars. Laundry tech. What don't you do?"

"See enough of you?" Will leaves the car and comes toward me. He slides his hand around my waist and kisses my neck. But hey, maybe he's buying time and currying favor while Tessa gets her kit back on inside? I clench my jaw, galvanized not to be such a pushover.

"So, what about the car?" I ask.

"Seems fine to me. I'll give it a drive before you go. Kinda hoping that won't be for a while, though." His grin says he's got extracurricular activities lined up. And some of them involve nakedness.

Maybe Tessa's not as thorough as she'd have me believe? I cut to the chase and go for it. "Tessa here?"

"Why?" Will shakes his head. "She never works weekends. She won't fix cars — she might break a nail."

I keep my grumbles zipped. "Looking tidy after the party. Did she help?"

"Contract cleaners, um...Iz. What's with the cleaning OCD? You submitting me for some hygiene test?"

I let out a breath. "I wondered. How are you in the party's aftermath?" I'm walking through the hallway, swiftly scanning through the lounge door doing army-surveillance with every step, yet trying to look completely normal.

"No damage — other than the incident with the snapper. Why didn't you return my calls?"

"I was marking." *Liar, liar. Tartan pants on fire.*

"How about we get some up close and personal time? Best way to end a Saturday night I can think of." His eyes sparkle at me. His dark shadowed jaw is more A-rated chiseled than a sculpture masterclass. I'd love to be in the mood to have him ravish me and throw my caution cape to the wind. But Tessa's proved to be my devil of discombobulation.

"Sorry, Will," I whisper. "I'm not in the mood. Jack's still in hospital and I was up all night. The party took it right out of me."

Shit. I hate to be a cock tease but the way confusion is rampaging around inside me, sex is the last thing on the cards. I'm fit for a cry and a tantrum, not lust.

"Any chance of a cup of tea?" I ask.

"Sure. And a hug. I'm great at those."

We walk into the kitchen, and when he closes the door, he turns me in his arms. His eyes hold mine steady and I feel the strain begin to ebb as his comforting, warm embrace engulfs me.

"Hey," he says, with more soothing power than a team of Florence Nightingales. "Babe. Ease that stress. You need to breathe and let Will hug it out." He holds me firmly. Some of the feelings ebb away. It's better. A little. But Will's still watching me oddly. "You're not acting pleased to see me. What's up? I can tell when you're not yourself."

"Dunno what you mean."

"Keep it to yourself if you want to."

I can't confess — that I came expressly to catch him. To fit him up. I check around me now and I'm still craning to hear a giveaway noise from a stowaway Tessa. She's completely done a number on me.

I stumble on the perfect get out of jail-free-card. "I came to find out about the photographer. What are the police going to do about it all?"

He watches me, then his stance relaxes. "All in good time, but first I'll give you the massage you need. Then I'll tell you all."

I decline the massage. As tempting as Will is. As soothing as his digits would be on my back—and other places—maybe there's something about having a blonde psycho Fruit Loop confessing past sex exploits with your man that puts a large bolt on the door of future bonk aspirations.

I can't get Tessa out of my head. I can't find a way in to discuss it without coming over as a large jar of nutter butter. I want this properly explored and I need time to hatch an approach.

Will pulls me into the warm, strong cave of his arms but I'm rigid as a frozen deckchair left in the garden in the snow.

"So. Photostalker? What's the news?"

"Tabloid snapper. He came to try for pictures of me and Ben. Personal effects were taken from Tarquin's car—he's been charged. I'm unsure as to why he wanted pics of me."

"At least he was caught in the act. Is Ben a decent guy? Is there substance to the story about him being a player?"

"No way. He's my friend. Known him years and he's sound."

"I have a friend's feelings at stake so I'll take you at your word. And another question—your maid, Tessa. How did you get her?"

"Why are you asking about Tessa again?"

He reaches to touch my shoulders and start a massage assault, but I resist. "Just interest."

Will narrows his eyes at me. "Has something happened? Is this why you're acting weird?"

I opt for a fabrication to justify my comments. "I saw her when I was out—all over a man. You told me she had a husband and kids but the guy she was with was young and the way he snogged her set my alarm bells off. Why would a married man and woman snog in a car like they were scared they'd get caught?"

"Trust me—that couldn't have been Tessa. You have it wrong. She's employed by the property company. She seems efficient. Though she rarely gets the dirty work done herself, as long as the place is clean, that's not my business."

"Something about Tessa worries me." I'm more warm and woolly than a huddle of hillside sheep. But at least this is my way of broaching things to see how Will reacts. So far, his responses confuse me. How could he say with certainty that Tessa wasn't where I saw her?

"Perhaps you should spend less time worrying about others. And more about me. I'm starting to feel neglected."

I rise from my seat, steeling myself to be strong and leave. "I've marking to do."

"Izzy. Have I done something to offend you?"

"I'm tired."

"You won't take a massage. You don't want to talk. You haven't touched your tea and now you want to go."

"I've a busy week lined up."

"We were going to schedule in time—experimenting. I want us to go to the room again together."

"Not this week, Will."

His face hardens and his body language reads of pissed-off man. "If that's what you want."

I nod, but it's not okay. I've put the first mighty spanner in our relationship's works. If there is something between Will and Tessa, I've driven him back into her clutches with my bipolar bender lady response.

"Why are you following me?" I ask as Will shadows me out of the door, hot on my heels.

"Car test, remember?"

"Leave it. I think it's fine."

"Next time we meet, I want full reasons about what tonight was all about."

I jump in the car and slam the door, but he's watching me with a weird expression. I don't answer his words because I'm too pissed off and perplexed at myself. Shit. That wasn't cool.

Not clever. And I shouldn't have come.

* * * *

Such is my confusion and lack of ability to settle that I head straight for Mo's after making such an arse of myself at Will's. I sense that there is precisely diddly squat chance of class prep or marking happening tonight. But blame Psycho Visitor's havoc.

I head through Mo's tiny garden, only noticing the shiny, new motorbike under the kitchen window once I've rung the bell and it's too late to reconsider. Maybe she's ordered pizza and invited the delivery guy for a slice? Then again... It's a posh bike for pizza runs...

I hear the ding-dong of her doorbell echo in the hall. My eyes return to the bike. It's brand new. Gleaming. Has Mo taken up biking? Or bikers, for that matter.

When she arrives at the door and only opens it a smidge, I immediately jump back in anguish. I've seen undone buttons and glimpses of lace.

"Shit, you've a visitor. A man!"

"Yes, fuck, Izzy. It does happen—don't sound so shocked!"

Yes, her bra is visible, but we're old friends and Mo's not mad at me, she's grinning. She has an ample chest that deserves to be appreciated. As much as I'm mad at myself, I'm full of joy for her burgeoning sex life.

She chuckles. "Yes. I. Really. Effing. Have." Then whispers so softly I can only lip read the words. "And. He's. So. Fit. Game. On."

"I'd better go."

"No, it's okay. Talk for a bit. Does no harm to let the fire pit blaze and sizzle in my absence. If you get me."

"You have a fire pit in the back garden now? You sure? You can't swing a cat round there."

"You're bloody thick at metaphors. For fuck's sake, Iz. I mean he's keen. Let's stoke up the passion. Waiting won't hurt him. In fact, I find it stirs him up nicely. Nice to think there's a baby-oiled, semi-naked man waiting for me stretched out like a starfish in bed!"

"Holy thunderbolts." I'm red as the gleaming bike's paintwork, next to me. In fact I think I'm slightly more scarlet and certainly more embarrassed. "Who is it?"

"Long. Arm. Of the Law." She whispers then snorts with laughter, then does her best to shush herself up. "Do you think he'll take me to a cell if I ask nicely? I want him to read me my rights!"

I gasp and put my hand up to my lips. "As in Rod the Plod O'Leary?"

She doesn't say a word. "Let's say Stalker Snapper may have done me a favor. And the law's arm isn't the only thing that's impressive and long around here." She's laughing like a drain now and my ears can bear no more so I run.

"See ya!" I'm back up the path like a rat up a particularly scalable drainpipe. "Gotta go."

"Call me tomorrow. We can have a rundown of what kinky cops do best. You can use it in your books. What did you want anyway?"

"Nothing that can't wait. Never keep a policeman hanging around. He might write you a penalty notice."

Mo grins. I sense a constable who'll be tired on his beat later. And who won't have to want for chocolate dipping sauce for a very long time.

"Bye." Shit.

Everybody's busy with fulfilled, unbuggered-up sex lives but me.

* * * *

No sooner have I reversed into my usual school car park space than there's a rap on my car windscreen that startles me. Will's green eyes stare down at me.

He opens my passenger side door without asking and slips inside like a particularly deft spy — but without any disguise or code words. His eyes stay fixed on the view from the windscreen and the dilapidated tennis courts — hardly a vista of choice.

"Stalking. Nice addition to your repertoire."

His eyebrows raise a millimeter. "Figured I'd follow your lead from Saturday. Unannounced and unexplained."

Touché, Batman. Fuck, he always has a better answer. It's one of the reasons he drives me mad with lust.

"What do you want?" I know I sound surly. Hell, I *am* surly. Surly and seriously peeved. Most of all with myself. As well as Twatty Tessa Sexpot.

"I'd love an apology for your *mucho* weirdness lately but as it's a Monday morning and, going by the bags under your eyes telling me you had as little sleep as me,

I'd say that's a fruitless hope. So instead, I wanted to mark a date in your diary for rampant, teach-you-a-lesson sex. I believe it's the best kind. Especially if it involves restraints and lots of spanking. I don't know what you were playing at, what contributed to it or why you haven't returned my texts, but my hand wants to make firm contact with your arse rather soon."

"Nice. You should get out more."

He glowers at me and his eyes become slits. "Woman, I swear, I could do your private parts a mischief right now. And it would be fucking amazing for both of us. Sadly, it's an arsing school day."

"Tetchy, Sir. Tut tut!" I know. I'm a surly child who can't even find a good comeback. But it is a Monday and the toaster broke again. *WTF?* Will I ever get a decent slice of golden bread again? With Jack AWOL there is no glimmer of hope.

My stomach rumbles as if on cue.

"Wednesday. Seven sharp at mine. Make sure you have a carb meal and plenty of glucose tablets before arrival. It'll be a long night. I have a lot to get out of my system."

"Said the septic tank to the plumber."

"For fuck's sake, I should shag you in the car for your lip, lady!"

My womb high-dives into the center of a perfectly formed lotus of synchronized swimmers. How does this man manage to do this—make my innards turn into a raging estrogen fest and have me melt with longing in a matter of sentences?

"What should I wear? Armor?"

"Your choice. Make sure you bring that whip. And the crop. We didn't get a proper chance last time. Believe me, I'll make up for it."

He clicks open the door and I think he's gone. Like all the best SAS guys do, he pops back unexpectedly and without a noise.

"What about tonight? Wednesday is a bit of a wait and I'm on a rolling boil already. Only so many polar showers a guy can stand."

"Can't. Busy. Other men to pester. I'm a busy temptress!"

His low growl makes me whimper, then as swiftly his demeanor alters completely. His tone becomes almost nice. "Thank you, Miss Tennant. That was most helpful. Have a very productive day."

I soon realize why, when Rogerson walks past like the lumbering he-hulk with a briefcase he is. Rogerson stares at Will and smiles. Then stares at me and pretends to. Subtle difference but I see it like a wild pig senses truffles on a Solstice morning. Bastard. And I'm not quite sure whether I mean my headmaster boss or my deranged, domineering lover. I can't help myself but die for Will's crazed maniacal touch.

But he's still a complete bastard.

* * * *

It's morning break when I learn the party popper-worthy news. Janey's been delayed in school but escapes to find me in the staffroom.

"Had to come see you!" Her expression and shimmering exuberance tell me it's great news before she does. And she doesn't confide at all — she presents the evidence on a wiggling finger with a shocking squeal.

"Fuck me backwards! Bloody love a duck — what a corker of a ring!"

She squeals a second time and I'm fearful it could shatter her crystal earrings. Then she jumps up and down until I stop her. "He asked me last night. Isn't it fab? The ring is a bit big, mind, but he's getting it resized. In Bond Street no less. God, Izzy. Can you believe it? I'm engaged to the man of my dreams."

We hug and hug and hug some more and I couldn't be happier for my most wonderful, beautiful friend in all the world. Her smattering of freckles crinkles as she grins with her sheer exuberance and delight.

"I'll need a debrief on details."

"Course. You'll get the full shebang."

We hug again. "Was it *très romantique*? Or hot and hungry sex please *à la mode*?"

Janey grins. "Bloody both, Iz. We don't want to wait long, either. And I'm thinking bridesmaids. All of you will be bridesmaids—maybe a bondage theme and fuck-me shoes?"

I'm laughing like a drain at that one.

"But I think you may approve of the best man? Now that I'm engaged, Ben has no secrets—he's told me you may have a thing going for a man we both know."

I blush but the hilarity of the fuck-me wedding shoes hasn't abated so I'm still grinning from ear to ear. "We might be friends. And I may have seen his willy a couple of times."

"Pfffft. Friends. Yeah. Is he the guy who's causing you to write like a lusty Agatha Christie on LSD?"

I raise my eyebrows. And hug her again tightly. "Will is my spark, my muse—and the man who drives me crazy. Especially when he's playing grumpy, angry bastard to sex us both up like he has today."

Janey's eyes widen. "Aren't we both the lucky ones?"

"Bloody lucky indeed."

Chapter Seventeen

I have to admit it—filming reality docudramas isn't half as bad as I'd thought it would be. I'm ignoring the camera and getting on with it—getting lost in the text and the students' experience.

The kids are progressing through our *Pride and Prejudice* study pretty well. I've had no bad attitude—interested, motivated girls. Who could've guessed?

I overheard that Rogerson had a prior word with all our young mentees, promising a celebrity party conclusion as wrap celebration, complete with a boy band and celeb DJ, so I'm guessing this tactic has worked. Or at least had a sobering effect.

Even Sophie is sounding interested and as if she's done her homework. The last time we achieved that was a one-page essay about 'My Favorite Things' in which she talked ceaselessly about her affection for false boobs and nail art. I'm feeling we've turned a corner. We're only covering Chapter Eight and I have high hopes for how they'll progress by the book's conclusion.

Ellen, a girl whose idea of a good read is the cover of *HotFussOMG* magazine, tells me, "I've finished the book. I like that Mr. Darcy is ashamed of his 'orrible aunt's rudeness. You can tell he's falling for Lizzie and he's not as stuck up as she finks, miss. Lady Cafrin is talking down to Lizzie and he hates it. You can tell he's a good suitor for her."

"Well done, Ellen. Exactly right."

If teachers had medals for breakthroughs, I'd be polishing mine now and shouting for joy.

I look up because I'm so taken with my moment of teacher's pride and it's straight into the shining, smiling eyes of Andy Regis. Shit, I'd forgotten about him — but he's taken my inner joy as a come-on. I'll have to put him right later.

He slides up to me when the break bell rings and after the crew have packed and are leaving.

"Hey. How's tricks?"

"Good. Busy."

"Enjoying the limelight? The camera loves you. Takes all my strength to keep from zooming onto your tits. That bra is epic."

"Hardly. I'd forgotten you're here."

"That's not flattering. I hoped I had more of an effect on you than that. Fancy doing lunch?"

"I can't. I'm backed up. And we're doing prep for our football mentoring lessons later."

"How about tomorrow?"

Jeez. This guy is thicker than a corrugated iron windcheater when it comes to brush-offs.

"Andy, I'm not sure it's a good idea."

"It's only lunch. And, if it helps, I'll bring colleagues. So it's not you and me. Call it peace-making."

"We're not at war."

"We're not in a place of love, that's for sure. I want to start over. Lunch, on the BBC expenses? We have a tab at the local five-star hotel? How about a gastro feast? How often do you get such offers?"

I smile. He does his smolder eyes. He's a great-looking guy. He's not my type at all. "Lunch only. Nothing further, ever."

"Just friends," he says.

"Friends. Deal."

So why do I feel like I'm going to regret it as soon as I've agreed, especially when he's whistling happily as he packs up his kit, then winks at me on the way out.

Mistake. Neon sign. Mistake.

* * * *

I bump into Dibian on my way to the canteen. We pass like ships in the night — ships that hold hands and gabble at each other as we move in opposite directions.

"Need to see you."

"Back at you! When?"

"Ten minutes. Behind the stage?"

"Sounds like a tryst, boss lady."

"It is. Lots to tell."

I see Will in the distance as I'm queuing for my salad pitta. I'm ready to go heavy on the jalapeños today. Salad and low-cal carbs are all well and good for the waistline, but a girl needs a bit of gusto to go. I hope I don't regret this move in the flatulence department later. Farting on camera isn't cool. And could lead to YouTube fame.

"Hey," says Sam the porter, as he passes with a trolley full of toilet roll. He picks his time for school comestibles logistics that's for sure. "How's Jack, Izzy?"

"I hear he's a bit improved. I'm going to see him after school."

"Send our wishes. And there's a couple of cards at reception—we did a whip round collection as well."

I smile at Sam. He's covered in tattoos and is built like a bulldog, but when it comes to heart, his is a thumping great marshmallow of soft mush.

"Take a selfie wiv 'im and send us a copy, will ya?"

"Course, Sam. Laters."

We may be a weird bunch at Netherfield but we're a weird bunch with love. Then I see Annie James standing in the queue to pay for her enormous hot dog—figures. She's wearing a spray-on dress with a split that cuts thigh high. Anyway—what I was saying before? With the exception of one mad whore with a sausage fixation. But, in the main, we aren't bad.

I look over and see that Will is seated at a table and talking animatedly with Tarquin. I wonder what they're discussing. I also wonder about the slick guy in the suit? He's handsome. He looks city chic metro sexual. He can't possibly be new staff—that suit looks pricey. I vow to ask later.

When dinner diva Doreen hands me my napkin-wrapped dinner and I get through the pay queue in record time, I dash down the corridor intent on maximum time with Dibs.

But when I get there—nothing preps me for her surprise.

* * * *

The lights click on, but it's still dim because we're in the darkened wings of the school stage. It's eerily quiet and I'm looking at something that makes my eyes widen.

"Hell's fiery pashmina! What the heck?"

"Look," says Dibian. "I wanted undisturbed. Top secret. What do you reckon, lady authoress?"

For a head of English—is that a word? "Digital imprint writer will do."

"Either way. You're up on Omazod. Get used to this! E-readers around the globe are accessing your novel as we speak. Speaking of which, you ought to get on to writing the next one. Time's a ticking. This is a new career and you have to spend time with hands on keys to feed the machine."

I hold my hand in front of my mouth and get nearer still for a close-up. "My—the cover's very racy."

"Your book is too, Iz. Are you sure you've read it? I had to go to bed and lie down three chapters in. And so it went the whole way through. I'm sure it's what's turned me into a high-octane sex bomb with Jack. You fueled my lust reserves."

"TMI." I want a gag, blindfold and earmuffs immediately. The gag's for Dibs. The others are for me. As for Jack, only a straitjacket or a chastity condom belt will do.

Dibian raises her eyes and bats those enormous lashes—they've grown. She's done some kind of enhancement there, for sure. And there's glitter dangling from each spider's leg of eyelash. Not a good look. "Sorry. But it's the truth. The man's impressive. Even in a nursing gown, he's got it."

"He needs to get to the sexual health clinic and get cream then."

I have never thought of Jack outside of his familiar janitor's coat. Nor do I ever wish to. I squeeze my eyes shut to remove the image. But I have to open them again if only to see my incredible cover.

"Who designed it?"

"I have contacts in publishing. It wasn't too expensive."

"Did they read the book?"

"No. Though I'm well connected with editors, I resisted. I could've pulled strings but I'm reliably informed self-publishing is where the innovative voices are raking it in, darling. I have a big hunch you'll do well financially out of this one. You're going to make a killing and I wouldn't want you to miss out. I have a confession, though. I did change your title." The cover is something to behold. The nude female figure has her back to the camera, but it's demure yet sensual in every curve. Her hands are bound. Her face is in profile. Is she sad or in sublime pleasure? It's hard to tell. There's a tiny glimpse of side boob. Just enough to get the juices flowing, I'd imagine. And there are instruments laid out beside her. Her legs are open but nobody can see from this view. Instruments of pleasure gleam in the foreground.

The title — *Pleasure's Edge*.

The writer — Raye C. Ryder.

"You're joking, right?"

"Why would I be?"

"I can't believe you've called me that."

"You needed an attention-grabbing moniker. I got you a peach."

I laugh nervously. My God. If my mother ever saw this, she'd disown me and opt for deed poll.

"Kara!" Dibian laughs low in her throat.

"You're a total slut."

"You're up already. There's been eight hundred pre-order sales since ten a.m."

"Fuck."

"You even have great reviews. Do you know how hard that is to achieve?"

"I deserve the reviews. For my new name alone. We're breaking boundaries. If Rogerson ever finds out, I'm toast!"

"Jack's ultra-keen to give it a read too. He's sworn to secrecy."

I fix Dibian with a warning stare—my friend and crazy boss with fingers in too many publishing pies. As much as this makes me falter and cringe, she's done an impressive job. I'd already approved mock-up graphics in an email but this is all so much more professional than I'd imagined. The book will garner attention. "Don't you bloody dare or the deal's off and I'm taking it down."

"Don't worry. I'm using it as bait. I'll spin it out as long as I possibly can. I'm enjoying piquing Jack's interest."

She takes down the glossy covers and puts them in a black leather artist's case. "If anybody asks to see my etchings, I plan to run for the car. Bye Ms. Ryder, you minx you!"

Something about this is worrying me. I'm on Omazod. I'm a published erotica author.

"Catch you later, Svengali Hicks.""

Holy orgasms.

* * * *

Jack is sitting up in bed in his paisley pajamas and he's wearing reading specs that make him look like an Oxbridge prof, while reading the sports pages with a hooded gaze. He's probably got a hotline set up with the local bookmaker's already.

"Jacko!"

"Izzy."

"You gave us all such a bloody fright."

"Meself included, girl. I thought I was going up to that big goal mouth in the sky. And it was nearly an own goal and an automatic suspension."

"Jack. Do you ever not think in football terms?"

He takes off his glasses and moves the papers to the bedside cabinet. "When Lady Dibian is around, it's rather hard to think straight or get a word in edgewise. Why the hell did you let her take over visiting duty? Were you trying to teach me a lesson, girl? That woman... I nearly called the nurses."

I'm laughing so hard now I nearly need a nurse button. Or a bedpan.

"Shit, Jack. I was under the impression you were keen."

"The woman doesn't stop for breath. And she rams those bosoms in places they aren't always welcome. Can't a man have peace even while convalescing? I missed all the races at Kempton thanks to her heavy breathing and hair stroking. It was intolerable."

"Sorry, Jack. Any news from the quacks yet?"

"Still a lot of tests to be done. But it's some sort of heart condition. They think medication will help but I'll need time off from work and to take it slow. My sister and her friend have told me they'll come and look after me for a bit."

"That's good."

"Dibian doesn't think so, but I'm pleased as punch they're coming—it's like the cavalry to stall her unwanted advances. She made it pretty damn clear she planned moving in for the kill. Kept suggesting she'd come and stay and keep me ship shape. Mata Bloody Hari, that one. I left her in little doubt it wouldn't work. But she insisted on going to mine to tidy for me getting home."

"And when are you getting back?"

"Tomorrow, maybe day after. I'll need to come back and forth for visits with the consultant but I'm okay to try going home. My sister's coming from Southend tonight."

He certainly looks more like himself.

"She's bringing her friend, Ada. She's the woman I told you about that makes the fish pie from heaven itself. She's won cake-baking awards five years on the trot and her Battenberg recipe has been patented via official channels."

"I have every faith you'll be in great hands, Jack. I wish you'd been honest about going to the docs. You didn't tell me the truth, did you? And it could've cost you dearly."

Jack's gaze skirts off and he fiddles with the sheets. "Sorry, duck. I don't do doctors. They never tell you good news. Gets me out of sorts."

"Sometimes they're essential, Jacko."

I hug him, enjoying the contact and the feel of him alive and vitally himself and his old ticker continuing to beat a steady rhythm.

"I ain't going anywhere yet. As long as you keep that ruddy Dibian out of my hair, I'll see a few summers out before I'm through."

I hand him the cards and presents sent by the staff and get out my phone.

"Selfie for Sam," I say.

And we both hug and do rabbit ears with gusto.

* * * *

Mum's at Uncle Cyril's care home, and he's in a wheelchair waiting when I get there. I'm late and can read in my mother's face that she's displeased but not owning up.

"Okay? Traffic was a nightmare."

"Can you bring round the car?" she instructs.

"Course."

Already I've missed her precise marker. God, I do love my mother but she makes me do a marathon of effort to meet her standards. Where my dad was a solid saint and savior with a heart of gold, Mum wields a heart of iron and rules from the highest shelf, where the ladder won't reach.

I fetch the car, and five minutes on we're settled for the trip. The journey is pretty hard going and quiet. Mum's lips are set in a hard line but it's worry, not a bad mood. She worries about Cyril—he's prone to occasional confused episodes, so taking him out of his supervised surroundings stresses her.

"Did you see the game last week, Unc?"

Uncle Cyril grins at me, but while at first I think he's got my meaning, I realize he's missed the lift and gone back to the basement.

"Sweets. Sure. They're in my pocket. Want a caramel or a mint, Izzy love?"

He still thinks I'm five. But he's the sweetest man alive—it breaks my heart to see his memory diminish and dim so.

In the confines of this situation—and even though I'm an adult and the one behind the wheel—I do feel like I am five. I could cry as easily.

"You still follow the Arsenal, girl?" he asks.

"Course, Uncle Cyril. Who else would I ever go to see? Still got my season ticket. Same seat. Same scarf and I wear it proudly."

"George Graham still doing us proud as manager?"

Shit. Just when I think we're on a level memory playing field, it happens again. Arsene Wenger's been time-machined out of the picture.

"Don't tire your uncle, Izzy. Keep the conversation simple and short."

Fucking Mother. She drains me. And it makes me sad to recognize that she's become an emotional vampire without meaning to. She's too stressed, too closed, too rigid. Will I end up that way? Is this what closing up your heart space does? Did losing Dad when she needed him most make her this way? Was she once free and easy? I find I can't remember.

We're at the cemetery in Barnet before too long.

It's tiny and packed. Grave after grave and so close together, it depresses me at every visit. No sense of space here. It's Cram-a-Corpse in action. I can't believe I've admitted that out loud in my head either. This is my father's final resting place. If I could I'd bring an excavator and dig him up and take him somewhere nice—with space and a view. And birdsong—Dad would love that.

We find his tiny plot at the back left.

There's dead flowers. From my last visit. I recognize the carnations.

"Izzy. Get rid of that old mess," orders Mother. I've barely got there. She can see my heels aren't the greatest for traversing the ground.

"Trust you to wear inappropriate shoes."

"Sorry. Hold Uncle Cyril for me and I'll sort it."

I get rid of the decayed relics and lay out the new array of floral tribute, in their plastic wrapping, on the ground and my mother tuts.

"What?"

"Do you have to be so messy?"

"It may be messy but it's organized. And I don't tend to bring along a pop-up floristry table everywhere I go. Look away if it offends you. I'm getting it ready for when I bring back the water."

I march to the wall tap and retrieve an empty plastic milk bottle to fill. I take my ire out by turning the tap on too hard and end up with water spraying over my tights and shoes.

"Shit!"

I can't believe I've sworn in a cemetery. On a visit to my dad's grave. How disrespectful am I?

But my thoughts are stalled short when I get the fright and surprise of my life.

"Hey, beautiful. It's only me."

"Will."

He's standing, watching me. In a dark overcoat. He's got on his suit from this morning—the overcoat is Daniel Craig in *Skyfall* and I feel my womb go wibbly. In a bloody cemetery—Izzy Tennant, thy name is harpy!

"What the hell are you doing here?" He's staring over my head toward where my ever-critical mother is awaiting me. Hell. Not good timing.

"I could ask the same of you. But I think I can guess."

"Now's not a great time."

"You want me to go?"

"My mother isn't the easiest. Time on death row is preferable to ten minutes of her death glare."

"I don't want to cramp your style. I was worried earlier. Our connection. I thought you were flipping me off."

"I did have something on. It wasn't a lie."

"I see that now. You going to tell me?"

I sigh. Then look back to Mum. She's watching us over her shoulder, and I can tell from her face that she wants me to go.

"It's Dad's birthday. We always come. Dad's brother. Mum."

"I won't stay. But call me later."

"Okay. Gotta go. She's in a mood."

He turns. "Izzy. I'm sorry for your loss."

"It was years ago." But my eyes are brimming with tears and I don't ruddy know why. Probably the soft edge in Will's voice. The fact that my 'sex man' has come here to my emotional no-man's-land.

He walks away and is gone in a matter of seconds. Shit! He followed me all the way here. He cared enough to check. I can tell by her expression that I've displeased Mother greatly as I head back. My dad would've been egging me on. I remember the way he'd cut in and put her straight. Guess the apple never falls far from the tree.

The flowers are soon arranged and they're a pretty display, given that I didn't buy the priciest at the supermarket on my way over.

We say a silent prayer then we're heading back. Duty done.

But I'm always struck by how far away from the real sense of Dad this place is. He was everything that was wonderful in my world. This horrible hole is a place, a dark crowded corner he'd never come to. His heart isn't here. Nor is mine.

"You at the game this week?" asks Cyril. "Get me a program, girl?"

"Course," I tell him. I always do. I've been bringing him programs for the last two years he's been in the care home.

His blue eyes are watery but still echo Dad's ready blue gaze.

"Go and see your aunty Doris," he concludes. "She misses you. She'll do you a roast, girl. You're too thin."

It catches me off guard. Doris is in spirit and Alzheimer's clouds his mind. Not knowing whether or not your loved one is dead or alive is surely the hardest curse of all.

Then he blows me away. "Will Darby. Glad to see he's coming around asking you for tips. Great finisher that boy. Always knew he had talent when I saw him play against us. His goals took skill and speed. You trying to get him to move to the Gunners, girl?"

I stare at my uncle. Amid the confusion he's right about Will, if wrong about the circumstances.

"Will's a friend," I answer.

And Uncle Cyril nods, winks and grabs my hand.

"Good girl. Tell him to give up the women. Used to see him in the papers gallivanting with the girls. A player can go astray that way. You keep 'im right, girl, keep 'im right."

"I'll try. And I'll tell him you rated him as a player."

I'm lost in thoughts of both Will and Cyril for the rest of the way home.

* * * *

"Who was he, that man you were with?" Mother asks when I drop her and Cyril back at the home and we've settled him back in his room.

"A guy from work. I left something when he gave me a lift."

I know she doesn't believe me. But what's the point? She wouldn't be over-pleased with me fraternizing with ex-footballers, nor would she have a clue about his kudos, so I don't try.

I love her, I respect her. But I don't connect. My mother doesn't know me. Her heart put up a closed sign when I was four. She went to see Dad in the chapel of rest and her hugs somehow stopped feeling real. She helped me to grow. But kept her heart at a safe distance. And it's a gap I cannot bridge.

She's not the only one who can play the calm outer shell game.

"A man from work followed you all the way to the cemetery? Must be more than colleagues."

"Some people go the extra mile, Mum." I turn to hold her stare and I keep my eyes on hers, even though it's hard. Her face is firm and unflinching, her mouth the only thing that gives her away. The chink in her armor that reveals uncertainty and sometimes remorse. "If they know you need them, if they connect with what matters, people can be the saving of you. It's about risking your heart and giving it a try."

I take her home.

But she doesn't say another word and nor do I.

* * * *

Will is at my front door.

Will Darby Dark Stalker and Man Who Won't Take A No.

I take a deep breath in prep even though I know damn well who stands outside the frosted glass—he has a memorable head. In more ways than one. And I don't mean that in a bad way. I've had boyfriends with weirdly shaped heads before, so I'm a fit judge. He has two very respectable heads and I've had experience with both. Fortunately, the one between his legs is hidden from public view.

"Hey."

"Hi." His eyes dance and flicker. Inside me something ignites, but I squash it with a fire blanket of restraint.

"I figured I'd play your card back at you."

"And what card is that? A big fat joker?" As you can probably tell, I'm not in jovial mood. Blame it on time spent with my mother. She often has the power to wring life out of me like a Chinese laundry tackling string vests. "I thought I was to ring you later. I haven't had a chance." I shrug. Shrugging is always a giveaway for acting like an arse but I'm too far gone to care.

"No nice to see you, Will? No thanks for dropping in?" His tone is as bleak as the look he spears me with.

"Let's say it's been a bad day. Come in," I invite him but I'm already walking up the hallway.

I don't let him sit down and get comfy before I get right in there with the main thought that's been on my mind. "Why did you follow me to the cemetery?"

Will doesn't answer. He takes off his overcoat — the same one from earlier — and carefully lays it along the back of the chair. Is he prepping an answer with such careful deliberation? I've never seen him act like a footman with OCD before?

"You did."

"I'm not denying it. I thought you were blowing me out. When I asked to see you tonight, let's say I got vibes and they weren't good ones."

"Well, your vibes were wrong."

"Are you sure on that?" He sits down then stretches his long legs out. He reminds me of a movie actor — playing the teacher part in his waistcoat and shirt. But is that the real Will? Can he ever fit the teacher mold or is he football star indelibly marked? I find I'm not fit to say.

"Since the party something's been off with us."

Shit. I am so not in the mood for a Tessa talk. *The* Tessa talk. I still haven't figured out how I feel about that one.

But when I look at Will, his face has that grim cast he has when some bad shit is up and he's trying ultra-hard inside to deal with it. Shit — that means he cares. This counts for him.

I chew on my bottom lip, trying to work out how to proceed. But keeping quiet and working out my words in advance hasn't done me so well so far, has it? Something inside me — gremlin revisiting the scene, most probably — makes me speak out.

"I had a visitor. She had things to say about you. Colorful things. It's been on my mind."

Will's eyes go from pained to puzzled. There's a healthy pinch of pique in the measure too. And pique — like paprika — is something that has impact and can't be ignored.

"Who, for fuck's sake? You can't lay that on me and not tell me who."

"She works for you."

Will ruminates. Then answers. "It can't be Mrs. Mayer, my ironing lady, because you've never met her. And please don't tell me it's Tessa."

I turn my back on him and put the kettle on to boil. I'd make us toast to keep the avoidance technique up but number one, the toaster's still fucked, and number two, I don't think either of us is ready for egg and soldiers at present.

Will's behind me in a second. His fingers gently touch the tops of my arms.

"Don't touch me."

"This is exactly my point. We go from totally at one with the vibe to distance and don't touch me. What's Tessa fucking said and done?"

I don't want to have this out. I don't want recriminations, accusations and lengthy debacle. I should never have said anything because, after time at the cemetery and Mum, I'm too raw for conflict. I'll cry. And I hate to cry. I hate this combative state and I resent that Tessa ever came into our lives and fucked a good thing up. Twatty bitch that she is. And I don't care that she's a blonde princess — I care that she's screwed up my little patch of wonderful.

I turn around, into Will's arms. "I don't want to go through this or argue. Maybe you should ask her."

Will is staring, his green eyes hard as emerald chips in a dark mineshaft.

He still stays mute.

"And that's all I get from you?"

I nod.

"I came," he says, clearing his throat, and bingo but I can hear the raw, jagged slice of emotion there — the way his voice drags from his larynx tells me there's cruelty in the mix and I might have caused that. "I came to ask if you wanted time together pre-mentoring. I know you're worried about it and I know you hate Annie getting one up. I came to offer to tutor you in advance to save face. I want you to succeed."

Will turns. He walks to his coat. And picks it up roughly and devoid of the initial footman finesse.

"But now that I've come here" — he walks up the hallway to the door and opens it — "I see I've wasted our time. As you were. Don't let me intrude."

Bang goes the door. And my conscience.

Chapter Eighteen

It's eleven and I've had a glass of wine on a school night—it's not my usual style but I'm peeved and can't settle to sleep so I log onto my computer instead.

My bad mood prevails because I've ballsed up my love life, my mother hates me and it's been a bitch of a day. Maybe a bit of gratuitous Facebook will soothe me? And I mean of the laughing at other people's posts variety, not the airing of my dirty doings online. Only I don't go for the big blue F. Something makes me head to Omazod and the e-book section. I gaze at my new Dibian-initiated author page and see my book in all its shiny majesty. I take a full minute staring at the arresting—if ballsy—cover and marvel that it's mine.

And that's when my shock of the night dawns. "Oh my ruddy, giddy, delirious aunt."

My insides go on fast freeze—fright or flight making me rigid with total gobsmackedness.

"I've sold frigging four thousand copies!" Bloody bat cocks. This is *big*.

There are reviews. Double figures reviews. They're top star rated.

I pick up my phone and call Dibian. There's no answer and I'm an impatient arse at times so I try again but still it's on answerphone. So I leave her a message telling her the skinny then I get back to reading my reviews.

One reader is asking when the sequel's due. It's been a day. What have we started? And how the hell am I going to write more now that Will Darby — the source of my every lust-fueled line of prose — has walked away and thinks I'm a total walking she-shit with bad balls on. Nice move Iz-bomb. Nice move.

Dibian hasn't called me back so I shut off the computer, then break a nail. I'd throw the laptop at the floor only that would totally kybosh my writing future. And right now that's all I have left. Will's gone, I've stuffed up. And even Dibian's lost interest.

* * * *

I've tried to talk to Dibian all day but she hasn't been in. I only find this out at lunchtime. I'm mildly curious about this, and wonder why she hasn't called or texted, but I shrug it away. I've been busy with filming and Andy wouldn't take a no about lunch.

"C'mon, Iz. Don't play hard to get with me, huh?" He smolders at me. His designer stubble is very Hugh Jackman, but sadly that's as near to divine Hugh as he's ever going to get. Maybe if he were closer, lunch would be a no brainer.

"Tomorrow then?" His tone is verging on an order, which causes my ire to bristle but, I'll be honest, I give in to get him to back off.

"Okay. Tomorrow. Lunch."

"Great, babe!" Shit.

I bump into Rogerson after I've left him.

"Ah, Izzy. It's about Dibian. She's taking several weeks' garden leave. She has an aunt who is unwell and it's going to be a long recuperation plus she's had to go to Stornoway."

"Where?"

"Stornaway, Scotland. Her aunt lives in a lighthouse."

I'm dearly tempted to ask Rogerson if he has shit for brains, but I remember in good time that he's my superior.

"Ah," I reply with deep certainty that Dibian's fed him a nice healthy portion of baloney.

Rogerson chucks me a total curveball, however. "I wonder if you'd act as acting head of department? This could be for several months, maybe even a term?"

I falter as the news trickles in. This is news!

"Me? Really?"

"Yes. She expressly suggested you. She said she'll be in touch very soon. Once she deals with the issue of her aunt's iron lung. So, how does that sound as a plan?"

I nod. Acting head. Me. Wowzer. I'm pretty darn chuffed. It's not every week you publish your first novel – did I mention that this morning sales are at ten k? – and get made acting departmental head of English. I'm wondering if there might be a badge or at least a small buffet of celebration in my honor.

"Of course I'm stuck on who else to ask. Abigail Montague would've been a contender but she's going on maternity leave."

Bastard! As if sensing I'm getting above myself, even if it's only in my head, Rogerson adds, "Only a temporary measure, mind. And a trial. No remuneration or change to your contract."

Aww. And just when I was enjoying my flight of fancy too. I'd settled in for the in-flight movie and opened a tin of gin and slimline tonic.

"I'd be very happy to oblige," I say, magnanimous voice fully employed.

I'm not deterred from imagining good things. A promotion is a promotion. And for once in my life I'm going to tell myself, hey, Izzy Tennant, you're doing well and life is good. You're rated at work. Even if Will never shags you again.

Because life is about positivity.

And that's when I remember Will all over again. And wonder what he'd say if I told him my news.

Shit. Fuck. Balls. A seagull's shat on my silver ruddy lining again. Where's my shotgun? Where's the pest controller? And make mine a double Jim Beam bourbon on the rocks.

* * * *

Next day, I do have a celebration of sorts. Andy Regis has brought me to the local hotel. If Miss Gaudy and Mr. Tasteless ever got together for a night of rampant passion, this hotel's interior theme would be their lovechild. It's so bad I need shades to get through the door. Heinously bad-taste statues and a thoroughly horrid shade of mauve, painted by somebody more accustomed to fairground decoration, are in stark evidence everywhere. Perhaps it's My Big Fat Gypsy Hotel? I realize I'm being über-judgmental and I try to banish taste snobbery, so instead I focus on the fun of it all and hope the staff aren't offended.

"Look at the willy on that cherub," I remark to Andy, but he's staring at the gilt mermaid nymph's GG bazoomas.

"With breasts that big she won't need the tail — she'll float."

"Shall we get out of the car and go and see what delights are inside?" Andy invites.

A man wants to wine and dine me, I shouldn't look a gift horse in its dentures. A cocky cock Andy may be, but right now he wants me.

"You okay, babe?" he asks, and puts his hand on my knee.

Shit. "I'm good. I don't have classes on this afternoon due to a fluke. So I'm good for three courses at least. Maybe even coffee with chocolates after, if you're well behaved."

"I'm hoping you'll be good for more than that, girl," he says like a lecherous uncle at a wedding. His balls are too far away from me to stun gun so I grind my teeth and ignore him.

Andy drives a great car. It's an Audi. A very *Guy with the Silver Tie* motor. He makes a fuss of showing me all the buttons and revving it a lot. Bless him, I fear he must have a very small penis and I try not to hold it against him. No personality and a mini dick are a curse indeed.

"Shall we go in?" I chivvy him on. "Kinda hungry."

"Me too. But not for food." He makes a lunge at me and I pretend to move away to admire the view.

"Let's eat then, babe. Don't go making me chase you."

Normally I'd give him a smart mouth answer. With Will I'd have voiced my jagged thoughts with ease. Only I wouldn't want to discourage Will, would I? The realization causes a leaden feeling inside me.

I cover my disappointment by coming over all *Famous Five* and I put my hands together and say, "Let's go dine!"

I'm ever so slightly appalled when he grabs my hand. And I feel I have to stop him right there.

"Andy, what happened to our friends understanding?"

"Aren't friends allowed to hold hands? Surely a bit of necking and a squeeze isn't out of the park? I get you won't let me tongue you but c'mon, Iz. Guy's gotta have a payoff."

"Um. You touch me and I might stab you with my fish knife."

His eyes are those of a man dying on the battlefield. If I had a bayonet I'd send him to Valhalla sharpish. "Fuck, Izzy, you know I think you're hot. Why hold out? You can even have lobster here if you want it. And champagne. They've put a room on hold and everything."

Wily. Fucking. Shit.

I shake my hands at him in frustration. "Andy, this wasn't what we agreed."

"I'm kidding, you daft goose," he says and laughs like the bird he's accused me of being.

"Honk, ruddy, honk".

"Only pulling your leg. Your face was a picture. What a wind-up!"

Hmmm. I'm feeling a Marge Simpson mood coming on, and my slapping hand is twitching to do something to his face.

"Funny. Let's eat."

I'm going to ramp up his expense account. And a tiramisu followed by Eton mess may well be in my future. Waistline beware. When you're out with a total knob — take solace in the sweet trolley. Mantra number one hundred and forty-nine. Food quality eases the side effects of an arsehole prat shit dinner date.

Now watch those calories tally.

* * * *

Andy is staring at me over the brim of his fluted glass. He chose champagne and made a show of doing a mouthwash to test. The waiter looked as unimpressed as a pedigree show judge that has encountered a dog's dollop. I know exactly how he feels.

"Beautiful woman. Fine dining. Expensive libations. What more could a man need?"

"Support trousers? A lobotomy — oh no, you've had that done before." I smile. I don't care if he thinks I'm rude. He's being such a cock I can't hold back.

Andy eyes me. I think he's trying to smolder but it isn't hitting the mark. "So. The room. Reconsidered?"

"You said it was a joke."

"Lied, doll. It's all there waiting for us. Even the condoms. Ribbed. Extra-large."

I laugh. I also push my plate away. My lobster is lovely. Messy, but jolly tasty and worth the expense. Oh yeah, I'm not paying, I remind myself as I dab my chin in a genteel fashion with my damask linen napkin.

"We haven't even had dessert, Andy."

"If you eat any more, there's no chance you'll get in the lift, babe."

Hardly gallant. I narrow my eyes at Andy and sip my top-price bubbles. "You often use expenses to shag women in hotel rooms?"

"Well, just the once but she was a minger. You're special, different — with a sass banter factor that drives me to distraction and a pert, round arse designed for hot tub love. Can't wait to see your curves in a thong, babe. The room on hold has multidirectional vibrating jets. And complimentary bubble bath."

I sip again and feel my eyeballs roving around to work out where the loos are. I wonder if there's a window big enough to squeeze through? I can always get a bus back to school. Damn it, I'd walk. Barefoot and over a cinder path if necessary. "What are you bloody like, Regis? Pack it in with the claptrap. The jiggyjig is *so* not on the cards between us."

"I definitely want you. I've had a raging monster in my pants since the party. When I met you I thought you were all right—tits could be bigger but your arse shape compensates—but, man. Every time I see you lately, Iz, my spear of lust gets rigid with need. While filming a scene in the library, it got too much—fortunately I had a change in the car."

I sip my champagne again and hide my revulsion. Then I laugh a bit louder. Some other guests look up.

"We're friends. And friends don't get raging below-the-belt reactions about other friends. The expense account seduction's wasted on me and I've been telling you this long and hard."

"Speaking of long and hard." He points below the tablecloth. "When you talk to me like you hate me, it brings the dog out of the kennel, babe. C'mon. Do it some more."

I feel something touch my knee and jump. The couple at the nearby table—the lady looks very nice and wears an eau de nil twinset—look perplexed.

"I'm off for a slash and to take care of urgent business." He disappears to the loo. Thank the Almighty.

We haven't had dessert but he's ruined my appetite for the rest of my life. I'm figuring we've both had enough wine. We should head back. I've a football tutorial with Will at the end of the day and if I don't sober up any he'll go dipshit.

I hiccup and the woman looks appalled.

"Sorry. Waiter." I'd click my fingers. I know it's very rude, so instead, I do a come-hither plea by batting my eyelids on fast tempo. The waiter appears in a flash.

"Mademoiselle?"

"Can we please have the bill and a cab called when you're ready. Delicious meal. Sorry my partner is so awful. He's a business acquaintance with a too-big expense account. He's a total bumrag knob. He bores the arse off me." I raise my eyebrows. "There's an open tab on our bill and a room that's been reserved for us upstairs that we won't be using. Please ask this lovely couple what champagne they would wish to sample and charge it to my partner's account? They may use the room as we're about to leave. With our compliments. Add it to Mr. McKnobhead's bill."

The waiter stares at me and I think he's about to tell me off. Then he gives me a wide smile and a wink. He scuttles to sort the bill sharpish. After a great many irritating restaurant visits where I've waited for ages for a bill, I now know the secret to prompt service – get pissed and be loose-lipped. Or maybe it's to enact a random act of kindness?

The couple nearby are squeezing hands and it warms me inside. Then that chill feeling rains down in a steady trickle that turns to a downpour on my fuzzy warm thoughts. I want that. I want somebody to take me out and treat me nice and squeeze my hand without being an arsehole in the process. If I could choose who it would be, it'd be Will. And I've screwed that up.

I can feel tears well in my eyes. The couple are watching again. And the woman looks devastated, comes over and gives me a packet of tissues.

"Are you all right, dear?" she asks me.

I sniff. And summon composure as Andy the Knob appears and stands poofing his hair out in the mirror by the door.

"Yes, thanks. My partner's an idiot and this was a mistake. You've set me a very inspiring example. Thank you, have a wonderful meal. We've left you a gift for disturbing your meal — the waiter will reveal all."

The waiter rushes over with the leather bill wallet. Andy returns and I'm smiling when I tell him I've already made our arrangements and I have to get back to school for some urgent forgotten business.

He's pissed off enough to start pouting, so I reach over and squeeze his hand. "It didn't work out. But look on the bright side. No calories for dessert. I've a Curly-Wurly in my bag — we'll share it in the cab. I might even snog you with tongues — I am pissed after all."

However painful the snog will be, it's worth it to have him pay for everything. And anyway snogs are less painful when you're as pissed as I am. Andy scribbles his name on the credit card chit without a glance.

I wink at eau de nil lady. She's crystallized what I want. And it's not lobster thermidor with a mini-dicked monster.

* * * *

Will, Annie and I are in the sports hall at five. He's clearly thoroughly pissed off at me. His jaw alone could crack nails if you got too close with a tool belt.

"Enjoy your lunch?" he barks in a low voice at me as he passes.

I ignore him. So what if he knows? Maybe Andy boasted.

"I've had better. I've had worse."

I'm sober. Three jugs of filter coffee and all the coffee Revels in the packet and I'm good.

"Will, you have such muscular legs," says my enemy Annie the Fanny. She's oblivious to the major negative vibes buzzing between us — but then, hey, what's new? Annie and Planet Self are one and the same. It's clear from a couple of things she's said that she's spent the afternoon in here with Will getting one-to-one tutoring. Nice touch, Darby.

I get my own back. "Enjoy your private lessons?"

"Definitely. Some people make things easy," Will replies and I feel slapped.

I stare at him in earnest, hoping for a guilty glance or a reaction, but Will pointedly ignores me.

So I clear my throat and resort to puerile behavior. "I could go to Rogerson and complain about unfair competitive advantage. This isn't about competing. It's about doing your best."

Will rasps beneath his breath, "Quit the banter. Let's get the job over. It's painful enough for all of us." Ouch.

The camera team are late and they rush in with Andy Regis winking at me. He explains, '"Hey, doll, recovered from the Irish coffee yet?" He tried to insist I have whiskey in my coffee this afternoon. I ended up having to get Carson to manhandle him away from my classroom. His words help me not a single inch. Will glares like Mr. Bad Wolf baying for a kill.

When Andy walks past and wiggles his tongue at me suggestively, I realize I've blown it with Will forever after amen. At least Annie will be pleased to have a free run at the man of her dreams.

"Right. Today is about fitness testing. Let's start with sit-ups. Then we move to lunges and squats! Get to it."

Will's become crazy tyrant dictator meets a drill sergeant—setting us a grueling prep that doesn't even go anywhere near ball skills. It's all full-on fitness bench press stuff to make me mourn. My thighs are quaking for mercy.

Annie makes sure the camera has a full-on view of her pneumatic tits and it's only then I notice Andy taking rather a lot of close-ups. For a guy who's wined and dined me, he's lacking in the loyalty stakes.

"Andy, why don't you crawl down her tube top?" I do wish I had more guile.

Will turns. Then moves like a shape shifter. Before I know what's hit us he's grabbed Andy by the scruff of the neck.

"Mate. Get this straight. In my classes—my rules. Sexist shit is out of the question. Get to the back of the sports hall and film from there or I'll take you outside and enforce it personally. And stop harassing the staff. Got my point or do I have to press it on you or kick it up through your arsehole?"

My, but my loins are moist. Andy's eyes narrow and his face screws up like a spooked spider monkey. For a short time I'm convinced they're going to jump on each other and scrap but they don't. It would've been especially galling to have both the man I want and the man I don't want brawling over Annie James' cleavage.

But then I'm freaked by the words I hear Will utter with threat-like menace, "Leave Izzy Tennant alone. Got me? Today wasn't your remit."

Fuck. Annie's looking between them and back at me, equally confused.

While the men are still giving it verbals and Will is setting them a boundary area as far back as he can, I join Annie. "Look, I don't want to compete with you. You can win—I don't mind. Have Will. He's all yours. Let's get this shit over as quickly as we can. Do what we need to do and finish, yeah?"

"You don't want Will? I'd got vibes at the party that you were both on."

"The spark died on us both."

She nods. "Very civilized of you, Izzy. Thanks for the heads-up."

Annie pulls her ponytail back and makes a show of redoing it. I know for a fact it's because it makes her boobs pop out of her top. It's like a cantaloupe show at the farmer's market. And I've never been a melon fan. Slimy, no thanks.

Will walks back to us and I make a show of wafting air up my top.

It's genuinely needed. I'm red and stewing after the workout and there's perspiration coating me like a Popsicle about to puddle. Whoops, but if I don't find myself flashing him a glimpse of the peek-a-boo bra I chose to wear. I try to hide it but I know he's shaken and stirred. What I didn't bank on was making him angrier yet.

"For fuck's sake, can anybody start to be even a touch professional in here! It's sodding well beyond a joke!" He walks past me and yells, "Twenty more. Get to it—

faster!" His face is livid meets thunderstorm. "Squats. Fast as you can. Get to it, Annie. Good job!"

He bends down to mark my sit-ups and says very low, so only I can hear, "You were seen, by someone who told me, necking Andy Regis in a taxi. Fucking. Out of. Order. If you ever pull stunts like that or go out with that walking knob again, there will be consequences. I want a full explanation in my office after this is over. Got me?"

I gasp between sit-ups. "It was a sympathy peck for services rendered and I was a bit pissed. Though I don't suppose you believe that."

"Enough! Do the repeats!"

I'm sit-upping like a metronome on fastest speed. It's crazy. I won't be able to get up or walk again by the end of this.

"Yes, Sir!" he shouts at me, and I yell it back as every muscle in my pelvis and thighs screams for mercy.

I feel like I've woken up in a Nam film. But my man's given me a glimmer that all may not be lost.

"Will... I want to say," I try but stumble on the words.

"Shut up, quiet. This is a workout, not a chat line."

"Sorry, Sir!"

"Do the time, Tennant!"

God, he's hot when he's like this. I find I want sex in this manner immediately. Hard and fast and taking all I have and shouting, attitude and yet more shouting on the side. I'm sweating and moist from every pore of my being and it's not the exercise.

"Yes, Mr. Darby, yes, Sir!" Private Benjamin got off lightly.

If I'd realized this could be so thrilling I'd've signed up for the Territorial Army years ago. I might be getting my arse slapped later. So why does that fill me with secret screaming joy? I can't work out our crazy fest but I know I love and crave it.

Beyoncé's back playing my soundtrack. My bad ass dirty bad boy's in the building. My sequel's back on track. *Yee-effing-ha!*

* * * *

I decide to take a shower in the girls' changing rooms before facing Will. Primarily, because I'm a total sweaty minger. Second, my legs are still shaking from too many squats and I lean back against the tiles to regain my composure and strength.

The water beats down on my head and I close my eyes, reveling in the soothing liquid sensation.

My man is mad at me. He thinks I'm an idiot.

Okay, maybe it was stupid to go out with Andy. Maybe I should've come clean sooner about Tessa. But it's hardly crimes of the century and it honestly doesn't warrant this level of stern, steely, poker-in-the-eye pissed off.

I towel my hair, dry myself, don my clothes and am coming out of the change cubicle when a hand is pressed firmly against my shoulder, slamming me into the door. I'm taken aback by the strength of the jolt.

"You need a lesson in making yourself scarce!" says a female voice behind me.

"Ouch, for fuck's sake!"

It's Annie. "You fucking understood me. What happened to our plan? Where's the recognition that Will is mine and you're a bystander, you silly, grammar-teaching bitch."

"Hey. Enough with that. It's grammar, punctuation, creative writing, text comprehension and critiquing skills to you. Anyway—what do you do? Fuck about with glockenspiels?"

I think I've touched a nerve, because she slaps me full across the face. I'm in total shock—having been assaulted by a mad nympho egotist percussion player.

"It was bad enough watching you make cow eyes at Will. Now you've got talons into Andy. First you flirt with him at the party when he'd been sleeping happily with me—then I hear from my mate at the Audley Hotel she's spotted my new man today with a mystery woman. You think you're so bloody sexy!" Annie flashes me her cell phone, showing a pic of me and Regis at the lunch from hell.

"Annie, Andy Regis is a desperate dog on heat without any charms to recommend him. Absolutely nothing happened—even the food was rubbish." Now I understand why Annie's mad at me and why Andy ceased his pestering for a short period. If I'd known I'd never have agreed to lunch.

Annie narrows her eyes as her lips thin. "Since you've gone after the man I shagged, I'm taking Will. I know you want him, it's obvious by how you are when he's around. So I'm having him as payback."

With a swift hand, I slap her back. It's totally uncalled for and a stinger that leaves a mark but I believe she dealt me and my camel's back the straw that tipped me into psychopath.

"Fuck off, Annie. And if you touch me or Will again, I'll brawl with you on camera. I will lay you out and make a beaded necklace from those polar-white teeth. So back off. And butt out. Wake up and realize Andy isn't worth it."

I walk off, tossing hair that's still wringing wet and sending a spray of droplets all over her.

I'm outta there. I think I contravened the teacher's etiquette code. But she started it. Mad bitch from hell.

* * * *

Will is at his desk writing. He doesn't look up when I enter. He does, however, speak without eye contact.

"Shut. The bloody. Door."

"Certainly, Sir." I do it with enough firmness to make it bang. I guess slapping Annie's got my gusto revved. "What does Sir require? To fight? To slag me off? To exercise his latent inner caveman? Or to act like a prick — please say option four."

Will stares at the wall behind me. Then he rises and paces behind his desk but doesn't come near me.

Fuck. He is livid. I itch to reach for the doorknob and bolt.

"I need to get a couple of things straight with you. Firstly Tessa."

"I'd rather you didn't... Primarily..."

"Enough." He raises a hand and I zip it in an instant. "I went round and had a word. FYI, the woman is delusional. She's going through a separation with her husband — it's taking a toll. She also has money worries. But the affair she alleges to be having with me is entirely fictional and exists only in her head. I talked about this to her and pointed it out. She is no longer in my employment but I'm not a total wanker. I have connections and she'll be cleaning for a friend. Does that cover our Tessa issue? Or do you want to turn it into another mental event?"

I'm still processing, so don't answer right off the bat. "The idea wasn't totally impossible. She was convincing. And direct. And," I add grudgingly, "you are quite attractive. As is she. If you like harpies."

He stares at me hard. "I'm also loyal, monogamous and off limits. I thought I was with you. I thought we were clear on the rules."

I don't reply. What can I say that will give me upper ground? Right, nothing. Epic fail.

"Until this weird phase, which we now know was caused by Tessa's visit after the party, I am the guy you run to for wining and dining. I'm the guy you ask to explain things when you come across something that freaks you out. I'm also the one you come to when you need sexual gratification. Day or night, FYI. Or support. Or to communicate what's going on in your life. Do you understand what I'm saying here?" He blinks at me with the patience of a head librarian teaching the new girl how to alphabetize hardbacks.

"Control freak. Check. You want a rundown of my life or will a tick list filled in daily float your boat?" Shit. I'm skating on the wafer's edge of the ice here but I'm fired and I can't help myself. He's acting a touch scary sex-pestish. Doesn't matter that I'm up for his adorable and earth-moving brand of pest sex.

Will strides to me. He clasps my face between strong palms.

"I saw you slap Annie in the changing rooms. Fuck."

"And how the hell did you do that? A bendy telescope?"

"I was bloody well in there in a cubicle. Waiting for you until she came in. I intended to screw you and have angry making-up sex in a new place."

I can't answer. I'm utterly agog.

"Nice job with the slap by the way. She's had it coming."

"Shit, Will. You do have a stalker side, you know that? First the cemetery, now you're sneaking in on my showers."

"I'm reacting to extenuating circumstances. First you go weird. Then you go out with Dweeb Dick the Lens Leech. The cemetery thing has still got me mad too."

"And what the hell did I do wrong by visiting my dad's grave on his birthday?"

I'm standing with my hands on my hips. His hands are still on my face and he pulls me close. Kisses my lips like they are coated in rare Madeira wine and he's an alcoholic with a raging thirst curse. He tongue teases mine, his mouth demanding. I return with open-mouthed fervor. His hands hold me so gently but firmly, an ache deep within me rises. I think he may have it bad—this man clearly has issues. With me. Ouch.

"Get this. You matter. You matter to me *a lot*. And yesterday you barely ate. I watched you. You raced around doing things for people and you didn't eat. No dinner. Barely any lunch. Then you go out and let an arsehole feed you and try to get you rat-arsed to get into your lingerie. Now do you know why I was mad fit to burst?"

"Yes. I think so. You want to be my nanny or my footman. If it means you do the cooking, the job's yours, no contest. Sign here."

"Be fucking serious!" he yells at me. "I want you to behave. To treat yourself with care. And to be my woman for good."

Wow. Now that's a statement.

With that, he pulls me into his gym cupboard but I'm not complaining. I won't even point out that I kinda saw this coming and I've gone commando in the hope.

I'm braless too. I throw down my bags and yank my Lycra blouse over my head. I don't care if he twigs. I've come prepared as my boobs spring free, ready to be sucked and teased.

"You've been heinously in error. But I'm a forgiving master."

I throw myself on his cock and release it from his trousers and boxers.

"I am not worthy of Sir's attentions. I beg your mercy."

He scrambles to lock the door, remembering we're in a cupboard in school and discretion does have both our contracts by the balls.

"I want to screw you. I want to possess you. And I want to do it *now*."

"Some would call it detention. I prefer to call it…dessert."

At least he's smiling again. And so am I. But if there's a CCTV cam that guards gym supplies we're buggered and in a whole stack of poop.

* * * *

I have a coaching session set up with Ben tonight. He says I'm improving a lot and I can not only head the ball about five times in a row but I can keep it up on my knee and I've managed a few flicks, when luck is on the rise and the wind is in the right direction. I'm very fortunate to have confidential allies in both Janey and Ben. I don't view my prep as cheating — more like home study.

It's only as I'm going to my car and because I'm late that I see them. I'm driving home and there they are — my English mentees. Sophie, Ellen and Lydia.

They're arguing. It's intense. Not fighting and throwing punches intense but full on, like a scene from a soap drama where there's deep words that reverberate and change the rest of the plot.

I find myself pulling into a lay-by and getting out of the car, walking back. But when I get there, they're laughing.

Did I imagine the argument? Am I being paranoid Patsy here?

"Miss, what are you doing here?"

"I thought you were having a fallout."

"Us?" says Ellen with a mocking expression like I've made a major gaffe.

I nod. Lydia looks unfazed. In fact she pulls a 'what's with her face' right at Ellen and Sophie. Suddenly I feel like I'm the idiot or the victim. And I'm kinda bitch-slapped by the move.

"It's real nice that you care so much, miss, but maybe you need to get a life of your own? This is kinda turning stalker teacher."

I reel at the comment but I don't argue. I look at my watch to hide my reddening face. "It's late. Any of you guys need a lift?"

They decline. "Nah, thanks, miss. We are allowed out of the house on our own. We're legal."

Ellen adds, "We're meeting some guys. And they're hot. A chaperone might spoil the party."

As I walk back to the car, I rewind mentally what I saw, doubting myself, wondering how I could get it so mixed. I see clearly in my mind's eye that Ellen was having a go, talking to Lydia as if she was telling her off and Lydia standing there, taking it. Yet she's denying it vehemently.

Am I right to worry? Are they pulling me a line?

I vow to burrow deeper. But for now... There's nothing I can do but let it go. Maybe they're right and I'm seeing things that aren't there—ghosts from my past. Specter shadows from my imagination, but I can't shake the unease.

Chapter Nineteen

Fi is staring at me from behind her science safety glasses with a face that tells me I have her attention. She usually only reserves this face for a new issue of *Science Geeks' Monthly*.

"That's totally incredible!"

"I know." We both stare at my tablet. The Wi-Fi reception in our school is surprisingly good, considering the building and roof are likely to collapse and if too many toilets flush at once, the water supply stages a protest. Which goes to show what they say about books and covers.

"You're number one in the erotica chart worldwide. Number one in UK romance. Top of the movers and shakers list."

"And look at the sales."

"Three hundred thousand. When are you buying me a gemstone for being a chief consultant?" she asks.

"How about a bag of midget gems between friends? I might even throw a party with cocktails. I'm bloody gobsmacked. Still hasn't sunk in."

"When will you get paid?" she asks me.

"I think Omozad pays monthly. I might even afford a new toaster at this rate. Maybe even a six-slice Italian jobbie."

"It's gonna be a rather nice payday."

"Fuck, Fi. Never in a month of Sundays could I have believed this would happen. And I don't even have the password for Omazod yet. Dibian's masterminded my publishing coup."

"It's bloody marvelous."

"Did I hear somebody call my name? Marvelous *c'est moi*! And how's my cherry lips this morning?" Alan's head appears and his face falls. "Oh shit, Izzy. Didn't realize you were here."

"Thanks."

Alan's appearance curtails our discussions. Fi puts the tablet back in its case, and her beau is none the wiser that as of today I am the most in demand erotica author in the country, nay, the world.

Given that I'm wearing a cheesecloth blouse and linen trousers, I'm feeling a tad more Miss Marple than Madame Nipple Clamp.

"See you later?"

"Definitely."

What a tangled web I weave. One nobody would believe. Only my good news and euphoria are about to be short-lived. There's something wrong in the state of Denmark and Jack's about to dish the crap.

* * * *

"When I got home, I knew something was wrong. My place felt off. Took me a couple of hours and then I realized. The clock was gone — the antique clock in the hallway. There was no tick."

"Your clock disappeared while you were in hospital? Was there any sign of a break-in?"

Jack's getting agitated now and I watch as he rubs his temples. "No, Iz, you're missing the point. This wasn't a burglar. Dibian's been in and had a trolley dash, stealing my things. She's stolen money from my drawer. There's also my coin collection and some antiques. Jewelry — I'm so gobsmacked. I've been with the police all morning."

Rewind. What the fuck? Hold on a minute, says my brain. All at once.

Jack's not returned to work since his health issue. Today, he's come in in his civvy clothes to see me with this crazy news.

"Jack! No way!"

"Yes way. I gave her my keys. She promised to collect pajamas and drop in some washing and collect the post and milk. I said I'd get you to do it but she was most insistent, saying you were too busy."

"I'm never too busy for you, Jack. She told me she had the hots for you and I should back out and give you both some space."

"Pish, tush and codswallop. The woman's a whoring thief!"

"Steady, Jacko. That's a bit strong."

"She's taken my Lilly's beautiful jewelry. There were heirloom brooches and bracelets."

I put my fingers to my mouth and gasp. I remember the jewelry. He showed me once, and it was top-notch stuff. The thought of our own head of department going to Jack's home and going through his possessions to cream off the good stuff — well, it makes me go cold and numb all over with shock.

"These were art deco twenties items she was bequeathed by her mother. Course she won't have banked on my having photographed and recorded them. I even have serial numbers of the notes she stole from my holiday money drawer. I don't use banks — never trusted them. Dibian's made off with about fifty thousand pounds."

I'm hearing his words but they don't compute with the Dibian I know. She's intelligent, kind, compassionate with a warm heart and ready wit. I know she's had a tough time lately, but stealing? Surely there's some mistake.

"Jack. Is there any chance you've misplaced the money? You've been on meds and in hospital."

"It's gone. I'm no fool, Izzy. Someone's rifled my effects and gone over my home with thorough attention. She had my keys and there was no forced entry. Dibian saw a chance and took it."

I still don't want to believe it could be true. "Bloody hell, Jack. She told me she had a thieving boyfriend who'd defrauded her. Said he used all her savings and left her in the lurch."

Jack shakes his head and sighs. "Maybe it's sent her a bit loopy? Though I'm not sure I'd believe a word she says. Dibian Hicks has sticky fingers and not from eating as many pastries as she does. I willingly gave her my keys and she's ripped me off. But she won't win. We'll get her for this."

"You need to go to the police," I tell him. But I'm hoping there will be some saner explanation. Could Jack have a close relative who's done the dirty and he's no clue? In my heart I can't accept that Dibian could knowingly have done this.

"Izzy, love. I've already told you. The police dusted for prints earlier. It felt like being in an episode of *Taggart* — enjoyed it better than a crime bestseller. We don't need to tell them. They're already on the case. They probably have her in custody already."

I suck in a breath. "Dibian's gone. Rogerson told me she's caring for a sick aunt but it sounded like a cover."

Jack's eyes widen as his mouth falls open. "She's taken off with my cash — plain and simple."

I whisper a confession because I don't want this to be happening or to be true. "She's got the access to my book's royalties. I've made half a million in sales."

Jack stares at me. "Bloody Nora, girl! We've been had and double crossing Dibian's not going to come back. I have to go and report these developments to Will Darby as a matter of urgency."

"Will? Why does he need to know?"

Jack rises to his feet. "Because he's the one who came to my house to ask me all the questions."

* * * *

I rush into Will's office, about to tell him all that I've learned about Dibian, but he shushes me with a full-on kiss, then a stalling finger.

"But…" I begin but his eyes brook no argument.

"I want you to move in with me. At the Grange. This is fucking killing me. I rarely get time to see you. It's driving me nuts. We're always ships that pass in the night and lately we've been more off than on. Please say you'll think about it."

Ruddy hell. Today is all about surprises. Will is staring at me. For an answer. And I can't quite believe he's asked me such a big commitment-related question. My Secret Sir is suddenly serious and it's alliteration a-go-go. Fuck.

"I will think about it. But first I need to ask you what you know about Dibian? Jack says you know where she is and she's a bloody thief and cash grabber who's run off with our money. Me and Jack have been scammed by Dibian."

"I can't tell you. It's confidential."

I boggle and stare as I take that in. "What? You want me to live with you and make big declarations and next you say you can't tell me anything about Dibian?"

"Exactly that. I'm not at liberty to discuss this."

"So you do know where she is?"

Will nods. "It's complicated."

"Fuck!" I rub my temples. "Today. Is not adding up. Did you know she's stolen? Do you realize she's a thief and you're concealing her whereabouts?"

"Izzy. This isn't my secret."

"You can and you will tell me, Will. Dibian's run off with stolen goods and money. Jack says you know where she is. She's in the process of defrauding me of rather a lot of money too. And I think she did it on purpose."

"I can't give you those details."

"Fuck. Will. Come on."

"I'm sorry, Izzy."

"She's taken money from me. She's probably halfway to Spain by now. Or Mexico. Where she can dress up as Carmen Miranda all she likes."

"She isn't. But I can't tell you what I know yet."

Will sits at his desk while I explain that I've written a book, it's done well and Dibian set the whole thing up. Only she has access to the account and she's disappeared.

Will grabs his coat. I can see the concern on his face, but I'm totally flummoxed. He stops as he pulls the door open, goes into his pocket and retrieves a key with a small piece of paper.

"Take this."

"The key to the Bat Cave?"

"And the numeric code." He nods. "If I didn't trust you, I wouldn't give it to you. But for now, I can't explain. I'll see you later. I have work to do."

"Where are you going? What's all this about?"

"Later."

He walks out and I'm none the wiser. Shitting hell. Is this any way to move in with a man?

I stare at the key in my hand.

Well… There might be good reasons to try it out for size given the facilities…

* * * *

I knock on Annie James' door. There's music on in there—Coldplay are singing about a *Sky Full of Stars*, and I'm pretty sure she thinks they're singing entirely for her.

"Enter," she says so I do. Her face falls when she sees me. She is like a walking and talking Lego person without the awesome personality.

"Oh. It's you. Come to slap my face again?"

"No. Sorry about that. Though you did slap me first."

"And you did deserve it."

"Ooh, bitch. Just when I try to forgive you, I realize you're a hellcat with acid in her veins."

It's at times like these I have to boggle that I am a grown-up. After all I'm a qualified professional teacher. Annie is too — allegedly. And she's a certificated guidance teacher too. Yet here we are having been in a fight in the ladies' changing rooms and we're going at it again, like twelve year olds having a rant.

"It's about Lydia Salter," I say. "I'm worried about her and she's in your guidance group."

I notice she doesn't tell me to take a seat so I take one anyway, uninvited.

"There are two girls in my class and I keep getting a feeling that they're not getting on with Lydia but it's always smoothed over whenever I challenge them."

"Maybe they don't want you interfering?"

"Look. We both know how seriously the school takes bullying and how we react at the earliest signs. Something doesn't sit right with me. Last night I saw them having a dispute in the street but when I challenged them, they denied it. Lydia is looking very gaunt and agitated at times, but she won't speak with me. I thought it was time to bring this to you. Maybe you could call home?"

"Izzy. I'll note your concerns. Leave it with me, but your evidence here is distinctly lacking. You're working on a hunch."

"Call it intuition."

There's something in her expression that tells me Annie's making the most of putting me down in the same deft way Lydia and the girls did.

"Don't you have to investigate an allegation? Isn't it wise to examine things in case?"

"I'll use my discretion. Leave it with me."

I get the feeling my concerns are being swept off the priorities tablecloth like stray scone crumbs. I figure I should chat to another guidance teacher for a second opinion or baseline.

"And while you're here…" says Annie. And I have a sneaking suspicion that this is the chance she's been waiting for. Bingo.

"I know what you've done," says Annie. "And I intend to tell Will all about it."

I roll my eyes at her and palm the air. "What have I done now?"

"You're Raye C. Ryder of *Pleasure's Edge* fame. You have a chart-topping book on Omazod. You're set to make a fortune. And reading between the lines — you're writing it about Will Darby. I'm not stupid, and I'm going to tell all the people who count, so you will never be taken seriously again."

I sit back in the seat.

"Don't be ridiculous."

Shit. I always knew Annie was a bitch but I never counted on her having keen intelligence or insight.

She shows me the tablet that's lying on her desk and flicks through pages. It's already loaded like she was reading it when I entered.

"'*His emerald eyes glint at me and dark lustrous curls graze my thighs as he settles himself. The muscular veins of his arms grab my attention as he braces his weight. My sex is a coiled ninja awaiting his assault when his tongue meets my clit. My mask and ball-gag won't permit words! This is a man I can't say no to!*' What do you have to say about that one?"

"Could be anybody. Why do you think it's me who wrote that?"

"Dibian told me you did. And that you used Will for research."

"You should keep taking your tablets—stopping meds gives you strange ideas."

"I'm going to tell Will."

"He already knows." I'm a crap liar but I tough it out.

Damn. I could hit the Omazod delete button but I don't have permission, thanks to Dibian. I'm sailing shitty creek with a very poopy paddle.

She licks her bottom lip. "I'll raise the issue with Rogerson. Is this the kind of extracurricular activity a teacher should present to the world?"

"Do you know, Annie, I never liked you, but I never had you down as a nasty-arse bitch. You couldn't get Will yourself, then you picked the wrong guy in Andy and used it as further reason to hate me. I'd feel sorry for you, because you really don't deserve to be done over by a tool like Regis. But in trying to spoil and sully and fuck up things for the rest of us you stoop too low. So what if I wrote a book? It's a fiction, a bit of fun. And it's been more successful than I ever dreamed. If you want to crap all over that and the fact that me and Will have a shot at a decent love life, then be my guest. I came to ask you about Lydia. I can't state strongly enough how much I think you should listen to me. If you want to try to balls my life up, go ahead. Why not up the headcount to two? Lydia and me. Do your worst."

I walk out.

And Coldplay is switched off by the time I'm closing the door.

* * * *

I've been summoned to Rogerson's office—it smells strongly of wood wax, so clearly Florrie the cleaner's had a mad buffing episode. Something about it takes me right back to the basement at Will's with a longing that shocks me and rocks me on my heels. Inside I quiver.

"Izzy. Take a seat."

He turns to the gazunder behind his desk and brings over a tray with an enormous candle as its centerpiece. It's multihued and must've taken nights of detailed work to create.

"Always wanted to pay my own homage to the leaning tower of Pisa. It's where my wife and I honeymooned. Anniversary present, thanks to your candle mentoring skills. I'm eternally grateful."

"Wow. It's big and beautiful. I know your wife will love it and the time and care you put in."

I hold back on my view that she'd probably rather have a lily bouquet, Belgian chocolates and a theater weekend pre-booked. But let the man deal with his own domestic bonfire.

I get up to go when he adds, "I asked you here because I need to ask you something personal."

Immediately I jump to the conclusion that Annie's already been before me. Bloody hell, that was quick. She's dobbed me in with the boss for my writing and for Will.

"I need to ask you to please show restraint with Mr. Darby."

"Sorry?" I'm trying to gauge what he knows, what's been said, but I can't.

"I know you and he are on friendly terms. But Mr. Darby is on a very pressing assignment and I'm asking if you could please accommodate me by permitting him space and not asking questions. He's going to be rather tied up. Please don't ask about it. Full details will emerge when the time is right.

"I won't ask. We're colleagues."

"Can I rely on you to stay away from him? In the short term and for the sake of the school? I know you spend time together. And that's fine. But he cannot be disturbed at school right now and your job depends on giving him space to undertake my instructions. Anyway, on another issue, a concerned parent contacted me today, intimating their daughter made an allegation you are taking too much interest in her social life."

Blimey. Talk about a curveball.

"What? I don't understand."

"Lydia Salter thinks you bother her. Asking if she is being bullied. Stopping her while she's with her friends out of school time."

"Yes. These things are true."

"You know the boundaries as well as I, Izzy."

"It's interested concern only. I wasn't pushing in my nose."

"She's off today. Her mother asks if you can please be mindful that Lydia finds your attention intrusive." Rogerson steeples his fingers. "I must ask you to consider this your first verbal warning."

I nod. I'm stunned. I've never been given an at-work dressing down or an advisory meeting in my career.

Shit. I'm gobsmacked. And I really must have got it all wrong.

* * * *

There's nothing like a back-off warning and a sense of shock and disappointment to carve the way for minimal foreplay and great frantic wild sex. So it must be, when I finally go to Hangley Grange that night for our last night of passion and to let Will know I've been officially warned off. I think he's somewhat stunned.

"The key," I tell him and thrust my bags at him. "Bring these to the playroom!"

I've never been a real dominatrix before. Well, I pretended for the party but tonight I'm taking full control. If I have to stay away from Will and not ask questions then I'm damn well going to go full throttle at all my sex fantasies and lay them bare in one full-on night of epic sex.

He's obviously been on the treadmill, because he's in his running shorts and track shoes only. His breathing is still in the exertion zone and there's a glistening sheen of perspiration on his pecs.

"And be quick about it!" I snap as I walk to our basement lair. He's beside me opening the door and sorting the keypad, still panting from his workout.

"Don't you want me to shower first?"

"Nope. You will obey all instructions. There isn't time. I've a lot of stuff to get through. Tonight I'm in charge."

He's looking at me oddly. "Okay. Mistress. I think. Go for it."

"I understand that you have something secret afoot. But I have things I want to do too — tonight's about my sex fantasies. I want all my boxes ticked."

The lights are dim in the playroom slash Bat Cave. It's as I remembered. There's something about the black fixtures and deep rouge color scheme of the walls that remind me of Moulin Rouge meets opium den in a bordello. I find I like it.

"Open the bags," I order. "The black glossy one is yours."

I sweep off my overcoat and watch as Will's jaw hits the floor.

"Shit," he says softly. "You've gone to effort."

"Indeed."

I'm wearing new patent leather thigh-length boots. They're pretty damn hot. They lace right up the front and right up the back and there's buckles aplenty. Put it this way—taking them off and putting them on will require three maids and a livery expert. Plus Harry Houdini.

"You like?"

Will comes toward me, as if to prove it. "I like."

"Wait. Do not touch the goods," I instruct.

I throw my coat on the leather chair at the door.

I'm wearing a sheer black cloak. If highwaymen wore negligees, then this would get the bonus ball. I'm calling it a cloak but it's more like a voluminous waistcoat, complete with a large hood. My arms go through it, but there are no sleeves. It's a sheer as a will o' the wisp. I think it's sexy as hell and it shows all the things I'm not wearing beneath. It's a bit Kylie round the edges but Kylie on a being very bad girl day.

All I am wearing beneath are leather pants. Similarly, the leather pants have a thong and they are covered in tiny buckles and zips. I've never worn leather knickers before—I find I like them. Even though I've not technically got a penny of my publishing money, I've spent a sizeable sum of money in the nearest sex shop tonight—I figure, after what I've been through, I deserve the treat. It's crazy to think I've made a million yet I have to be careful because it may never be mine.

I have three other leather and lace outfits. One decidedly dominatrix spandex number. Plus a bra and pants covered in Batman logos. That will be my *pièce de résistance*.

The bra I am currently wearing has a foundation structure of leather but it's inset with peekaboo lace, and the cups are pointed and PVC. With shimmering steel pointy bits.

I watch as Will sucks in a breath.

"Holy jeez, babe."

"Tonight, I'm in charge. You have the knowledge. But I have the power."

Will's voice is dry with desire. "I'm getting those signals. Whatever you want, babe."

"Kneel by the bed," I order him. "Give me the bag first."

From the bag I take out my kit—a whip, three crops, a tickly duster thing that caught my eye, nipple clamps—I cheated there, as Janey left them at mine. There are also balls for a certain part of me and a mask. The big sausage-style dildo implement was on special offer and I felt a little sad to leave it behind on its own.

"Christ on a bike. Did you rip off a sex shop?"

"Silence. Aren't you going to open your gift?"

I watch him, while holding my own first toy of choice. It's the cane from my forfeit—I've still not returned it. And I dearly want it to have some fun before it goes back.

Will looks in the shiny black bag I've brought him. "Ah. Okay. Right."

"What are you waiting for, Batman. Get them off and get those on."

Dominatrix Izzy. I think I'm going to be good at this.

* * * *

Will is wearing a leather sex pouch. He suits it very well. He's also wearing a lot of baby oil and he's finger-licking good. My very own Will Darby McNugget.

I have him cuffed and chained to the bed — arms and ankles. I also have him blindfolded.

I can see he's ultra-nervous and I'm loving every delightful, loaded, clock-ticking second. I sense it's going to be a long night.

I take the lit candle and pour wax upon his chest. It's very near the nipple but misses. He growls, but does not protest.

"Good boy! You make a very good submissive."

"What book are you reading now, Mistress? I'd suggest this one's gone up the scale a notch too far toward loopy loo."

I snap my crop down across his thighs and hear the jangle of chains and cuffs as he tries to bolt and flinch from the surprise punishment.

"Mistress will be kind if Will is a good boy."

I kiss him, enjoying the taste and feel of him. Reveling in the moment, I can feel his tension and I'm pretty sure he doesn't like being restrained. He's a guy who likes to be in control.

"As much as this is okay, I don't suppose we could have straight vanilla sex now?" he asks.

"You dare to disagree with your Mistress' orders?"

"Just sayin'."

Again the candle wax becomes my plaything, only this time it's close to his stomach and he shouts out with surprise. I reward him with labored attention to his mouth and ardent kisses. He is shaking beneath my touch and I realize this isn't fair. He isn't in the zone, he wasn't prepped and he didn't ask for this.

"Don't you like being a sub?"

"It's okay but—"

"Would you like me to stop?"

"Not if you mind."

I sigh. Then take off his mask. His eyes are earnest and he looks somewhat relieved. "If it's important to you—"

I find I'm not that bothered. It started out as a giggle and a chance to try out all the things I'd read about, but, in reality, if he's not into it, neither am I.

What I am into is the way he makes me super-hot seeing him in those tiny leather pants.

I unlock the cuffs and ankle straps.

"Vanilla sex has its place."

"Nothing wrong with vanilla. As long as there's spice on the side," he answers, and in a deft flick, he's on top of me. I'd been planning to give him mind-blowing attention to a lower part of the anatomy, but he's beaten me to it.

"Sir always likes to take the lead."

"In these tight leather pants, babe," he answers, "I'm in danger of an embolism. Let's get this moving, shall we?"

Chapter Twenty

It's all well and good having sex in a good dozen different ways in a room expressly designed for sin and experimentation. But there's one thing that's liable to darken proceedings—and that's introducing the elephant that's currently in our room.

Namely the fact that my erotic author identity must be properly discussed before Annie does it for me.

I kiss him as we dress each other. We don silky robes, then head arm in arm to the kitchen. "About my book. It's doing really well in terms of sales, now. You were pretty important in helping me find material but I had started writing it before I met you. Don't worry, nobody knows you were my sex mentor."

"I know all about it. Read it too. Didn't think you could get away without me investigating?"

Come again? I stare into his green eyes. And try not to be distracted and mesmerized by a glimpse of bare chest and pecs—they must take a lot of gym work to hone. I shake my head slowly. "You know?"

"Yeah. Pretty sexy too."

"Who told you? Dibian?"

"No. Ben did. I'm flattered—after all you've touched on experiences we've shared. It's very well written. And hotter than a jalapeño sandwich with hot sauce. Eaten in a sauna straight from the barbecue. Makes me proud."

"You've bloody read it? You knew and didn't say? And now I have to bloody well wait until you decide you can finally tell me what's going on with this Dibian thing?" I'm pushing my hair back and trying to regulate my breathing. At this rate I'll need to ask for a paper bag to blow into.

"Dibian is a subject that will be fully explained when I'm given clearance to do so. As for the book, I've only read some of it." He grins. "It's a great read. I fancy the hero and heroine myself."

I laugh and prod him. Then I give him a push and he yanks my wrist and kisses up my arm in a move he does oh so very well.

I feel myself heat to inferno level from my blushes. "I can't believe you read that and never told me."

"Izzy, babe, we've shared wild jungle sex in many ways and tonight you found a new fascination for straddle bars and BDSM sex toys. Why get all coy and girly about me reading your fantasy book?"

He has a point.

"Saying it out loud is different."

He grabs my fingers and kisses each one at a time, then makes a delicious feast of the pinkie by sucking it in a scurrilous manner.

"There's somewhere else we haven't tried. Could feature in a sequel. The whirlpool?" He crooks a finger — he has the power to make me quiver and I all but leap at him.

"Thought you'd never suggest it. Add a chocolate fondue pot on the side and it's pretty much ultimate fantasy nailed."

His eyes light up and he yanks me in his wake. My perfect man — dark secrets and all.

* * * *

It's funny how in life, when you tell a lie about something, the falsehood becomes a divine prophesy that the lie you told will bite your behind and leave marks. Well, that's happening tonight with my car.

When I came unannounced, I pretended car trouble. As I head up the drive to the Hangley Grange gates, my car sputters then stalls. I try the ignition but it's dead.

"Shit. C'mon."

I scratch my head and flip the bonnet switch. But my car maintenance knowledge is as basic as my skills in advanced knot-tying. I can call the AA or maybe even have Will look? Sounds like a plan.

The driveway avenue here is a winding fairy-tale woodland affair with small lay-bys, where rhododendrons create quiet corners. I'm whistling as I walk but stall as I round the bend in the drive where the house is in clearer view. It's Tessa. She of the crazy, deluded fantasies. She of the long blonde hair and claims of experience in Will's bed. Psycho nutter in spiked heels. I gasp as Will walks out to meet her and they talk. When his hand goes to gently touch her arm, my stomach takes a disorienting dip.

I thought she wasn't working here anymore?

I lurk, sniper-style, behind a rhododendron. I'm unseen in the dim light and my eyes widen as I watch.

She's walking into Will's house with him, her red sports car parked near the entrance—it wasn't there when I came out. It's as if she must've been behind the property when I left. Will told me she no longer worked here. Will said there was nothing between them.

So why is she entering Hangley Grange carrying a suitcase? And why is Will greeting her like she's number two in the queue?

I've spent the last two hours having sex with my man in his house. And the next woman was in the wings for the main event. It causes me a pain in my heart to see him talk to her, then gently place a hand on her shoulder. I can't watch more because there's a raw feeling in my stomach like the flu bug that made me puke.

I return to the car, my pace increasing with each step and my head crammed full of my questions. I don't feel ready to confront them—maybe I should? I get into the car to find my phone. I turn over the ignition on the off chance and the car starts. I drive away at speed and in such a state that only half a mile down the road, I wrap the car around a ruddy lamppost with a heavy metal *thunk*. The bumper's hanging off and there's a massive bash in the bodywork. It's drivable, but only just. Will has another woman and all I care about is fleeing this place for good.

I feel as dented as my car.

Will's a liar and he's dead to me. He's a cheat.

* * * *

Rampant hurt doesn't cover my feelings. Inside me is a churning, dark pool of pissed-off rage. I can't believe Will is two-timing me. I know for a fact he's lied. I've swallowed his lines and he must think I'm easy to hustle.

I'm so gutted about it all I can't bear to discuss these events. Not even with my closest pals. I cry and drink a bottle of wine as a nightcap but next day throw myself into work and developing a full avoidance strategy and anti-Will emotional shield.

"Still no news on Dibian. Will's not in today," says Jack when he pours me my tea. Jack is back at work on a trial basis — it's his first day in. There's more emphasis on tea than actual manual labor but it's great to have him back.

"Hold on, girl. You got an asbestos throat or something?"

I set a new tea-drinking speed record, because Will's not in and I want to seize my chance. I leave a note in his office in an envelope and the deed is done in under ten minutes.

It reads,

We're over, Will. I saw Tessa. I don't want to talk. Leave me the hell alone. Bullshit is your specialty. Keep your key and put it somewhere painful.

The key he entrusted to me is now in two bits, thanks to a hacksaw and a dose of revenge.

Now attached to the biggest piece is a cardboard tag that reads,

For Tessa. Your next in line.

* * * *

I almost walk right into Lydia Salter on my way back from Will's office.

"Um. I think it's best we don't talk. I got your message." I begin to walk past, but Lydia reaches out a hand to stop me.

"I'm sorry. I came to find you to apologize. I lied and I've felt terrible ever since."

"What for? Making sure my boss told me off for taking an interest in your welfare? I'm sorry you felt I was poking in my nose."

Lydia shakes her head. "I tried to cut myself — self-harming, the doctor calls it. I've been doing it since the stuff with Sophie and Ellen started but hiding it from Mum. She surprised me in the shower and saw the marks. I thought by lying about you and making it your fault, I could ditch the blame. You were right. You've always been right."

I stand still staring at her. Lydia's okay. I was right. She's okay. But she might not have been. Thank God this has all come out.

I try to take in the enormity of what she's told me. "Lydia. Why have you been hiding this?"

"I wanted to be accepted. I know they weren't being kind but I wanted a gang. I was sick of being a nerdy, clever geek."

God. It's like listening to a tape of myself at her age, recorded for hideous posterity. I badly wanted to fit but did at the expense of my trust. I almost ended up with a broken neck. How low is self-esteem when you're prepared to take those odds?

"Lydia. I'm sorry. Thanks for the apology."

"I am sorry I pushed you away." She's crying, so I comfort her and rub her hand.

"I'm glad you're here to tell the tale. How are you going to cope with seeing these girls again? Aren't you back at school a bit soon?"

"They're being talked to now — Mum came in to see Rogerson. I said I wanted to come back. I can't avoid it forever. When Miss James called to say you'd been worried about me, Mum asked questions and I felt cornered. Then she came into the shower. I was so embarrassed but I couldn't evade admitting that something was wrong. She saw the wounds."

"You're alive. That's what counts." I hug Lydia. "Why was it so hard to tell me?"

"Like an idiot running to teacher?"

"I meant what I said." I stare at her long and hard. "Like you, I made a big mistake when I was at school. I fitted in with the bullies by not speaking out. I nearly came unstuck — we both need to go and thank Ms. James for stepping in."

"Thanks for telling my guidance teacher. She helped sort this out."

"Come on. Let's go and find Miss James then. Thanks and apologies all round."

And that's not a phrase I ever thought I'd hear myself saying. But I'm very glad Lydia's come through this.

* * * *

Lydia leaves after we've done the necessary and Annie slides a note into my hand as I go to leave her office. I stall, shocked, and stare at her, wondering what she's doing and what this is about.

"From Dibian." Annie's features are pinched as she stares at the envelope in my hand.

"She's been in touch?"

"There's a meeting shortly and you'll know the full story soon enough. The letter arrived in my pigeon hole and I intended to pass it straight to police. There was an entreaty to give it to you. Look, I'm taking a risk here so please give it on to the cops when you're done. Dibian's in custody already so it's evidence."

"Shit!" I raise my eyebrows at this news. "I'll make sure the police get it."

"There's a nice computer fraud sergeant called Tessa who came to interview me when I first had suspicions about Dibian."

"You reported Dibian to the police?" I say it slowly because I'm struggling to process this revelation. "Wait, Tessa — *is a policewoman*?"

"I knew Dibian was up to something so I voiced my concerns to Rogerson. Dibian was always at work, in her office, at night on the computer, sometimes weekends. I'd agreed extra overtime with Rogerson to develop an orchestra workshop. When I caught Dibian lurking in the admin office after hours when she'd no business to be there, my suspicions arose."

"So where did Tessa come in?" I'm still struggling to work out why she's moonlighting as Will's maid or if that was all a cover for their liaison.

"Sergeant Tessa Davenport came from Scotland Yard to interview me. Initially I thought the case had gone cold or maybe I'd imagined it. Tessa has told me today that Dibian's been apprehended and charged. And you should tell her about your letter. I'm trusting you to do the right thing."

How crazy and weird and messed up has life become? My pulse is racing and I'm finding breathing normally tricky. I want to back out and run to sit down quietly to absorb this but I don't. I stand my ground. I struggle to find my voice. "I'll get this to the police. Thanks, Annie. It seems you've done a lot of things right lately."

I need to find out what the hell's been happening directly under my nose. But first I need to read what Dibian has to tell me.

* * * *

Dibian has sent me a letter. With the username and password for my Omazod royalty account. The letter is briefish but written in her familiar fountain-penned flourish.

Izzy, I'm sorry for what's happened. Please pass on to Jack how much I regret what I did to him too.

You've probably guessed but there was no fraudster boyfriend. No amount of excuses or words can wipe away the shame of what I've done.

I'll say only this — I never meant to use you or Jack but I do find temptation hard to resist. I knew you had a bestseller on your hands and Jack was too trusting — I couldn't stop myself, even though I'd been defrauding online for years.

The police are on to me. It started as an experiment — I'm good with computers and great at numbers. English teaching isn't my only flair. Then it became habit. I've amassed a fortune — with good reason.

My sister lives in the States and has a rare cancer with no insurance cover. I've been funding her care. Yes, it's no excuse, especially when I've taken so much. When you found me crying in my car I'd had bad news about my sister's worsening health. I'd promised myself I'd give up the online racket. I wanted to stop but it was an addiction. Like I said, I have a problem.

You'd be surprised how easy it is to get into a system and secrete away a company's cash. I knew you were writing the book before you told me, I'd been reading it on the server. I always knew you had something special.

You were a friend. It's over now and I'm glad they've stopped me.

Dibian

The day's end bell rings and I've a staff meeting. I shove the letter in my pocket and go.

The staff meeting is in the library and I'm there before anyone else arrives. I have so many questions and I need time to myself to collect my thoughts.

Why has Will lied about Tessa? And what the hell's been going on — from Dibian's hidden thievery to the realization that our school is a tangled web of intrigue?

Fiona marches up and sits next to me with a loud exhalation. "God, this place has boarded the loony express. Have you heard? It's everywhere. Even the radio. And officially nobody's told us yet."

I purse my lips, summoning the strength to say it. "Dibian's been charged with fraud."

"And the rest! Massive fraud — using the school system to access the local authority's bank accounts, I heard. She's been nicking left, right and center from a lot of people for a long time. The story makes for juicy copy. They're saying there were piles of money stacked inside the grand piano in her living room! Can you believe that? And to think I used to lend her change for a coffee in the canteen. Sheesh, some people take the piss! Wanna read the story?"

The strangled gasp I've tried to keep inside because I long to cry escapes without permission and it's loud. I hold back the tears but I'm gulping in air. Fiona grabs me into her hugging arms.

"Shit, Iz!"

My voice is shaky with hurt when I whisper, "The grand piano—I sat admiring it in her room. I asked if she'd duet an Elton-George Michael number for a laugh. Shoulda been a rendition of Abba's *Money Money Money*. Was I a willing dupe?"

"Should've been *I Fought the Law and the Law Won*. She's going to go to prison for a very long time, babe. And you need to realize it's got nothing to do with you."

"I trusted her. What kind of crap judge of character am I?"

"She was charmingly believable, doll. Don't beat yourself up. You weren't the only one to fall foul of her sticky fingers. Somebody told me they saw her nicking the silver cutlery at Will's buffet by sticking it in her Carmen Miranda skirts!" Fiona shoves a piece of printed paper in front of me. It's a leaked news article about Dibian that's already appeared online.

I scan the text and have to go back and read whole sentences again because the shocks derail me. Her fraud amounts to millions. What she took from me and Jack is nothing compared to her aspirations as a fraudster. I'm speed-scanning the print to glean more.

Scotland Yard's fraud squad have arrested a North London secondary school teacher in connection with the theft of embezzled funds from the authority's education service and assorted companies. Her haul of at least two million pounds is the biggest in UK online fraud history perpetrated by a single individual. Victims include local authorities, travel firms, a hotel company, online banking accounts and a department store chain.

My eyes fall on a name lower in the story and I stall. My heart beats fast as I replay the words and realize I can't take more in. These developments have corrupted my head's programming.

"Scotland Yard's fraud inspector Will Darby successfully led the covert operation within the school."

Fiona's voice is right beside me but I don't absorb her words. "Once a footballer, now William Darby, secret star of the Yard."

"Will is a chief fraud cop," I whisper, processing what's happened as I speak it aloud. "Tessa works with him. It was an undercover sting to catch Dibian. Was I being investigated too?"

The article falls from my grasp and Fiona retrieves then reads it, "One time pro footballer Will Darby scored fast-tracked detective promotion post-football after trailblazing in a pilot scheme partnered with FBI fraud experts. Scotland Yard continue to develop such partnerships to great acclaim. Darby's track record is unparalleled."

I stare ahead in iron-clad disbelief, then I see the man himself walk through the doorway. He's tall and grim-faced in his dark suit, with slicked-back hair, and inside me there's a maelstrom of stormy disbelief.

I'm angrier at his lies than I'm ready for and I grip my bag's rim so tightly it hurts my palm.

"Lies and more lessons on who not to trust," I whisper.

"You okay, Iz?" Fiona asks, and she touches my arm.

"Never. Fucking. Better."

Who am I kidding? Anger is so much easier to swallow as a bitter pill than heartache.

"Is it me or does Will look like a total policeman now I know?" I ask her.

"He's the same to me. You don't look okay." Fi watches me oddly. As if I've styled my pet chihuahua's hair with a set of rollers and tongs. If I had either to hand I'd use them to inflict harm on the inspector who's come to visit.

Will looks tired. I don't know whether to be concerned or gratified. Why have I been so ruddy effing thick? Has any of what I've been experiencing of late been real? The realization hurts like a throbbing ache that won't abate.

He walks past me without meeting my gaze so I speak out. "Sir? Nice undercover performance. You played us a blinder."

He flashes me a steely warning glance and his jaw clenches. I find I want to kick him somewhere painful but Tessa enters the room and Annie's by her side and they're talking.

"Oh, look. You've brought your cheerleading squad."

"Izzy. Stop this now," Will commands.

The police, Rogerson and the guy I saw Will with in the canteen the other week stand in a group. Annie comes to my side and slips her hand over mine. She squeezes when I hand her Dibian's letter with my other hand. She nods, then gives it to Tessa who flashes a hesitant smile.

Tessa approaches. "Izzy, I'm sorry about my visit. I thought you were going to blow our cover and took action. Got the rap for it, too, from the boss. You didn't deserve to get so caught up in things."

"You're right. Maybe some of you could've told me the truth."

"Couldn't risk it. We were close to a collar," Tessa answers.

"She is his colleague," Annie explains. "Not Will's girlfriend. I know when you're jealous — can read it a mile off — I've had plenty of practice." My eyes search Annie's for truth, because I find, right now, I'm not sure who to believe. "Tessa's got a partner. Let it sink in."

I force on a sarcastic face. "Cagney or Lacey? I don't give a stuff."

"She's into girls. How many ways do I need to say your man is still your man? For fuck's sake, girlfriend, wakey-wakey!" Annie walks off.

Will stands nearby and doesn't make any move to communicate. There is not a flicker of a glance or a glimmer of emotion. I feel like the biggest idiot ever to breathe, so I say nothing.

It's over. He's only involved in 'the job'. I was a mere casualty of crime busting. Bugger if that's not shit, so I can't hold my anger.

"When were you going to confide?" I challenge him but Will is still tight-lipped.

Rogerson throws me a dagger-spiked glare and even Tessa looks like she's about to go *Hawaii Five-O* crazy and cuff me against a wall. In a blink, they've closed ranks to protect their hero.

I refuse not to have the last word. "I guess you were on work experience. The FBI may think you're hot shit but I'm left less than impressed."

* * * *

"So you see," says Rogerson, summing up like a vicar at a turgid wake, "the BBC were here undercover for *Crimewatch*. Their staff are covert Scotland Yard. This was a huge sting and an important case." He steeples his fingers, and I figure this will be the biggest deal of his entire teaching career. "Miss Hicks not only defrauded the London Borough of Barnet's education department, via cleverly linking into their management accounting system and syphoning off money, she also had an Internet fraud scam going with a whole string of companies."

Will sits behind a desk, in front of a Scotland Yard logo, looking like Batman without the suit or gizmos. He's a policeman. An inspector. And he was never a teacher, he used that as a suitable foil for his undercover machinations.

"I can't believe he kept it all secret," I'm muttering.

Fiona flicks me a shush glance and some of those in the front stare to see what I'm on about. They probably think I'm having a flush.

Will briefly slides me a silent *quiet* command. Shit. It's Daniel Craig complex come to life. And I'm a Bond Girl gone bonkers.

I should've guessed it was too much to dream. The bottom would fall from my fantasy relationship – it always does. I should stick to books – and teaching. I'm passable at those.

Will stands and inhales. "I want to offer Netherfield Secondary School my sincere apologies for the duplicity and undercover surveillance necessary in this case and the impact our actions have had on individuals at the school. This is a major case – Netherfield played a key role in securing our success. Scotland Yard is immensely grateful."

I stand up. I say nothing. But I walk out.

The sex room in the basement wasn't a dungeon or a playroom but a cell. A place that should have been padded because it's certainly affected my mental health. The handcuffs were his day job. And I was sap enough to fall for the emerald eyes and smooth lines.

I can hear Will's sum-up as I walk out. "We appreciate your involvement in this project. The mentoring footage will not be used by *Crimewatch*. Police will no longer be based at Netherfield and as of today filming is officially over."

Amen to that.

Good bloody riddance. I feel kicked in the privates and my heart's been shredded and pulped.

* * * *

It's the next day — life must go on. Lydia and I take the stage at Assembly. Lydia takes a seat behind me and I go to the microphone center stage.

"To you, I'm Miss Tennant from the English department. But I'm more than a teacher — a long time ago I was a school pupil too. One with hopes and dreams and dramas and comedy moments as you all have. And regrets too. I'm not here today to talk about English, you may be relieved to know. I want to talk about how we treat people, and how we deal with the way people treat us can make the biggest difference of all. I urge you to think about facing the bullies around us. And letting your guidance teacher know if it happens."

I tell my personal story about my teenage brush with emotional abuse. How I so badly wanted to be accepted I agreed a dare with a forfeit — to befriend a girl I knew from chemistry. How we met at night in the park to be accepted into the Cool Girl Gang—but neither of us realized we were being set up to be humiliated then beaten up as entertainment.

"I ended up in traction. I nearly had a broken neck—I was lucky. The end of this story is that Colleen ended up in hospital twice. The second time, after an overdose. She couldn't face living with what the bullies had done. Fortunately she didn't succeed. Think about it—if somebody doesn't treat you with respect, tell your guidance teacher. It's why we have them."

Lydia comes over to the mic, her heels starkly clacking as she walks. I'm so proud of her.

"I want to thank Lydia for handling her own issue this week with bravery, courage and clarity. She realized she hid the truth because she thought she could handle bullying alone. Fortunately, she realized not letting her teachers help her was a mistake. By telling your guidance teacher and parents you enable us to put measures in place. She has come to tell you her story. I commend her actions."

Lydia stands and reads out a piece of her own creative writing—it's a Lydia-fied version of Cinderella in which Cinders questions her treatment by the ugly sisters.

She summarizes, "We *have* to speak out. The only fairy godmother is your decision not to settle, and to enforce change. Tell your teacher—she can help. Mine did. And my thanks go to Miss James and Miss Tennant." For a girl who struggles to summon the confidence to communicate, she's done herself and me proud.

Tears well in my eyes as the applause rings out around the assembly hall. And even as I've said the words I realize Will would say he played a guardian role while he worked among us. And Annie started the process for justice when she spoke up to challenge Dibian's behavior. I push the thoughts away. But I don't feel like any hero here—I was doing my job. Which makes me think.

At the end of Assembly, Rogerson tells the pupils that all filming is now off and explains that Mr. Darby is from Scotland Yard. The fraud stories in the newspapers are true and Netherfield has seen justice served.

As I walk down the stage steps, I'd like to believe him.

But, like Lydia's story, life lately has a fairy-tale feel. The bubble's popped and I'm left feeling empty. When I get back to my class there are three missed messages from Will on my phone. I power it down. As Lydia reminded me, time to change and move on.

* * * *

I'm sitting in the school's sensory garden because it's deserted and, while I have lunch on my lap, the last thing I want is food.

When I see Jack wander in to find me, my heart dips. I'd thought I could skulk here—turns out there's no isolation and misery time at Netherfield Secondary.

I hit stop on my iPhone music player. I've been playing Adele songs—the morbid, toxic life-in-tatters mega-mix on repeat. It's a nod toward self-indulgent self-flagellation over a relationship gone wrong.

Jack sits down beside me on the bench, undeterred by my mascara tracks or the massive lavender bush that always attracts the bees. He's a brave guy. I still don't comment. I solemnly take my sandwich out of its foil and bite it. It tastes like a cardboard fusion shit medley but I do my best at feigning enjoyment face.

"You can't do pretend, girl. Never could," Jack opines.

"Don't know what you mean. Can't you go and pick holes in somebody else's life mess?"

"Don't be so dramatic, girl."

I want to spit the sandwich back out again but I won't dismount my high horse. So I force down the arid crust.

Jack takes out a greasy aromatic sausage roll and my stomach growls with longing. Comfort food of the highest denominator. He looks at me with a sidelong Jack-ish glance, then splits it in two and hands me a half. The pastry flakes and lands on my trousers but I don't care. I want to sniff the sausage like a coke addict.

"Get that inside you."

"Cheers."

"Don't want you fading away. Apparently most of my stuff is coming back—Dibian's handed over her spoils. It's been impounded as evidence but it's out of her clutches. Your money will be sorted out too."

"Good news. That's novel. Wonder when the birds will crap on that too."

"Glass half-full if you please. Or I'll leave and take my sausage roll back."

I take a bite. Sometimes sausage roll is the best and only Band-Aid salve worth sampling. Good old Jack.

"Can we just not talk?"

"Will called me from Scotland Yard this morning and gave full details. When you're ready to know about it, you can ask me."

"I don't care."

"Izzy. Your book is big news, I hear. You're going to be a very wealthy woman. Somebody has to claim the payments eventually."

"By all accounts Rogerson is keen on me going for head of department, I'll have no time for writing. And I've had my fingers scorched by writing heat, above my temperature range."

Jack doesn't talk of what I've written. We've never had that conversation. Which is good. He's like the dad I never had. Erotica conversations would make my toes curl.

"He's coming into school later."

"Who?"

"Detective Inspector Darby. The man you're faking doesn't exist."

"Don't want to know."

"He's still Will. We fell for his charms because he's a good man."

"He's no charms for me. He hid the truth about various things. He wasn't honest or upfront plus he got his lines blurred. For a policeman he broke rules himself."

"Said by the Maverick of the English department."

I parry back with a death glare. I do not want to talk this over. Ever.

Jack wipes himself down to eradicate the pastry crumbs. "Remember Ada, the cake supremo who makes the perfect pies? Turns out she's taken a fancy to yours truly. It's never too late, you know. Sometimes you have to take a chance. I think I could make a go of this if she'll let me. Believe me, her haddock bake's better than a Thierry Henry hat-trick."

"I'm pleased for you, Jack. Truly. She's a lucky woman."

"Trust me, one bite of her steak and mushroom lattice pie and I was smitten. I'm the one who stands to win most." Jack stands and stares down at me, blocking out my sunlight with his bulky form. "For God's sake, girl, what I'm trying to say is, you're cutting off your nose here. It was more than his job was worth. If your allegiances meant you inadvertently told Dibian the truth, he'd have been sunk. He was investigating us all, not just you."

"He told me falsehoods. There are too many question marks and I can't see past the lies. I think he may have a woman on the side too."

Although I've had a mini epiphany with the Annie truce, I still wouldn't put it past her to have lied about Tessa being a lesbian merely to get back at me. After all, I did tell her Will was gay.

"Oh, well. That paints a different color of sky. And craps on the ship's mast into the bargain. Well, I'm to pass on a message — Will says he wants to see you. He's tied up in London with casework but he asked if you'd call. You won't return his calls — he's asked me for direct access."

I've finished the sausage roll and now it feels wrong inside my tummy. I could well be throwing up into a flower bed for the second time in my life. And that thought makes me want to howl. "I won't. You don't know the full facts."

I roll up my own lunch and foil and fire it into the bin with a great aim.

"Goal!" Jack declares and punches the air lightly. But the mood doesn't fit. Usually I'd laugh but I can't. My laughter chip's corroded. Nothing's funny.

And nothing but Miley Cyrus singing *Wrecking Ball* full blast hits my spot on how I feel. I have it bad for a man. I've been through all this crazy shit at school and yet the thought of being taken for an idiot again in my life hurts me.

"I came," Jack tells me, "to tell you I'm proud of you. You sorted young Lydia out with a good outcome. You have to stop beating yourself up about Dibian. You seem to forget that you have a lot of wonderful friends — crazy, some would call 'em — but loyal works too. Did you know they went an' bawled Will out on your behalf?"

I suck in a breath. But Jack's always had the innate talent to get to me.

"Who did?"

"Fiona, Janey. That woman who runs the chocolate shop with the enormous —"

I interject, "Mo."

"That's the one. Dressed him down good and proper."

I hadn't realized they all knew about my dangerous liaison. But, while I'm at it, I still have issues with the Dibian thing and how it came to pass. "I still feel guilty, Jacko. After all, I introduced you to her. I feel responsible for what she did."

"She was her own worst enemy. You've a good heart and saw the best."

"I admire you and should have protected you at a vulnerable time." It's been going round my mind in a crazy loop of guilty mind corrosion.

"Izzy. I got off effing lightly, girl. What if she'd inveigled herself into my life and tried to pair up with a sad, old, lonely geezer? What if she'd taken me for a ride? I was lucky."

It still doesn't take the sting off my wounded trust. That I took Dibian so readily at face value. My prior experiences haven't helped to educate my choices.

"It's because you trust that you're the treasure we know you to be. I know it. Your friends know it. One bad apple and all that."

I sigh and finger my temples. "I've been foolish of late. Will's no exception."

"Tea at mine? Tea and a truce? And we won't discuss events. I have Hobnobs — half-covered chocolate kind. With the sports pages."

I nod. Some things — not many — but some, I can still rely on. And Jack's the rock to which I cling. The kind of man you can trust.

* * * *

There is a good side to *Class Wars* at Netherfield being stalled, a.k.a. called off, and revealed as a clandestine ploy to catch a thieving rat teacher.

Firstly, the fuss and extra work abate and I can get on with being a teacher. Secondly, the kids will knock off the exuberance and quit trying to outdo each other in the fashion, hairstyles and spray tans department. But mostly I get to see Andy Regis slope off with his camera, lenses and assorted tripods.

He salutes me as he walks past, but doesn't approach. I'm guessing he's a copper too. Which makes his double-crossing even worse. I'm piqued enough to confront him.

"So it wasn't a BBC expenses account? And trying to date two women at once is just one of your foibles?"

He sighs but doesn't answer.

I continue, "I always figured you were a crap cameraman. Sometimes your camera was upside down. Annie's well shot of you."

"Cheeky cow. I am BBC — this will be shown on *Crimewatch* primetime next week. I'm ex force. Scotland Yard. Fraud Squad — trained with Will. Hicks got too greedy. Great book, by the way." He winks at me. "I'll pre-order a sequel. Great to know what women want. Be even better if you could put a word in for me with Annie. She was hot."

"Hell will freeze over first. And the hero of my next book won't be police."

"Dunno. Will has it pretty bad for you. He swore he'd tear my head off if I went near you again. Said he'd use my balls for penalty kick masterclasses. He's been pissed off about some expenses account gaffe I've made — don't remember anything about an old couple when we had our meal? Booked a free room on my expenses, thievin' old codgers."

I'd like to be flattered about Will but I'm too raw.

I'm cheering about the expenses rumble.

Andy was always a dick. I never figured on Will being one too.

Tarquin, on the other hand, does not take the weasel's route of trying to skulk off. He's more than happy to come up for another Yank-a-Hand demonstration in how to paralyze a writer–cum handshake.

"It's been a pleasure working with you. There's a chance we may come back for filler filming later. I believe we'd be interested in having you come in at airtime — perhaps an interview, as she was your department head and friend? I'll let you get your head together on events."

"I think I'd rather forget it's all ever happened. We never did get to share that raspberry pastry," I add. And, damn me, I wish I hadn't. Why did I let my brain even go there? I don't want a revisit.

"Then I must pop by and rectify. Soon. I'll be in touch. Adieu then. Do think about that interview—you're a key witness."

The BBC slash Scotland Yard leave the building.

I'd like to say I'm happy. But, given the circumstances, I'm sad.

It was Netherfield's hope of a bright new shining future. It ended up crapped on by life. And eye gouged. Like a *Game of Thrones* season ending that's left the star players buggered, bullied and beheaded. And I'm left discombobulated and traumatized.

* * * *

"Come in."

I'm answering a knock on my office door, but nobody appears. So I shout for the visitor to enter again, this time more firmly.

Mickey Peters appears around the door. His Mohawk hairdo looks like it hasn't been brushed this week. I'm somewhat shocked. I haven't seen him around much since I bawled him out in the car park. I think back on how much has happened since then. And how my car is barely holding itself together, having wrapped it around Totteridge street furniture. Shit. I need to get that sorted or buy a new car. My Omazod statement arrived this morning so maybe there's hope?

"How can I help?"

"Jack Carson sent me, miss. He wants your 'elp, miss."

"What with? I'm in the middle of something."

"Didn't say, miss." Peters sniffs. It's a filthy habit of his, yet so characteristic. I know he'll never stop.

"Get a tissue." I hold out the box and he takes one, then pockets it. I simply follow his lead. I lock the class door and he's sniffing as he goes. "Use the tissue, Peters. They're not on ration."

He shrugs, then blows and we proceed. Not talking. Just the clack of my heels on the parquet. Accompanied by the occasional sniff.

* * * *

"Fuck."

I'm saying it out loud and Peters is still there but I don't care. I should've seen this coming. Jack's in cahoots.

"You may go," Jack tells the boy.

I walk into the basement and Will's drinking tea with Jack. My heart goes crazy tempo when our eyes meet. It's clear Jack's got me here under false pretenses, so blow me if I'm staying to have them gang up and give me crapola.

"Not you!" says Jack. "This time, lady, you're gonna listen and listen good. And not to me." He removes his keys from his janitor's coat pocket and shows me them pointedly. Then he locks us both in the room together. With a bold click and wobbling jowls and a glower, he stitches me up good and proper.

"So?"

"Hi would do," says Will.

"Is there any point to this? And why are you back here when you only came to do Taggart does *High School Musical*?"

He shakes his head as his jaw flexes and his eyes narrow. "It's not as cut and dried as you're assuming."

"Look. Can we make this discussion brief because I've marking waiting. You came, you got your collar. You fulfilled your jurisdiction and got a shag into the bargain. Can we leave it there?"

"Izzy. Does everything have to be so ruddy black and white with you?"

"Yes. I don't respect liars, Will."

"I never lied to you. I was doing a job."

"Did you use me as your motive to get a way into the English department?"

"Initially I wanted to question you. It's why I approached you in the car park. Believe me, I got so much more than I expected."

"Did you fail to tell me any of that?"

"Detectives don't break confidences. We were something entirely different. I would've told you in time. There was rather a lot of drama in the mix as it was."

"Oh, and now I'm a drama-seeking missile in this?"

He stands to full over six feet height and paces the room. Must be said—a three-piece suit looks phenomenal on him. "You're the only reason I'm back. And whether or not you believe me or want to hear what I have to say is up to you. I want you to hear the truth, then I'll go."

He hangs his head and watches his shiny dapper shoes. The suit gets my juices frantically flowing. Betraying juices that they are.

"Been in court?" I ask.

"No. Been for an interview. Got the job. At Hendon Police College."

"My, but the job offers keep stacking up. Do you collect them?"

"Look. I didn't come here for a war of words. I wanted to see you — *needed* to see you and urge you not to believe all the crap you've read and assumed about me. Yes, I'm a police detective inspector. Yes, I came here undercover. The thing is, before I even started proper pro football, my sights were on a police career and the dream didn't fade. As soon as I left football, I took a criminology degree. Did well, then fast-tracked onto the force graduate track. Until now, I've mostly kept my head below the parapet, media-wise."

"Why are you telling me all this?"

"To say I came here for work but I fell for the place, and for you. And I had genuine reasons for my issues when we met — I had major surgery for testicular cancer. It left me shell-shocked. Freaked out and trying to get my life back. When I met you, I knew I was meant to come here."

"Oh." My mouth forms an 'o' of surprise. "Sorry. About the cancer."

"We never got to a point where I could explain — so I will now. The surgery was successful in stopping the disease. But it left me having problems in the sex department. I came out of it alive and vital and wanting to go back and do my job and live again. And you treated me like an out and out arsehole rather than a patient on the edge. All I could think about was shagging your brains out."

"Shit. You make me sound like a night with Fanny Fish Market at Lonely Man's Quay bordello."

"Gimme her number — I might look her up." His forehead wrinkles. "If you'll let me finish," he states forcefully. "I met you and I realized you were the most exciting, daft, infuriating, passionate and wonderful woman I've ever met. And now I'm certain I love you."

"I don't need to know anything. You're out of here, aren't you? I'm sorry about your cancer but it's none of my business anyway. You're a copper and you were just here doing your job."

"I did a degree in criminology when I was at Spurs, Iz. I'm not the moron footballer womanizer you think I am. And if you really think what happened with us was just the job, you're a bigger fool than I've realized. I thought we connected, Izzy."

"And what about Tessa? She wasn't a cleaner—she was a copper too. Why did she warn me off?"

Will moves to me, staring hard. "She thought I was ballsing up the case. She called me out that I was getting too close. She knows my job means everything and kept warning that if you knew the truth, you were the kind of honest person who'd spill the beans to Dibian. Didn't we count? I'm not shagging Tessa—she doesn't do blokes and I don't do women who can beat me at arm-wrestling. Have you seen the guns on her? She may wear wildcat heels by day but at night she's a gym-a-holic with a weights and protein drinks habit."

I don't need all this info. I really don't. I need to sum up and move on as I risk getting entangled with Will all over again. "Look, you and me was a nice diversion. A thrill ride. Like a dark-covered, tantalizing erotic paperback. Overpromised under the covers. Ended up hyperbole masked as substance."

"Spoken like an English teacher."

"Most of the time I'm a good one. In plain old English, didn't meet expectations. Read the book, bin it."

Will moves to open the fire door from Jack's lair, the one that says 'Push In Emergency Only'. I know damn well that going out that way will cause the sirens to go off. Maybe even the fire brigade auto summons — is that such a good idea? He always was the kind of guy to go for the big action scene, not giving a shit about consequences or danger.

And ain't that secretly why I loved him to bits and let him have full access to every private scared piece of my heart?

I can feel the tears well in my eyes at the realization.

"Will. You shouldn't have come. It's over. Plain and simple over."

I put my hands on his and push the door.

And I run out, stopping only at reception to say that it's a false alarm and we opened the door in error. Mistake but well and truly concluded.

Chapter Twenty-One

I have to go back to my class for my stuff, then collect my bag and coat from the staffroom. By the time I get out of school, Will is waiting at my car. Leaning on my car bonnet, to be more precise, and inspecting the damage I've done to it.

"Is this legal?" he asks when I reach him.

"Don't tell me. You're going to report me to traffic division."

"No. Well, maybe later. Look, can we talk?"

"We did and I don't honestly have time."

"*Make* time. I made time for you when you were sick. It may not be cool to call in past favors, but I'm prepared to grab anything I can. I need to explain things."

I gulp. "I don't want to fight with you, Batman. My Joker suit's in the wash."

"There's every need for you to know the gaps in what happened to detonate our chaos. Even if you have given up on me, you need to know about someone in your circle who isn't what they seem."

"Yeah. Dibian. I did get the point of the meeting. Well done, et cetera. Hope you get an honorable mention. Can I go now?"

He reaches out and gently grabs my wrist. "Can we talk in the car?" He's looking over his shoulder, and, right enough, there are kids gathered by the tennis courts staring our way.

I unlock the car giving a long sigh. "Get in!"

"Remember the photographer who crashed our party? He was onto the story about the fraud. The case was completely embargoed and hush hush and he nearly risked a big reveal that might have meant we'd lose the collar."

I nod at him but, although it's interesting, I'm not entirely sure why Will is telling me all this.

"Tessa came on strong with you because she thought you had loose lips. I told her you could be trusted — despite what you think of me, I trust you totally. Anyhow, I identified Flo was the root of the leak. She tipped off the papers."

Fuck. A Duck.

"Flo? My flatmate Flo? You can't be serious."

"She recognized me from a picture to do with another case and knew I was police. Must've researched it through her newspaper contacts. She hoped for a scoop on a big story. We had to do a deal — it could've gone badly wrong and she's been warned off. She wanted a payoff, surprise, surprise. She's the reason the story broke so wide today."

The heavy feeling in my heart gets another kick of disappointment while it's down. "I've always worried about Flo. Don't suppose we'll stay flatmates for long. It's water under the bridge — lease is up soon."

"I want you to move in with me. I was serious about it before and I still am."

I start shaking. I'm in a bit of a state as the enormity of what I've heard sinks in. I feel like a mug and it transports me with speed to the days of being bullied. Three people who've been close parts of my life have all been revealed as imposters or liars — Will, Dibian and Flo. It takes me right back to my fourteen-year-old nerdy self. My shoulders wobble, tears begin. Not an ideal moment for a 'will you live with me?' confession.

"Can I hug you? For a minute?" Will asks.

I nod. And I know, around me, my car's in a total state. Five chocolate wrappers are not the svelte goddess image I'd yearned to project. But I hadn't banked on Will carjacking me after I'd stuffed two choc flakes down my throat in fast succession at the wheel earlier. Let's say, now that I know the full skinny on how things stand, I could well be adding a full upper tray of a Thornton's pralines box to the melee.

"You weren't a teacher at all?"

"I have trained police cadets if it counts. I knew enough to teach sport. And I don't know if you realize but I once played a sport myself."

I jab at his chest with my finger but he just smiles and uses the pad of his thumb to wipe my tears.

"Was it really your mother? When we were in the pagoda? Was that crapola too?"

"We had a squad debrief booked — sorry for lying. I heard what you said in Assembly — Janey made a video on her phone. It took huge courage. And it made lots of sense to me. You make me proud."

I blink at him.

He continues, "It's no wonder you think I've deceived and hurt you. That wasn't my intention. I couldn't be as honest as I wanted. And I do think we have what it takes and we could be a great team—we've so many more uncharted sexual exploits to share it's a crying shame to blow me out now. It'll be the shittiest blow of my entire sex life."

But I can't answer. I'm on a roll now—thinking back in the past to try to work things out. "Who was the guy talking to you in the dinner hall the other week?"

"Gordon Mather. Scotland Yard ops director. There's a job at Hendon if I want it. It's not the job that makes me think twice about staying—it's you. And there's another job I've been offered. Schools liaison and youth development—at Arsenal. They phoned me up and asked. Does your team deserve that, or will you hate me forever?"

"Stick with police work. Or I might have to kill you."

He laughs and I join him. "I'm not leaving the force, even for your beloved Arsenal. It's what I love. Well, that and you."

"Will, please don't base any of your life decisions on me."

"Fuck, Iz. Is this how we're going to play it? Back off, pretend we don't matter?" His jaw flexes and his tone bites me harder than I'd anticipated. This has hit him hard. I see it in the way he looks as if he hasn't been sleeping and the lines around his mouth.

"We're over, Will. Best kept that way. We had a fling but I wouldn't want you to change your career based on anything to do with us. Be careful in what you decide."

He turns fully in his seat and accuses me, "*You* are what I want. Jobs don't matter. I want a try at us. I want that woman who fires me. Cancer tried to stop me and failed. Why would I let a little thing like a derailment kill us? You helped me to come again. You've shown me my future. I'm fighting back, Izzy. For you."

His words have gone deep, to a dark, private part of me. And I sigh as I suck them in and process. I make up my mind. "Then come with me. You've seen the crazy erotica Izzy. You need to see what lies deeper."

* * * *

We end up in Highbury. At Uncle Cyril's flat.

We enter. Seeing the chintzy sofa chosen by Aunty Doris and paid up on installments, plus all her assorted holiday glass ornament collection, causes a formidable lump to gather in my throat. From daffodils in spun glass to poodles, she followed the theme through diligently. I find I love each piece a tad more than the last.

"Uncle Cyril's. He hasn't lived here for two years now. He's keeping it for me." I walk to the balcony door and unlock it. We stand outside.

"Fuck. Ah. Now I get it," says Will.

"I used to stand here with Dad. And Uncle Cyril. When I was little. They kept my hand tight in case I got near the edge but I was always craning to see. To see my team."

I don't have the words for the hugeness of this conversation so I keep it brief. But Will sees the site that once boasted Highbury's grandeur—Arsenal's birthplace and home. Once the stadium of my dreams—once a living, breathing monster of a thing that I loved beyond all ken. Now slain—the East and

West Stand exteriors remain but it's mainly a site of new crazily priced housing and a garden.

Uncle Cyril had a ringside free view of the emerald green, floodlit pitch and the red-shirted warriors of our hearts.

"Quite a flat. Must've been something."

I nod. "It was. Still is to me."

"No wonder you grew up a Gooner." He slides his arm around my shoulders and he holds me close. His lips are on my cheek and he turns me in his arms to kiss me long and deep. It's a kiss I've needed for a long time—his kiss of return and welcome. How can this man have this effect? He fires me, moves me, and fills me with such comfort and joy.

I don't say anything. That lump in my throat is a tennis ball. I can almost feel Dad's hand around mine—holding me against him, and the tightness of his chest as he'd forget to breathe during play.

And I would give everything I have to be back with him and Cyril. So we could hear the roar of the match. I could always feel the excitement and see it dancing in their eyes. From that time I was hooked.

"Dad died when I was four, just before primary school. Mum and Cyril never talked about it. For years it was a big black hole, never discussed."

Will is watching me. I know he can hear the jagged emotion that clogs my throat and the tangle of barbed wire emotions that keeps me fettered and chained up inside.

"I never let my feelings out." I flick a few tears away with my finger. "It's the family way. I've always clammed up and kept it tight. Like when I was bullied—don't tell anyone, just deal with it. But when I met you, I felt a connection and I wish I'd told you and been honest. Instead I did my Izzy thing – backed off and used comebacks. I wanted to know you better since the first day we met. You scared me witless. Wish I'd known how to play it better. I want you. I want to be with you – there I've said it. And it's not about crazy sex, it's about finding the one who makes you whole."

Will takes my hands in his. Mine are shaking and I don't care that he knows.

"I've wanted you since that first day. Smart sass and bad attitude. Every time we met, I saw the spark that lit the room – and the shadows. Your distance. You're so wonderful you have no idea, but you scare me like a wild horse that's always about to kick me in the gonads."

"I lost young, Will. Later I made mistakes, got beaten by bullies at school. So I've learned to tuck my emotions deep. You've given me the full package – you are like the missing link that could fix the broken bits inside me. Your potential frightens me – I'm scared I don't deserve you."

He lays his head against mine and, inside, angel choruses sing. "It's me who doesn't deserve a single bit of your intense searing light. I'm the one with the baggage. The cancer. The dark moments. The shadow on the future."

"You're the only man who's made me feel secure this way. Except Dad."

There's tears – horrible, messy tears – and they're running fast down my face and proving that my mascara is a bag of shit and needs to go back to the shop.

But Will wipes the mascara river away. He tugs me closer and envelopes me in his marvelous, reassuring embrace. "I'll give you everything, my Izzy. All of me.

If you'll have me. If you'll run that risk. I'm far from perfect. But I'll try to be the man you deserve. I want to try."

He kisses me so fully my heart is fit to burst. He holds my face in his hands like a movies move. I feel a sudden sensation I can't even explain. It's like my dad's back here. And he wanted us here. It's as if he's brought me here for this express reason.

And I'm crying, but they're good tears because the man of my dreams is holding me, kissing me and declaring his passion. How lucky am I? Really?

"If you want to buy the flat, I'll look into it," Will tells me. "I have plenty of money from back in the day as a player."

"Uncle Cyril may be a bit infirm but he's made the flat mine by right. I don't want your money, Will Darby. I want your hand to hold. And the great things you do to me in bed. Do you know I even had Ben teach me how to do twenty keepy-uppies on my knee with a football? I can keep the ball going on my head like a pro."

Will pulls me to him, in his enveloping embrace, and I melt into his arms and chest. "Your uncle Cyril still keeps this place, even with no Highbury view? Uncle Cyril is the kind of guy I want to be. I want you to be you." Will smiles at me. "Come on, Iz. Let's go home. I've unpacking to do. We've argued for too long. It's time to let it go."

"Unpacking? Can't you think of anything better? Don't you even want to see my ball skills?"

"Somebody ruined the key to the fun room. You'll have to settle for the vanilla monotony of a bed."

I smile and try for an innocent tone. "I kept a key copy. I'm not a total moron!" My hand goes to my bag. "If I can find it under all this other shit!"

Will fakes looking pissed off but I can discern the grin that lurks beneath. "Shit, woman, my hand is itching to give you something to think about!"

And we're running. To the lift. To the Range Rover.

To life. Started over. As we jump inside the vehicle I wink at the man I love and he winks right back.

"Life with my Batman. My Secret Sir."

"Our love's a beautiful game of two halves — you and me." He looks down and I gasp when I see that there's something new on his arm.

"A tattoo? Fuck, you didn't!" It's a Batman logo and my name is beneath. I glance at the tattoo again. "What would you have done if I'd walked away?"

He grins. "Used handcuffs... Since I know you like them. Besides, you're a sensible woman — I trust your instincts."

We're driving faster. "Watch the speed cams, Darby."

"Copy that. Handcuffs is a great suggestion." Will growls beneath his breath, but he's smiling behind the glare. My auto-lust button responds to his dark leashed danger.

"Consider me under house arrest."

"We'll deal with your sentence shortly."

"Thank you, Sir," I answer and we both grin. "Please be punitively severe."

"I intend," he says softly, "to teach you a lesson you won't easily forget."

About the Author

After winning a lovely boxed pen for writing a poem about the beach in a school competition aged eight, Judy Jarvie decided the writing game promised untold exciting treasures. It took her a while to turn that poem into any full length work that anybody would want to read so in the meantime she worked in Press and PR in London until she moved back to Scotland and realised she'd been spurning her one burning love of writing love stories. So she gave in to the call to do it and has kept going ever since. Now the writing keeps her sane and happy and dreaming up new heroes on a regular basis. She lives in a village in Scotland with her husband, two very special daughters and a crazy black cat who all keep her out of trouble and cause a fair bit in return.

Judy loves to hear from readers. You can find her contact information, website details and author profile page at http://www.totallybound.com.